There were dark curtains over the windows, trapping the stale air inside. Five other men in ski masks and dark clothing were crowded into the cabin. Out of courtesy for my presence, they pointed their machine guns in my direction.

"Christ!" I sputtered. Sam looked at me without a flicker of recognition in his eyes.

The man with the furry face spoke. "Who are you?"

"Jane Lanier." My voice was trembling. I hoped I wouldn't wet my pants. "I got a call a few minutes ago that led me to believe Brute Mortimer was in great danger." I avoided Sam's eyes and looked into the cold ones of the stranger.

He puffed on his cigar while he considered my answer. "You're too late. Somebody already shot him."

"Oh," I said, my voice forlorn. That explained the blood on the deck. "Is he dead?"

The man shrugged. "Who called you?"

"A little old lady."

I felt a gun smack me on the back of my head, and I lurched forward. The edge of the table broke my fall.

"I'm not kidding!" I protested. The gun cracked my skull again, and the room started to fade to black. I heard someone say "Kill her. We'll dump the body on the way back." The last words to filter into my consciousness were Sam's.

"I'll do it."

City of Suspects

KATY KING

WORLDWIDE®

TORONTO • NEW YORK • LONDON
AMSTERDAM • PARIS • SYDNEY • HAMBURG
STOCKHOLM • ATHENS • TOKYO • MILAN
MADRID • WARSAW • BUDAPEST • AUCKLAND

For Lu Anne Vaughn, Arlene Sachitano
and Jennifer McBride.

Recycling programs
for this product may
not exist in your area.

CITY OF SUSPECTS

A Worldwide Mystery/May 2010

First published by Oak Tree Press.

ISBN-13: 978-0-373-26709-5

Printed in U.S.A.

Acknowledgments

I have a city's worth of people to thank for helping with this book! First of all, I have the best agent ever—the marvelous and talented Janet Reid of New York. I'm also grateful to Billie Johnson and her team at Oak Tree Press. I'm very proud to be associated with such a fine publishing firm.

The Harriet Vane Chapter of Sisters in Crime has been enormously helpful, especially in regard to the parade of experts who make guest appearances at the monthly meetings. Medical Examiners, arson investigators, private investigators and homicide detectives are all frequent guests. Special thanks to: Dr. Karen Gunson, State Medical Examiners Office, Sgt. Larry Welty, of the Oregon State Police and all of the other star speakers.

Thank you also, to Lt. Glenn Chastain of the Oregon State Police for your insight on police procedure and to the Portland Police Bureau for opening up the central precinct one chilly December morning to welcome the Harriet Vane sissies for a tour.

Writers sometimes have to draw outside the lines in order to color the story and I claim all errors as my own, despite my access to these top-notch experts. And all villains are fictional, of course. Jesús Borboa came up with the name of our sinister black hatter. Thank you, Jesús. Thanks also for the constant support of my co-workers: Grant Higginson, M.D., Bonnie Widerburg and Mellony Bernal.

I deeply appreciate the enthusiasm from my family and friends during this writing adventure. Lu Anne Vaughn and Arlene Sachitano, my fellow mystery writers, thank you from the bottom of my heart for all of your constructive feedback and encouragement over the years. Jennifer McBride, you are brilliant and fabulous. Thank you for poring over every page to make the book as good as it possibly could be. Eileen, I know you helped too! Tom Engle, I'm grateful for all of your technical and computer assistance. You are a genius. Kelly Garner, Jennifer Webber, Gina Mattioda and Cheri Tebeau-Harrell—I treasure our friendships and your unwavering support.

Thanks also to my wonderful family, my parents, Gail and Tim King, my sisters Judy, Sally and Jane, my brother-in-law Matt Padrow, and to my nephew and niece, Tim and Emily. But thanks most of all go to you, the reader. I'm so happy you bought this book!

Now strap yourself into Jane's leaky Cabriolet and get ready for a ride!

ONE

RAIN FELL OVER PORTLAND, Oregon the night of October 28th. It swelled the Willamette River, stripped the trees of their leaves, and sent tears streaming down the copper face of Portlandia, the six and a half ton statue that guards the city from her perch on a government building. A few blocks away I sat on a chair in the lobby of the Marriott hotel, waiting for a tardy client due from the Portland International airport. It was nine forty-five p.m. and my head was full of room price trivia from the brochures I had read to pass the time. I stood up, put on my coat and picked up my purse. For the third and last time, I stopped by the reservation desk to see if a Robert Riley had checked in. He hadn't. I took one last look around the lobby then rushed out the automatic doors. A soggy valet went to retrieve my car and I remembered belatedly my umbrella was tucked under the nice and dry lobby chair.

Maybe the man's plane crashed, maybe he was hit by a Tri-Met bus on his way over to the hotel. I hoped so. Otherwise there was no good excuse for wasting my time and getting my hair wet. Although it was late, Mr. Riley was not my last appointment of the day. I was one busy private eye. I still had to meet a new client at my office at ten. I dug into my pocket for the valet's tip and came out with a buck and the note I found under my office door earlier in the afternoon. I glanced at the note. My instructions were to meet the client at ten o'clock to discuss an urgent matter. "Urgent" was underlined in black ink. I couldn't decipher the signature. I folded the note and put it back in my pocket as the valet drove up with my car. His face was twisted into a grimace. My Cabriolet convertible has a leaky roof that allows me to shower and drive at the same time. I handed the valet a dollar, and a wadded up napkin to dry off. Then I jumped in my car and headed over to Tenth and Morrison.

I have a tiny office in the Galleria building. Built in 1910, it had originally housed the first department store west of the Mississippi. In 1976 it was renovated to become the world's first vertical mall. A sign says so when you enter the building. The first three floors are devoted to retail space and offices are located on the fourth and fifth floors. I rent a piece of mall history on the fifth floor. My working quarters are a bit shabby, the heating system is downright frail, but the rent is cheap, just how I like it.

Tenth Avenue was fairly deserted for a Friday night. Even the doorman in front of the Governor hotel had abandoned his post. I slid into a parking space a block away. The windows of Jake's restaurant inside the hotel face the Galleria building across the street. If I had time, I'd be having a drink at the bar while on the lookout for my mysterious client. Unfortunately it was almost ten. I turned off the ignition and flicked off the headlights.

A taxi turned the corner and pulled up in front of the Galleria building. I paused with my hand on the door handle. A fat man got out underneath the glare of a streetlight. He was Hispanic, probably in his late fifties, with a mean as hell expression on his face. His hair was parted on the side and slicked back. A pencil thin mustache was sketched on his face. An overcoat draped around his bulky figure. He was dressed in dark slacks, spectator shoes and gloves. He turned, reached for a silver briefcase, then slammed the door. The man looked around, sneered at no one in particular, and darted into the building.

This had to be my guy.

I opened up my glove compartment and pulled out the gun that I reserve for meetings with mean as hell clients. It's a .38 Special. A dealer in Albany sold it to me out of the back of his van for 250 dollars. So far I haven't invested in any ammunition. There are certain times of the month when I'd be tempted to use it. I put the gun in the pocket of my raincoat and got out of my car. I was immediately drenched by a hail of rain. I hurried to the crosswalk, sidestepping puddles even though the dampness had already soaked through my tennis shoes. A great gust of wind blew, bending the trees that lined the avenue. The dead leaves sailed from the branches and floated down the flooded sidewalks. I was cut short at the corner by a MAX train that slid to a stop in front of me. The doors swung open and I caught a glimpse of steamy windows and empty seats. A dirty word was traced on one of the windows. It echoed my thoughts exactly—this was no night to be out.

The prospect of money made me do it. I had spent most of the day at my desk typing reports on the computer, listening to the rain and waiting for the phone to ring. I have a few regular clients, mostly law firms, but I can't always count on enough background checks and witness interviews to cover my expenses. And then there are the no show types like Robert Riley, so sometimes, I trail a cheating spouse to make ends meet. I'm not fond of being a peeping Thomasina, but scruples don't pay the rent. My lack of scruples earned me 800 dollars from Janet Groves this week. I had the sad task of informing her that her husband of twenty years was dating someone that age. She dropped off my check today on her way to meet her divorce attorney. While I was at the bank someone had slipped the note underneath the door.

The MAX doors closed and the train slid away. I crossed the street, went in the building and wiped the water from my face.

I looked around in case the client had decided to wait for

me. The first floor was quiet except for canned music and the sound of the fountain encircling the side base wall of the escalator. The metal gates in front of the darkened stores were padlocked and the chairs in the nearby deli were stacked on top of the tables. The last employee probably left the building over an hour ago, but the escalators were still running. Art, the sixty year old security guard, isn't much on energy conservation except when it comes to his own. Most likely he or the badge on duty, was hunched over a newspaper in one of the empty cafes upstairs.

I walked over to the bank of elevators and got on one. It lurched to the fifth floor. I stepped out in the foyer and walked through the double security doors, which were wide open. Normally they're locked but it looked like the guard was really taking it easy tonight. Lucky for him there was no one around but me to complain. And since he had caught me in an elevator with a boyfriend once, I didn't feel like telling on him. I turned the corner and walked down the empty hall to my office. A small sign by the door read "Jane Lanier, Private Investigator". I expected my client to be standing there but he was nowhere in sight.

I unlocked the door and pushed it open. The room felt damp and chilled. I reached for the light but something swirled in the darkness. God, I wasn't alone! Panic shot through me. I yelped and reached for my gun as a pair of hands locked around my neck. I was slammed against the wall. Stars exploded in front of my eyes. I tried to yell "help" but the only sound in the room was the swish of my flailing arms.

My knees buckled and I collapsed. My attacker fell on the floor with me, his hands still savagely twisting my neck. I peeled his pinky fingers off my neck and bent them away from his hands. They broke and my attacker released his grip with a cry of pain.

I patted my coat frantically, trying to find my gun. My coat had twisted and the gun was pressing in the small of my back. He grabbed my neck again with his good fingers. I cupped my hand and pushed upwards on his nose with everything I had.

The man gasped. Hot breath hit my face as his body sagged on top of mine. I was dimly aware that the fingers around my neck had loosened and I could breathe again. I pried them off and shoved the man away from me. He rolled over with a thud. My fingers grasped the gun in my pocket and I whipped it out, frantically pulling the trigger in the direction of my assailant. Click, click, click. When I emptied my imaginary rounds I stood up on shaky legs and hit the light.

The man crumpled at my feet was not the fat man that I had seen on the street—it was one of the new security guards. His pockmarked face had been battered and his yellow hair was matted with blood. With a cry I fell to my knees and checked his pulse. He was still breathing—but barely. I looked at the nameplate clipped to his pocket. Peter Sundstrom. What the hell was he doing in my office? And more importantly, why the hell was he trying to choke me?

I jumped up and grabbed the phone on the reception desk so I could call for help. There was blood on the white receiver. Repulsed, I dropped it back into the cradle and flung open the door that connects the reception area to my private office. I stopped dead in my tracks, confused. The fat man was in my office. I moved closer.

He was seated in the visitor chair and the top half of his body was slumped over my desk. His face was resting in a pool of blood. A big pulpy hole gaped at the back of his neck. His beefy hand clutched at the edge of my desk calendar as if to hold onto one more day. A thick gold ring was wedged on his pinky finger.

"Oh God!" I breathed as I lunged for the phone to dial 911. The operator came on the line as I picked up the clammy wrist of the fat man. His Cartier was ticking but his heart sure wasn't.

"I need the police and an ambulance. I've got a gunshot victim here and another man who is injured," I barked into the phone. I looked at the security guard in the other room as I gave the operator my address. He was breathing in a ragged fashion. I hoped to God that he wouldn't die on me too.

"Hurry!" I urged. I hung up despite the protests of the operator and turned back to the fat man. What had happened here? I looked around my office for some clue. The place isn't big. The reception room holds an old couch and a coffee table with some back issues of *TIME* I had stolen from my doctor's office. The security guard was sprawled to the right of the entry way by the coat rack.

I turned back to my office area. The window faces the parking garage across the street, beyond that a tiny slice of the west hills. The room itself looked undisturbed except for the poor bastard on the desk. Not that there was much to disturb. I don't keep many personal items in my office. Normally when you walk into someone's workplace, their knickknacks tell their life story; cheesy family photos, awards, dried flowers and crap like that. Too revealing for me. My office is like a motel room—impersonal, generic, and garage sale furnished.

Plucking a tissue from the box on the bookshelf, I walked over to the filing cabinet and pulled it open. I keep research files inside. As far as I could tell they hadn't been touched. Client files are on computer disks—those are kept under lock and key in the bottom drawer of my desk. I walked behind my desk, crouched down, and gave the drawer a tug. Still locked. The wastepaper basket by my desk was overflowing and confetti from the three hole punch littered the floor. Couldn't blame the killer for that mess. I stood up. The computer is on a table behind my desk, facing the window. It was turned off. One thing caught my eye—the books on my windowsill were knocked over. One of the bookends was missing. It was a stone replica of Rodin's The Thinker.

I looked back at the body and shuddered. I had seen a murder victim before, long ago, when I first worked the police beat at the *Seattle Times*. I didn't know the person but I thought of him often through the years. This guy was different. I had seen him living, walking, and breathing just minutes ago.

Who was he? What was he doing here? It seemed to be in my best interest to find out before the police did. I gingerly slid my tissue covered hand into the pocket of his overcoat. I touched an envelope and pulled it out. A twenty fluttered to the floor. The envelope had been ripped open and it was stuffed with cash. I bent over, picked up the money and put it back in the envelope. With a shaky hand I returned the wad to his pocket. Quickly, I felt through his other pockets. I found a plane ticket. I took the tissue and squeezed the sides of the United Airlines envelope. I could see from the printed information inside that Mr. Federico DeOrca had been destined for a flight to Los Angeles at midnight, then on to Mexico City.

I stood up and looked out the window. A pair of headlights flashed at me from the parking garage across the street and then the car eased out. I put the ticket back in the man's pocket and went to the hall to wait for the police. On my way out I noticed that The Thinker was tucked into a corner by the door.

It was bloody.

TWO

"STATE YOUR NAME for the record," Detective Dermott said as he turned on the tape recorder.

I opened my mouth to speak as a police officer stepped behind Dermott. He aimed a Polaroid camera at me and snapped a picture. I blinked before I spoke.

"Jane Lanier." I glanced at the picture the officer dropped on the table in front of Dermott. It was in the process of developing and I could see my pale and ghostly face spreading across the photo. I looked awful. My long reddish blonde hair was wet and wind styled. A streak of blood was smeared on my cheek. Self consciously, I reached to rub it. I noticed that a bruise was forming on my neck as well.

"Do I need an attorney?" I asked. We were downtown in an interview room at the Portland Police Bureau Headquarters. After the police arrived at my office I was handcuffed and taken here for questioning. I suppose things looked a little suspicious—what with me holding a gun, the stiff on the desk and the guard on the floor. I was treated accordingly. My gun was confiscated and someone checked my hand for gunpowder residue. Then I was brought to this room.

It was windowless, stuffy, and it smelled like aftershave and sweat, the sweat possibly mine. The walls were gun metal gray and decorated with a couple of dry erase boards. A mirror covered one of the walls, probably a two way. I wondered who was watching me on the other side. I turned away from my wan reflection. A table dominated the center of the room. Detectives Dermott and Vance were seated directly across from me, taking my statement.

"Not unless you have something to hide." Detective Dermott answered, looking up. His pen was poised over his paper, waiting for me to spill my guts.

I shook my head. My ex-lawyer was also my ex-boyfriend. I'd go to the chair before I called him. "No, I'm ready to talk." I took a sip of water from a Dixie cup.

The police photographer snapped another photo and left me with Dermott and Vance. I knew Dermott by sight; he lives in my apartment building in Northwest Portland. He's a tall white guy, mid thirties, clean shaven, with dark brown eyes, short dark curly hair and a lean, muscular build. He looked good in the Levi's, boots and suit jacket he was wearing tonight. Not particularly friendly though. I've seen him in the laundry room a couple of times, washing his dainties.

Detective Vance was a middle aged man with a ruddy weathered face, watery eyes and Jell-O-like chins. His shoulders and arms strained the fabric of his too small blue suit. He had a Santa shaped physique with a paunch that rolled over his belt. He ran his hand through his short gray hair and I caught sight of a wedding ring trapped on his puffy yellowed finger. His tired and friendly demeanor made me think that he would be playing "Good Cop" to Dermott's "Bad Cop" tonight. I briefly wondered if they took turns playing the role. Bad cop would be more fun.

"Where are the bright lights and rubber hoses?" I asked Dermott, the bad cop, in an attempt to break the ice. The shock had worn off and I was starting to feel somewhat uneasy. The handcuffs were removed soon after I arrived at the station but I doubted I had been crossed off the list of suspects. I glanced uncomfortably at the two way mirror and wished myself home.

"We just want to ask some questions," Vance offered,

chomping on a piece of gum. He had the rough voice of a long time smoker.

"Let's get back to business," Dermott cut in. "Miss Lanier, I need your age, address and occupation."

"I'm 32 years old and I'm a self-employed private investigator." I watched as the two men exchanged looks. Private investigators are not held in high regard by law enforcement officials, especially in Oregon. Until recently it wasn't even necessary to have a license here. I recited my address irritably. Dermott copied it down without comment. If he recognized me from our apartment building he didn't show it.

"Go over the events of the evening. No, the entire day. I want to know everything. Who you spoke to, what you ate— don't leave anything out." I thought about it for a second, then retraced my day. "I got up at seven, took a shower and then I made toast. I ate in front of the television. The *Today* show was on and Martha Stewart was making jewelry out of pumpkin seeds. Normally I go for a run, but I skipped it today because my running partner was out of town for a conference. I blow-dried my hair, put on my make-up and got dressed in what I'm wearing now." I looked down at my black raincoat, navy blazer, white tee shirt, jeans and tennis shoes, then continued. "I went to the office about nine o'clock and checked my messages. I had a call from my mother who lives in Seattle, and from a client who wanted to pick up a report. I had done some surveillance work for her. I returned the call to my client and we made an appointment for two in the afternoon. I spent the rest of the morning on the computer finishing up a report for one of my law firm clients. I ran to the library at noon to do some research, then I grabbed a hot dog and fries at Robertos, a restaurant in the Galleria. My appointment came by at two o'clock to pick up a surveillance report I had done for her. She dropped off a check and I went to the bank with it. When I came back, there was a note underneath my door.

I couldn't make out the signature, but the person said it was urgent and they wanted to meet me at my office at ten o'clock."

I stopped, fumbled through my coat pocket, pulled out the wadded note and dropped it on the table for the cops to read. As they did so, I took a deep breath and tried to get my hands to stop shaking. Dermott looked up and motioned for me to go on.

"I spent the rest of the afternoon doing errands. I took my car in to get an oil change, I mailed some bills and an invoice, then I picked up some information at Election Headquarters for a friend of mine who's running for the House of Representatives. I delivered the packet to her campaign headquarters then I joined some of the volunteers for a beer and a burger at the McMenamin's on NE Broadway." I deliberately left out Maria Manley's name. It was her first race and I knew that she did not need the distraction of a murder investigation at a time like this. Election day was less than two weeks away.

"I went to the Marriott Hotel around eight thirty to meet a client who was supposed to arrive from the Portland airport. He didn't show but the folks at the desk will remember me. I waited there until nine forty-five because I figured his plane must have been delayed. Then I left for the appointment at my office. I arrived about the same time my client did. He showed up a little before ten o'clock in a Rip City cab. He was carrying a briefcase—which wasn't there when I found his body. Anyway, I watched as he went in the building, then I got out of my car and followed him in. I was only a minute behind him but I didn't see him when I went inside. The first floor was deserted. Normally, the security guard makes people sign in on a clipboard after hours, but I didn't see anyone on duty. I took the elevator to the fifth floor, then I got out and went to my office. I unlocked the door, stepped inside and shut it. When I reached for the light I was attacked."

I stopped talking. My gut started to quiver from the memory of it. "May I have some more water?"

Detective Vance stood up. "Yeah, I'll get it." Detective Dermott turned off the tape recorder and scribbled on his pad. Then he looked up and stared at me intently with his dark eyes.

"What?" I said, somewhat defensively. He shrugged. I squirmed in my chair until Vance returned a moment later with another tiny paper cup full of water. He handed it to me and I swallowed it with a single gulp.

"Anyway, my attacker grabbed my throat. I was able to get away by breaking his pinky fingers and slamming my hand into his nose. I turned on the lights. That's when I realized it was the Galleria security guard. I ran over to the phone on my reception desk to call for help. But it was bloody. I didn't want to touch it. There's a phone in my private office, so I opened the door to use that. And then I saw the body. You know the rest."

"Is that everything?" Vance asked.

"Yeah." It was everything except for the little matter of me searching the corpse. If he wasn't going to say anything, then neither was I. I squirmed in my chair some more.

"Can I go home now? I'm exhausted." I wasn't feeling like a big, tough PI, anymore. If they didn't let me out soon, I'd start crying for my mom.

"Hang on a second. Let's have you run through your day again. Maybe we missed something."

It's easier to tell the truth a hundred times, than to lie twice. Lies don't whisper, they scream. My sister Bonnie told me that. She works as a detective for the Seattle Police Department. Her advice was invaluable when I was working as a reporter. I've used the technique myself under the guise of fact checking. I was annoyed to see it used on me. Still I repeated my story. When I was done, Dermott started the questioning.

"Have you ever met the deceased before?"

"I've never seen him before tonight when he was dropped off by a cab. I couldn't make out the signature on the note either so I literally did not even know his name."

Dermott gave me a disbelieving look. "Let me get this straight. You showed up for a late night meeting with a strange man and you didn't even know his name?"

"Give me a break," I snapped back. "I need the money. I can't afford to turn down clients without hearing what they have to offer. Besides, I brought a gun."

"It was unloaded," Dermott reminded me, like I could forget. I made sure the boys knew that when I turned over the weapon. I thought back to the moment when I had fired the empty gun at Peter, the security guard. If the gun had been loaded there would be two men dead tonight. I pushed the thought away.

"He didn't know that," I said. "Who was that man anyway?"

Vance cleared his throat but Dermott spoke first. "We don't have a positive confirmation at this time, but we think we know. Ever heard of a man named Federico DeOrca?"

An inexplicable chill ran through me. Had I read something in the papers? I started to feel sick again but maybe it was just the overpowering smell of Vance's aftershave.

"Vaguely. Refresh my memory."

"Local guy. He owns a chain of Mexican restaurants and a couple of other properties. Laundromat, trucking firm." Dermott paused. "He was also tried for murder a few years ago. Somebody shot his business partner."

The words hung in the air. My eyes darted to Vance for an explanation.

"He wasn't convicted," Vance explained with a sigh. He picked up his coffee cup and drained it.

"What happened?" I asked.

"Mistrial," Dermott answered. "A juror took off and the evidence disappeared." Dermott looked at me like I had something to do with it.

I flinched. "So?"

"We need your help. Can you think of anything at all that

might be of importance? What about the briefcase DeOrca
was carrying? What did it look like?"

"It was silver, I think. I didn't get a close look at it. I was
a block away." They made me describe where my car was in
relation to the cab.

"Anything else?" Dermott asked.

"No. But I want to know how the security guard is doing."

"He was taken to University Hospital. He's still unconscious."

I felt like the wind had been knocked out of me. I didn't
know Peter well—he had only been working at the Galleria
a few weeks. With the exception of Artie, the old fart who
caught me in the elevator, the guards tend to rotate on a regular
basis so it's hard to keep track of them. I met Peter because I
had locked myself out of my office one day and he came up
to let me in. I introduced myself and we chatted for a few
minutes. I remembered him telling me he was working two
jobs so he could go back to school. He was a farm major or
something like that. I told Dermott and Vance this.

"Is he going to be okay?" I felt concerned, even though
Peter had tried to twist my head off my neck. He seemed too
young and stupid to be responsible for DeOrca's murder. And
why would he kill someone who broke into an office? There
had to be some simple explanation.

"Too soon to tell," Dermott answered, leaning back in his
chair. His eyes fixed on mine as if he was trying to read my mind.

My head started to throb from all that probing. "If we're
finished here, I'd like a ride back to my car."

Dermott reached over and stopped the tape recorder. "All
right. We need to get your statement typed. Once you sign it,
you're free to go."

Thirty minutes later I scrawled my signature on the
bottom of a five sheet statement. I was too bleary eyed to
read it carefully, but it looked like what I had just said. Vance
volunteered to give me a lift. I followed him to the elevator,

then to an unmarked patrol car in the underground parking garage. We got in. Vance started the car and drove up a ramp. An attendant waved at Vance and the yellow arm guarding the entrance swung up.

"I can't believe this happened." I leaned against the door. I was wiped out and my gut still hurt from all the stress. My eyes started to water and I sniffed. No way was I going to start bawling in front of a cop.

"You going to be all right?" Vance asked gruffly, as he turned the corner.

"Yeah, as soon as I get to the bottom of all this. I've got to find out what happened. I won't feel safe until I know."

"Better leave this to us," Vance warned.

I didn't answer. Instead I looked out the window as my skin prickled with goose bumps.

We headed north on Tenth Avenue, past a grocery store, the YMCA, and the Multnomah County Library. I pointed out my car. It was parked in a lonely spot, in the block between the library and the Galleria building. The lights in the restaurant of the Governor Hotel had been turned low. It was late. Vance pulled up behind my car and left the motor running. I unbuckled my belt.

"Did you know the victim?" I asked on impulse.

"I did," Vance admitted. Even in the dark, I could see his jaw tighten. "He was not a good guy."

"I guess not." I opened the door and got out. Intuition told me that there was more to the story. Before I slammed the door shut I leaned in. "Do you think he shot his business partner?"

"I think you better be careful." Vance answered curtly, cutting off further discussion. "Good night."

I thanked him for the ride and shut the door. Vance waited in his car until I got into mine. Then he pulled away and drove past me. I started my car and rolled my window down for some air. It was well after midnight. The rain had formed in puddles around the cracks and crevices of the sidewalk and the wind was gasping in short breaths. I thought of the kid I hurt and I wondered if he would make it through the night alive.

THREE

I WAS EXHAUSTED BY the time I got home and crabbier still since I couldn't find a parking space. I live in NW Portland and there are five times as many cars as there are places to park. After twenty minutes of prowling for a space I gave up and parked in the lot of Trader Joe's market. I ignored the tow warning and hiked the nine blocks home to my apartment. When I got there I wished I had picked up a super sized bottle of Tylenol. I had a hurricane of a headache and I needed something for it—like a day job where the clients don't get killed.

I live at NW 25th and Lovejoy in the Hillside Manor Apartments, a white building with a green awning at the entrance. The rent is pretty pricey—725 dollars a month for a one bedroom apartment. Two years ago I only paid 450 a month. The shops and trendy restaurants that line 21st and 23rd Avenue have gotten more upscale—in effect raising the rents for the whole area. At one time this neighborhood was home to students, artists, and retirees. The most popular coffee shop was a place called Quality Pie. The food was delicately flavored with grease and the service was surly on a good day. I loved it. Now the streets are littered with gourmet coffee chains and restaurants that serve things like apple brandy marinated chicken breast. I miss the good old days when food was fried.

I unlocked the security door at the front entrance to the building, checked my mailbox, and walked down the hall to my apartment on the first floor. I unlocked my door and pushed it open as my neighbor Stan Oscram bounded down the hall in a neon orange jogging suit. He looked like an over-sized traffic cone. Stan is forty something with a big nose that he likes to stick in my business. He looked at me and then at his watch. I noticed that he had picked up a big bag of Cheetos during his midnight run.

"Late date, huh Jane?" He leered at me expectantly like I would spill out some juicy details. Although I don't know much about Stan, I strongly suspect him of being a pervert.

"Yeah, yeah," I said sourly as I went inside my apartment and shut the door on his disappointed face. I need to move.

I took a look at my mail and groaned. All of it was addressed to Jim Lerner in Apartment 2-8. He lives one floor above me. At this moment he was probably gasping at my Visa bill. Oh well. I'd trade bills with him later. I ripped his bill open. His balance was $59.99. Maybe I wouldn't trade. I set the bills and my keys on my desk and went to the kitchen for something to eat. What I needed now was a big bowl of Cap'n Crunch and a twelve hour nap. It felt good to be home.

I poured my cereal, added full fat milk and ate it standing up by the sink. When I was done I washed it down with a straight shot of Jack Daniel's, then I took a scalding bath and went to bed. I didn't sleep well. I dreamt of DeOrca. He was whispering something in my ear but I couldn't hear it—his throat had a hole shot through it.

I woke up with a start and looked around the bedroom. I was alone—as usual. I got out of bed and checked the closet to make sure. No skeletons. I looked at the clock. It was after twelve. I had slept the entire morning away and I still felt sapped. I took a deep breath and went to the bathroom to take a shower. I think better when I have clean hair.

I was blow drying my hair when the phone rang. I ran for it, but when I picked it up all I heard was a dial tone. I set it down and looked at my relic of an answering machine. I had three messages. I have voice mail for work but at home I prefer the old fashioned way of phone messaging. I pushed the play button and went to my bedroom to get a robe. No need to flash the neighbors.

The first call was from my friend Maggie. She had heard about the incident on the eleven o'clock news and wanted to know if I was okay. The second call was from a college student selling circus tickets. The third call was from Elana DeOrca.

"Jane Lanier?" The voice was hushed and somber. "This is Elana DeOrca. I'm sorry to call so late, but Sam said it would be okay—and that I could trust you. He gave me your number. The police were just here to tell me that my husband was killed in your office. We need to talk. I'll try you again tomorrow." The phone clicked off abruptly.

I stood still and thought of the blood on my desk. I hadn't even stopped to consider whether or not DeOrca had a family. I replayed the message. Sam who? I wondered as I went to the bedroom to put on some clothes. I knew a lot of Sams.

I got dressed and went to the window to peek out. The clouds hovered, threatening to break open over the apartment building across the street. I was about to turn away when I heard the scream of a fire engine. I opened my bedroom window and leaned out. Cold air caught my face. I listened intently. The sound of a siren faded several blocks away. I shivered and shut the window.

I called directory assistance for Elana DeOrca's phone number but it was unlisted. I moved restlessly about my apartment trying to figure out my next move. A man had been murdered in my office. Why? How? I made some hot chocolate, went to the living room and sat down in my overstuffed chair. It's my favorite thinking place. From it I can see the flags waving on the Fremont Bridge through my kitchen window. I looked out that window and thought back to last night.

Peter the security guard had meant to kill me, I was sure. But why? Did he know it was me? And how did he get his head bashed in? Did he fight with DeOrca—or someone else? And why did DeOrca come to see me in the first place?

Unanswered questions were making me feel freaky. I pulled my coat from the closet and picked up my keys and purse. I had to do something or I would go crazy. I decided to swing by the Galleria. Maybe the killer had decided to return to the scene of the crime.

I left my apartment and went outside. The rain had stopped, leaving the air crisp and damp with the faint aroma of smoke. Bonfire season. I put my gloves on to warm my hands and looked around for my car.

The streets were lined, bumper to bumper with cars, but I didn't see the Cabriolet. I remembered then that I had left it in the parking lot of Trader Joe's last night. Hopefully, they didn't have it towed. I turned and started to walk in the direction of the store. A police car with flashing lights zipped past me.

When I got closer to Trader Joe's I found out why.

Black smoke filled the sky. Two fire engines barricaded the parking lot. An ambulance pulled away from the sidewalk with its sirens screeching as I arrived. A crew of firefighters were hosing down a row of flaming cars. One of them used to be mine.

"OH MY GOD!" I gasped, panicked. I stepped forward, into the path of a police officer. She turned around. Her sweaty face had a stern expression.

"Step back!" she ordered. "I want you to get across the street. NOW. It's not safe."

I made my way across the street. A cop was taking statements from store employees wearing red aprons. Several shoppers clutching grocery bags were chattering in excitement to each other about the accident. I sank down on the curb next to a middle aged bald man in a red apron.

"What happened?" My voice sounded strange to my ears. This couldn't be real. Across the street a firefighter trained his hose on a blazing basket of groceries.

The man looked up. His face was flushed and his brown eyes were bloodshot. A cigarette was shaking in his fingers. He flicked the ash into the street.

"Hell if I know. I was inside unloading potatoes, and I heard a big explosion. It sounded like I was back in Nam. That car on the end…" He paused and pointed to my car, now a charred metal skeleton. "…caught fire and it spread to the other cars in the lot. The police think it might have been a bomb."

"Was anyone hurt?" I held my breath.

"A customer. He was loading his car with groceries when the fire started. He was cut by the flying glass. The ambulance took him away."

I put my head in my hands. I felt sick. Was this my fault somehow?

"Are you okay?" a female voice asked.

I looked up. The cop who had ordered me across the street was standing there. She was young with short, dark hair, her face flushed from the heat. A gun bulged from the holster on her hip.

"One of those cars was mine," I squeaked. I knew I sounded pathetic but so what?

"Which one?"

We both looked over at the lot. The firefighters had the blaze under control, but the area was still hazy with smoke.

"The convertible." I pointed it out.

"No kidding!" She whistled. "Officer Crebs is going to want to talk to you. C'mon."

I stood up and followed her across the street. A television reporter inserted himself into the action, trying to get the story from one of the cops. The cop stopped talking as the policewoman and I approached. Our eyes met. I recognized him from last night. He was blonde, late thirties, with a stocky build and tired blue eyes. He had taken a Polaroid picture of me before I was questioned by the homicide detectives.

"What's going on?" He asked the cop I was with as he

moved past the reporter. The reporter, a baby faced kid in an overcoat two sizes too big for him, looked a little pissed off.

"Crebs, the convertible was her car," she answered, jerking her thumb at what was left of my vehicle. The blast had ripped out my car's right front door and the rear door was penetrated by metal shards. My convertible top was reduced to black shreds.

"It's you," he said to me.

"Yes," I admitted. "I'm having a really bad week."

"Do you know why anyone would blow up your car?"

I shook my head miserably.

"What exactly was in your car?"

"A spare tire, an overnight bag with a nightie and undies, a tennis racquet—" I glanced at the trunk of my car. It had a hole in it big enough to ram a grocery cart through it. "And a bomb, would be my guess."

"Any idea how that bomb got there?"

"No. And I still have no idea as to why a murdered man turned up on my desk last night."

"You better come down to the station with us," Officer Crebs said. "Dermott is going to want to talk to you."

Numbly, I followed him and the other cop to a squad car parked a block away. The grocery clerk I had been talking to watched, bug eyed, as I got into the back seat of the police car. He probably thought I was being arrested. Unfortunately for me, this wasn't my first time in the back seat of a police car. Trouble seems to be my sidekick.

Both officers were quiet during the ride and except for an occasional squawk from the radio, I was alone with my thoughts. Was someone trying to kill me? What for? Maybe I was supposed to die instead of DeOrca. It was too much of a coincidence to have two attempts on my life in two days. I closed my eyes and tried to think of more practical things. I'd have to fill out my insurance forms, get my office cleaned up—and call the mysterious Sam for Elana DeOrca's phone number. I slapped my head. Officer Crebs looked over but didn't say anything. I gave him a foolish little smile. I remembered which Sam Elana was talking about now. How could I forget Sam, the security store man? Oh well, I'd deal with him later.

Crebs pulled into a parking spot in front of the Central Precinct on Second Avenue. I followed him and his partner to the double doors and went in. A sign in front warned: "Notice! Prohibited items. Violators subject to arrest. No weapons of any kind, including firearms, knives, slugging or striking instruments, alcohol." This place would be no fun at all. We stopped at the front desk, and an officer behind a glass partition checked my driver's license and issued me a visitor's pass. The female officer left, and Crebs and I took the elevator to the thirteenth floor. I noticed that there were no buttons between the first and eleventh floors.

We got off the elevator and walked towards a set of double glass doors that read: "Detectives Division". Crebs unlocked the door and I followed him in. To my left I could see stacks of in/out boxes for the different divisions on the floor. I read them quickly; sex crimes, fraud, domestic violence. Looked like most of the deadly sins were covered. Several "WANTED" posters were tacked to the wall nearby. I resisted peeking through to see if anyone I knew had made the dishonor roll. We walked past the photo gallery to cubicle land. The salmon colored cubicles were about four feet tall, with a view of the downtown area. I could see the Morrison and Marquam bridges outside, with a cruise boat sliding through the distance between them. Crebs moved through a maze of cubicles until we stopped at Dermott's desk. He had a phone cradled next to his ear and he was rubbing his forehead. He had obviously been up all night. He looked like shit: tired eyes, stubbly chin, same outfit from yesterday. Crebs pointed to a chair stacked high with papers and then muttered something about me being Dermott's problem now. I looked at the chair and sat on the edge of Dermott's desk. Might as well make myself comfortable.

I picked up a photo of a smiling blonde from Dermott's desk. I was surprised that Dermott had a girlfriend. With his personality, I had him pegged as more of a loner type.

Dermott slammed down the phone and snatched the photo from my hand. "Get your ass off my desk—"

"There's no where else to sit," I replied irritably. "And I'm not here for the fun of it—someone is trying to kill me." I told him about my car.

"Do you think this might be connected to the murder last night?" I asked.

"You tell me." He was still pissed.

"I've already told you everything I know. It's time for you guys to get on the ball. How's the security guard? Have you been able to question him?"

Dermott stood up. "I want to talk about that—but not yet. Wait here. I'll be back in a minute."

I leaned against Dermott's desk. He returned a few minutes later with a middle aged African American woman with flecks of gray in her close-cropped hair. Her look was all business; brown suit, sensible shoes, crisp white blouse. I'll bet her underwear was even starched. She was carrying a notebook.

"Detective Vance isn't in today, so Detective Garrett will be filling in," Dermott explained. Detective Garrett gave me a stiff smile and a once over. "Let's go to a conference room. I think the one near the captain's office is free."

We followed Dermott out into the corridor. We walked past a holding room where I could hear someone yelling their guts out. A sign outside the door read: "Please leave prisoners handcuffed." There was an open holding room next to the occupied one. I glimpsed a bare cement cell with a bench. Thankfully, Dermott kept walking. He stopped at a small con-

ference room, opened the door and gestured inside. It was furnished with a table and several cushioned chairs. A large
window afforded a view of the downtown traffic. We took our
chairs. It was different from the stark windowless room of last
night. Dermott got straight to the point.

"Did you kill Federico DeOrca?"

I glared at him. "I don't have time for this, Detective. I
already told you how I found him. If you don't believe me then
book me. Until then let's be reasonable. Have you ruled out
the security guard?" I threw Peter Sundstrom to the dogs.
Maybe he wasn't so innocent after all.

Dermott gave me a deadly stare. I didn't flinch. Garrett was
taking notes.

I hoped that she was writing something along the lines of
"Lanier refused to take any crap from Detective Dermott."

"For the most part, yes," Dermott said testily. "But we
can't ask him any questions now. He's in intensive care."

"Oh." The news sobered me. Dermott paused for a moment
to let the news sink in before he continued.

"Do you want to tell me how your fingerprints got all over
DeOrca's body?"

He was exaggerating. "They weren't all over. I had to
check and see if he was okay."

"By going through his pocket?" He glared at me.

I kept my mouth shut. He was guessing. There was no way
he could know for sure. Even if I had left a print he couldn't
have run it through the Automated Fingerprint Information
System so fast. Still, the next time I frisk a corpse I'm going
to wear gloves.

Dermott leaned back in his chair. "You can tell me or you
can tell a grand jury."

"I'm not a murderer." I sputtered. "I'm a poorly paid
private eye."

"So what was a man like DeOrca doing in your office?"

"Hell if I know. Maybe he was looking for somebody. I specialize in missing persons cases."

"Is that all you do?"

"No. In this business you need to diversify or you'll end up eating cat food. I also work as a subcontractor for a law firm in Portland. Research, interviewing witnesses, grunt work. On my own I've tracked down a couple of dead beat dads, I've done some background checks, served some subpoenas and now and then I work as a loss prevention consultant." I stopped for breath. "We went over my work experience last night. Since then my car's been blown up. I'm tired and I'm cranky. You don't want to hear my story again. What's going on here?"

"What's going on here is a murder investigation. And you better cooperate unless you want to be number 59 for the year."

"Number 59?" I looked at Detective Garrett. "What's he talking about?" She shrugged and Dermott answered.

"Murder victim 59. That bomb in your car was a professional job."

FOUR

DAYLIGHT WAS STARTING to wane by the time I left the station. Although Dermott and Garrett refused to go into a lot of detail, I was led to believe it was no ordinary fire cracker that cooked my car. I found a pay phone on the corner and called my insurance company, then I called a cab to take me to a car rental place. I needed a car, that was all there was to it. Private eyes don't take the bus.

I waited for fifteen minutes. The Rip City cab arrived, and I walked over and got inside. The inside of it was coated with plastic, just like the police car. I gingerly sat down on the edge of the seat. The driver glanced in his rearview mirror.

"Where to?" he asked as he flipped on the meter.

"Hertz Rent a Car on Third and Pine, please."

The driver was a big guy with white hair and yellowish teeth. A dusting of dandruff had fallen on his shoulders. He hummed a happy little song to himself as he maneuvered through traffic. He looked like he might be a talker.

"Hey," I said, leaning closer. "You might be able to help me out with something."

The driver looked up. "Sure, doll. What is it?"

"Did you hear about the guy that was murdered last night?"

The driver's brows knitted in a frown. "Yeah, it was in the papers." His voice was suspicious.

"Well, it happened in my office. I'm a private investigator." I paused and the driver waited for me to continue. "The man who was murdered was dropped off in front of my building in a Rip City cab. I was wondering if you might have heard something."

The driver was quiet for a moment before he spoke. "I dropped the guy off. The police already came by to question me. I don't know anything. I picked him up at a bar downtown and brought him to the Galleria."

"What bar?"

"The Starlight Lounge. Not a place for a nice gal like you."

I decided to take that as a compliment. "Do you remember if he was carrying anything?"

"A briefcase. I offered to put it in the trunk but he wanted to hang on to it. It was a fancy one with a combination lock on it."

"What color?"

"Uh, silver metal."

"Did the guy say if he was going someplace? To the airport maybe?"

"He didn't say. He was real quiet—like he had something on his mind. I didn't bother him. In this business you have to get a handle on that. I don't talk unless the other person starts the conversation. Some people want to be left alone."

"You have a good memory," I remarked.

The cabbie laughed. "Not every guy leaves a fifty dollar tip for a five buck fare." His smile subsided as he pulled in front of the car rental place. "Too bad about what happened to him. It's a crazy world."

"Yep," I said absently as I paid him five bucks and got out. "Thanks. You've been a big help." I waved away the change and he tipped his hat at me. I turned to go into Hertz.

The Hertz Rent a Car office has a large window facing the street. I could see a sleepy looking kid shuffling through forms at the counter. I went inside and rented a couch on wheels, making sure to sign up for all of the optional insurance. The clerk and I exchanged "you sucker" grins as I handed over my Visa and he handed over the keys.

I left the car rental and waited for the teenage attendant to get my car from the parking garage. My next logical step was to visit Sam to find out more about the DeOrca lady before we spoke. She probably could use some answers and I was fresh out.

I looked up as the attendant zoomed down the ramp and screeched to a halt in front of me. I handed the kid my receipt and got in the car. I hoped the woman didn't think I had anything to do with her husband's death although I do admit the circumstances looked a little suspicious. And how did Sam figure into all of this?

Sam Madsen owns Portland Protective Services, a security consulting firm that installs surveillance equipment and alarms. The place has a storefront in the Hollywood district that sells closed circuit cameras, stun guns and those fake food items like Campbell Soup cans that you can store your valuables in. Sam is an ex-private investigator who moved to town a few months ago. I dropped by his place when he opened, to check him out. We kind of hit it off. Since then he's managed to steer several clients my way. Mostly crazies with no money. I hope I have the chance to return the favor some day.

I started the car and headed towards the Steele Bridge to cross over to northeast Portland. It was starting to get foggy out and the headlights of the oncoming cars seemed to hurl through the mist. I made a brief stop on fast food row, also known as Weidler Street, and picked up two tacos from Taco Bell. I ate them as I wound my way through the Irvington neighborhood. I like to admire the big houses in the area. Most of them were constructed in the building boom before World War I. I passed several three story houses. They became smaller as I approached the Hollywood business district.

Portland Protective Services is located between a dry cleaners and a bakery. A sign in the window advertised a special on stun guns. Might have to get myself one. I parked in the lot and looked at my watch. It was a little after six. I hoped I would have a chance to catch Sam before he went out to drink his dinner.

A muscular guy with a goatee looked up from a cash register with narrowed eyes when I walked in. "We're closed," he informed me as he punched a button on the till. "If you want something you'll have to steal it." I glanced around the shop. It was stocked with a displays of things like fake book safes, bionic hearing devices and mace. The place smelled like new carpet.

"That's okay. Actually I'm looking for Sam. Is he here?"

The burly guy stuffed a wad of cash into a bank deposit bag before answering. Apparently he didn't think I was much of a threat. If he knew how poor I was he'd make me wait outside.

"Yeah, just a minute." He disappeared through a hallway behind the counter. I amused myself by looking at a miniature microphone disguised as a bug. He returned a minute later pulling a leather jacket on.

"Sam's in his office. You can go on back."

"Thanks." I went around the counter and followed the hallway to the back of the store. It consisted of a small room with bars on the windows. There was a table heaped with newspapers and donut boxes. A beat up old beige couch was next to the wall. Sam's desk faced the doorway. He stood up as I came in.

Sam is one of the coolest guys I know. He's a tall man, Native American, in his late thirties, with dark hair slicked back into a ponytail. He was wearing a black suit with a black tee shirt underneath. When he reached forward to shake my hand I noticed the outline of a shoulder holster beneath his jacket. He motioned me to a chair and sat down behind a large dented green desk that was surprisingly tidy. The only object on it was a picture of himself next to a boat. Behind Sam I could see a computer that had an outer space screen saver on it.

"Hi, Sam," I said as I sat down on a metal folding chair.

"Jane, what can I do for you?" Sam said, as he leaned back in his chair and put his boots on the desk.

"I wanted to talk to you about Elana DeOrca. She left a message on my home phone that you had given her my number. You probably already know her husband was murdered in my office. You didn't plan that just to irritate me—did you?" My voice was a little more shrill than I intended.

Sam smiled and shook his head. "Course not," he said softly.

I melted a little. "What did DeOrca's wife say to you on the phone?"

The smile slid off of Sam's face. "She said that she needed to get in touch with you right away. She sounded pretty upset. The police had just been by to break the news to her."

"Did she say anything else? Like why her husband might have come to see me?"

"No, nothing like that. I just gave her your number. It's in the book." Sam gave me a quizzical look. "You don't know why DeOrca came to see you?"

I ignored the question. "How do you know the DeOrca family? From what I hear they're kind of a notorious bunch."

Sam tilted his head to the right. "We're neighbors. Freddie DeOrca owns the dry cleaners next door. He stopped by when I first opened and we talked. Went out and had a few beers. After that he started to throw a little business my way. He also has a trucking business and some restaurants. The guy had his fingers in a lot of pies. He complained to me about some recent break ins. I wired his warehouse with an alarm system before it burned down."

"Great alarm system," I commented. "The fire was pretty recent then?"

"Only works when you turn it on," Sam replied, unperturbed. "The fire was very recent—less than a month ago. He had a large warehouse in the River District that went up in flames during the middle of the night. DeOrca lost two large trucks full of cargo that were supposed to be delivered to his restaurants. The place was insured for over two million bucks."

"Which restaurants did he own?"

"A chain called El Mesa Del Rey. He started out with just one place but now he has restaurants all over the Northwest."

"Hmm. This fire—it sounds like arson doesn't it?"

"Maybe. Maybe not. The Fire Marshall said that the fire started in the kitchen area—a coffee pot was left on or something like that."

"Sam, do you know why anyone might want to kill DeOrca?"

Sam's face turned blank. "No."

"All right. Well, I better be going." I stood up. "Do you have a number for Mrs. DeOrca? It might be easier if I can get in touch with her instead of her trying to track me down."

"Sure." Sam flipped through his rolodex and copied her phone number down. He handed me a slip of paper and I slipped it in my purse.

"I appreciate this. You're a big help—for once."

Sam chuckled as he stood up. "I'll see you out. I'm ready to call it a day." Sam grabbed his coat, turned off the lights and we walked out to my car.

"Nice boat," Sam said as I unlocked the door of the rental and got inside. "I didn't figure you for the skipper type."

"It's a rental, Sam. Somebody blew up my car this afternoon."

A strange look passed over Sam's face, then he bent down to speak in my ear. For a moment I thought he was going to kiss me good bye.

"Be careful or they'll kill you," Sam whispered. He stood up and shut my door with a quick motion then turned to walk to his car.

Who would kill me? Chilled, I watched him drive away. Fear was starting to gnaw at my nerves. I turned on the headlights, started the car, and headed back into the fog.

FIVE

I DON'T CONSIDER MYSELF a sissy but I slept with the light on that night. I woke up early, threw on my sweats and drove to Lincoln High School to do a few laps around the track. When I was done I thought I was going to die. I go to the gym with my friend Kelly a couple times a week, and recently we've taken up running. I hate it but it seems necessary what with a phantom killer on the loose.

Once home I jumped in the shower and listened to the phone ring as I rinsed the shampoo out of my hair. The answering machine clicked on and I could faintly hear a very familiar voice.

It was Henry Sullivan, a reporter for Channel 7. I was not surprised to hear from him. His nickname in the news circle is Mr. Ambition because he'll go to great lengths to get a hot story. He's the kind of guy who would sneak into a wedding dressed as a bride if the groom was the target of his interview. It's only a matter of time before he'll be crowding Dan Rather out of his anchor chair.

I turned off the water, dried myself, and wrapped a towel around my head turban style. Henry was saying something like "So call me" when I picked the phone up.

"Hi, Henry."

"Jane! You're home. I was just leaving a message. I wanted to know if we could talk about the incident in your office."

"You're not outside are you?" I felt slightly panicked as I tiptoed out to my window. I pulled the drapes aside a bit to see if the Channel 7 van was parked outside. The last thing I needed was to be on the news with nothing on except for the towel around my head.

"No, but I can be there in fifteen minutes."

"Actually, Henry, I'm not giving any interviews—on the record." I said it as nicely as possible. He had done me a big favor recently by highlighting a case I had solved involving a runaway. The publicity had been good for me, generating a few leads. I didn't want to alienate him. Besides, he was very, very cute.

"Oh." The disappointment in his voice made me soften a little. I was ready to cave in when he asked me out to dinner.

"A business dinner?" I was skeptical. "Are you going to bribe me with chocolate cake? You must think I'm easy."

"Not at all." Henry assured me. "However, my sources tell me you're single—"

"Sources? You mean you saw my name and phone number on the wall of the men's room?"

Henry laughed and we made plans to meet at eight. I hung up and returned to the bathroom to blow-dry my hair. A good mood was washing over me all of a sudden.

I got dressed and walked to Jamie's restaurant on Twenty Third Avenue for breakfast. It was a crisp and cold day—apple crunching and leaf kicking weather. The trees lining the street were ablaze with leaves of reds, oranges, and yellows. A single perfect, gold one fluttered to the ground. I stepped on it and picked up a copy of the *Oregonian* from the corner newsstand.

Jamie's was packed with the Sunday bed head, brunch crowd. I made my way to the counter. Several of the patrons were wearing wrinkled sweats that appeared to have been slept in. The neighborhood regulars, including myself, treat the restaurant like their own personal kitchen except this kitchen dates back forty years. It's a fifties style joint, complete with a jukebox, a black and white checkered floor, and a shiny red moped bolted to the wall. The specialty of the house is fried cow. Minnie, the waitress, looked over at me as I hoisted my butt on a stool. Her arms were laden with pancake plates and she was smacking a big wad of gum. "Be with ya in a minute," she called.

"Great," I mumbled as I opened up the paper. The Sunday *Oregonian* is a thick edition loaded with slippery coupon inserts. I thumbed through, reading the funnies first, then the Metro section. I gasped as a headline leapt at me; "Man Found Shot in PI's Office." A grainy photo of Federico DeOrca stared out at me with fish-like eyes. I shuddered. There was a picture of me too—an old file photo taken two years ago on a bad face day. The zit on my forehead looked like a third eye. They must have gotten it from the *Seattle Times* or the DMV. I quickly read the article. The details of the murder were outlined but there was no mention of the missing suitcase or the condition of the security guard.

Minnie came over and leaned on the counter. "I read that story in the paper, Jane. I didn't know you were a private investigator. Must have been awful to find the body." She pushed a frizzy black strand of hair behind her ear, revealing a dangling skeleton earring. Minnie is big on holidays. At Christmas time she wears a Santa hat and jingle bells on her tennis shoes.

"Yeah, it was gross." I didn't want to think about it before I ate. I ordered coffee, scrambled eggs, fried potatoes, and toast. Minnie paused after she scribbled down my request.

"My uncle is a private investigator. Maybe you know him. Name's Eddie Dickerson."

I cringed. I did know him. I met him last summer in Seattle at the Northwest Private Investigator's conference. He's in his mid forties, stringy hair, and he introduced himself to everyone in James Bond fashion as "Dickerson, Eddie Dickerson." I have a particular dislike for the man ever since he took my polite indifference as lust.

"Sure, I know him. Nice guy."

"He's available. Just got a divorce."

I choked.

Minnie laughed. "Just kidding. I know what he's like. In our family we refer to him as Uncle Dick. He comes in here sometimes. I'll try to warn you first."

"I appreciate that, Minnie and my tip will reflect it."

Minnie gave me a knowing smile then she hollered out my order to the cook. I went back to the paper. The article had said DeOrca had been charged once with murder. I needed to check that out. I looked at my watch; it was nearly noon. The library opened at twelve o'clock. I could swing by the periodical department and do a computer search. The *Oregonian* newspaper database was sure to turn up more info on the infamous DeOrca.

I ate breakfast, left the promised big tip, and returned home for my car. No sense in burning off all the grease I had just consumed. I drove downtown and snagged a parking spot in front of the library.

The Multnomah County Library is a massive four story structure built at the turn of the century. The iron gates guarding the door were open. I ran up to the door and took the marble stairs to the third floor Periodical room. I had to wait ten minutes for a computer but I was richly rewarded when I logged on. There were several references to DeOrca. Most of them were within a four month time period in 1988. I copied the names of the newspapers and the corresponding dates, and moved to the microfiche carousels in the rear of the library.

A librarian helped me to find the microfiche cartridges I wanted. I loaded the most recent onto the machine and turned the levers. A year's worth of headlines whizzed past my eyes. I turned the knob more slowly until I found an October article detailing a warehouse fire on the DeOrca property. The Fire Marshall had not determined the cause of the blaze but damages were estimated to be two million dollars. Interesting but not bloody. I popped out the cartridge and inserted one for 1988. I scanned through the first part of the year until I came to an article dated February 17, 1988. It was entitled: "Portland Businessman Murdered at the Starlite Lounge."

I read the article. Everett Crombie, a forty-six-year-old Caucasian man, was found murdered in his office at the Starlite Lounge. He co-owned the bar and also served as the manager. A janitor discovered him at three o'clock in the morning after the bar had been closed. I fast forwarded the microfiche to the next week. The headline announced: "Man Charged in the Murder of Business Partner." A blurry picture showed DeOrca being led off in handcuffs. Detective Vance could be seen on the edge of the photo. The article said a gun with DeOrca's fingerprints and those of the dead man, was recovered in a dumpster in Gresham. DeOrca was indicted and the trial was set for November. I buzzed through the microfiche to November. "Mistrial!" The Oregonian declared. A juror had disappeared the day the verdict was to be read. In addition, the murder weapon had been "lost" in the police evidence room. The judge was forced to declare a mistrial and DeOrca was released. One other detail caught my eye.

Everett Crombie was killed by a single gunshot wound to the throat.

SIX

I MADE COPIES OF the other articles to read later and left the library. What was the significance of the shot to the throat? I wondered as I got in my car. Maybe Elana DeOrca could tell me. I opened my purse and looked for the phone number Sam had given me. It was gone.

Damn. I thought as I dumped the purse upside down. I remembered tucking it inside last night...

I started the car and set out in the direction of NE Portland. If Sam was in his office I could ask for it again—but I really hated for him to know I lost it. My second option was to try the DeOrca-owned dry cleaners/laundromat.

The sign hanging from Sam's shop read "Sorry Closed". I looked over at the Suds and Duds. There was a big cleaning special sign taped to the dirty window. I could see a woman with big, teased blonde hair, and fake and bake orange skin leaning against the cash register. It looked open. I got out of my car and went inside.

The clerk was reading a copy of *Cosmopolitan* as I walked up to the counter. She finished an article on "The Ten Best Ways to Turn on Your Man" before she noticed me.

"Hi," she said in a bored voice as she set down her magazine. "Do you have your claim ticket?"

"I'm not here to pick up any dry cleaning. I need to get hold of Mrs. DeOrca." I handed her my business card.

She looked at the card and shook her head. "Sorry, can't help you."

I took ten dollars out of my purse and laid it on the counter. The clerk put her magazine on top of it and looked around. There was no one in the laundromat except for a young mother putting clothes in a dryer and a kid eating detergent. Neither paid any attention to us.

"I don't have her number, it's unlisted, but I can tell you where to find her," she said under her breath.

"Good," I said as I pulled out another five and laid it on top of the Cosmo woman. "What can you tell me about Federico DeOrca? He owned this place, didn't he?"

"Lower your voice." She pulled a radio out from under the counter and flipped a switch. Sounds of AC/DC filled the room in accompaniment to the thumping dryers. Personally, I thought the dryers sounded better. "DeOrca was one of the owners of this dump. He's dead, ya know."

"I've heard that. Who are the other owners?"

"Just one. I don't know his name but he's been by with Mr. DeOrca a couple of times lately. I heard old Freddie refer to the guy as his partner. He's got dark hair, wore fancy clothes, buff. I think he made Mr. DeOrca a little nervous."

"Why?"

"Oh, I don't know. He just seemed a little uptight. That's all."

"Do you know his name?"

"Nope."

"What about Mrs. DeOrca? Is she involved in the business?"

The clerk gave me a hard look. "She doesn't do laundry." The door of the laundromat opened and a bald guy walked in with a basket of dirty shorts. "'Scuse me a sec—I gotta help this customer."

An office door opened in the back by the carousel of dry cleaning orders that were covered in plastic. "Rita!" A portly, red-faced man dressed in a shirt, loosened tie and slacks, stuck his face out. "Has the truck arrived yet?"

"Nope," Rita said as she made change. The man came out of

his office. His shirt was wrinkled like he had slept in it. He went to the window and stared out. Beads of sweat dotted his forehead.

I took another five out of my purse and laid it on the counter. "For my order. Thanks," I said. Rita picked up the money and slipped it in her bra. Then she took a pad, scribbled a few lines, and pushed it toward me. It read "On 33rd Avenue, turn right on Klickitat. It's the mansion at the top of the hill."

"Good bye," she said firmly.

I left.

SEVEN

THE HOUSES ON Alameda ridge overlook the city. It's a nice place to visit but I couldn't afford to live there. The neighborhood is like a club—you need a million dollars or you don't get membership. A former governor used to live there. So did a murdered mobster.

The DeOrca residence is the grandest of all the houses on the ridge. It was built in 1915 for a railroad tycoon and it sprawled over an entire city block. The front entrance of the house is bordered by marble pillars and statues of angels with frozen smiles frolic in the surrounding gardens. I climbed two sets of stairs to the door and rang the bell. I felt like I was visiting some kind of museum for rich people.

A security camera was aimed at the door. A red light blinked at the base of it. I flashed a smile.

A maid answered the door. She was a white woman, about seventy, with a poodle perm framing her face in a fluffy white halo. The black uniform she wore hugged her love handles. Sensible lace up shoes completed the outfit.

"I'm looking for Mrs. DeOrca. Is she here?" I handed her my business card.

She took it and gave it a doubtful look. "I can't read this dear, without my glasses. Is she expecting you?" Her tone was loud.

"Yes." I lied. "Is it okay if I come inside?"

"You'll need to speak up, sweetie. I can't hear you." She pulled the door open. "I'll let Mrs. DeOrca know you're here."

I stepped into the entry hall and took a look around. A big

round polished mahogany table stood in the center of the hall. There was a grandiose floral arrangement of white lilies on top of it. A card tucked into a plastic pitchfork read "With Deepest Sympathy." Beyond the table I could see a marble staircase rising to meet an enormous leaded glass window on the first landing.

"Why don't you wait in the living room." The maid gestured to a room off the entry hall. "It will be just a minute."

"Great."

She shuffled off and I walked into the living room. It had a fireplace big enough to stand in if one were the Joan of Arc type. Oriental rugs covered the floor and antique furniture was arranged in conversational groupings. A grand piano stood at the other end of the room next to three windows covered with crimson velvet drapes. The windows afforded a panoramic view of the city. I moved closer to get a better look. As I did so I noticed there were two holes in the glass. I reached up to touch them.

"They're bullet holes." The voice was cynical and crisp.

My hand dropped and I turned around, startled. A woman had entered the room. She was probably in her early forties, her skin surgically smooth and her body coat hanger thin. Glossy dark brown hair fell to her shoulders. She wore a form fitting black dress and a pair of diamond earrings flashed at me from her ears.

"Oh." I moved away from the window with my hand extended. I'd ask about the bullet holes later. "I'm Jane Lanier. You must be Mrs. DeOrca."

"Call me Elana." She shook my hand and gave me a social smile. "I'm glad you came by. I've been wanting to talk to you. Won't you sit down?"

"Thanks." I crossed the room and perched on the edge of a chair named after a dead French king. Elana sat down on the couch and leaned forward.

"Something strange is going on." Her voice was almost a whisper. Duh, I thought. I bit my lip.

"I know. I'm very sorry. This must be a great shock—"

"Yes, it is." Elana interrupted. "I can't believe that someone killed my husband. He's too mean to die."

Her words hung in the air, crystal clear. I laughed nervously, not sure what to say. The woman was obviously on some sort of medication.

She continued to think out loud. "Jane, did my husband say why he had come to see you? It's very important I find out. It might help me make sense of all this."

"Not really. He left a note on my door Friday afternoon while I was out of the office. The note said he wanted to meet with me that night at ten o'clock. He said he had an urgent matter to discuss."

"Hmm." Elana mused, wrinkling her forehead. She stood up and walked to the window.

"Well, do you have any idea at all of who might want your husband dead?"

"Everyone." She looked at the city of suspects below her.

"What?"

"He was not a nice man."

I was starting to get that impression. Still I needed to narrow down the suspects and Mrs. DeOrca now topped my list.

"Did you kill him?"

Elana turned and dismissed the idea with a wave of her hand. "No. I was at a fund raiser when my husband was killed. I have two hundred witnesses. And I had my photo taken with the president of the organization. I'm covered. But you were right to ask me." She gave me a look of approval. "I certainly had reason to do it. My husband was cheating on me. It's common knowledge."

"Why did you put up with it?"

Elana sighed. "What does it matter now? He's dead. And I want you to find his killer."

Was she offering me a job? I couldn't figure her out. By her own account her husband was dead and deserved to be.

"What about the police? Have you talked—"

"The police don't care." Elana interrupted. "My husband was a murderer, a drug dealer, a cheat and a louse, and those were his good qualities. Why should they care?"

"Why should you?" I shifted in my chair. "I mean if he was that bad…"

"He was." Elana assured me. "But I'm worried I'm going to be next." Her gaze drifted to the bullet holes in the window.

"Tell me about the bullet holes."

"Somebody shot at me. Last night." She spoke without emotion.

"You're kidding! What did the police say?"

"I didn't call them." She looked at me with a grave expression on her face. "I'm alone on this—and I have my reasons. That's why I need your help."

Curiosity kept my rear end glued to the chair. There are plenty of reasons why a citizen might avoid involving the police in a situation like this but most of them aren't good.

"Who would want you dead?"

Elana was still for a moment. "I can't say."

Can't or won't? I wondered. "Look, Mrs. DeOrca, I don't know what your husband was doing in my office. But I'd like to know myself. You don't need to tell me that something strange is going on. My car was blown up yesterday. I really can't believe it's a coincidence."

"Then they're after you too." Her face was white.

"Who are they?"

She lowered her voice. "You won't see them, you won't hear them, and you can't kill them. It's a business without buildings and all the employees are faceless. Their sole mission is to make money and anyone that gets in the way turns up dead."

"Did your husband get in—the way?"

"I think he did. He cashed a large insurance check for the corporation. He was supposed to turn the money over to the business but it was stolen from him before he could do it."

"Does this business have a name?"

"An unofficial one. It's known as Widows Inc."

EIGHT

"WIDOWS INCORPORATED?" I instantly had a vision of a widow-making factory with Barbie dolls in black dresses and hats packaged with a coffin for Ken. I made a face and shuddered.

"You have no idea—" Elana began. She stopped as a teenage boy entered the room. He was wearing ripped jeans that sagged on his scrawny frame and a tee shirt. There was a shadow of dark stubble on his shaved head but not on his face. His green eyes flicked quickly over me then he looked at Elana.

"Mom, I gotta get out of here. Can I borrow your keys?"

"No," Elana said with an edge to her voice. "I want you to stay in the house. Besides, you know you aren't allowed to drive anymore."

"Mom…" He protested, scraping his dirty hiking boot on the carpet. "I need air!"

"No." Her tone was final. The boy sniffed indignantly, looked at me, then swaggered out.

"Who was that?" I asked. The sound of his heavy boots could be heard thumping upstairs.

"My son, Sean." She sighed. "I don't know what to do with him."

"Is he taking his father's death hard?"

"Yes, though Federico was his stepfather. He never knew his biological father. He died when Sean was small."

"Ah. Well. Now about this widow making business—what else can you tell me?"

"I can tell you it exists," she said simply. The poodle permed maid shuffled into the room. We both looked up.

"Mrs. DeOrca." She bellowed in a loud voice. "The policeman is on the phone again."

Elana took the news calmly but I winced on her behalf. Thank goodness it wasn't her gynecologist on the line.

"Thank you, Frieda. Tell him it will just be a minute." Frieda nodded and left. Elana looked over at me. "I think this might take a while, Jane. I hope you'll look into this matter for me. I'm prepared to pay you generously for your time."

I thought about the body on my desk and the smoldering hunk of metal that used to be my car. I had to get to the bottom of this mess anyway and I might as well get paid to do it.

"I'll come back tomorrow. I think we need to discuss this further."

"Fine." She looked grateful. "The funeral is at noon. You're welcome to stop by afterwards."

"If I'm not intruding, I'd like to attend the service." My sister Bonnie once told me that killers like to show up for funerals and to observe anniversaries.

"That would be fine," Elana said, rising from the couch. "Now if you'll excuse me, I need to take this call."

"Sure. I'll see you tomorrow." I stood up.

Elana left the room, her heels tapping quickly down the hall. I couldn't resist taking one last look at the view. I moved to the window and traced my fingertips around the bullet holes in the glass. Outside I could see dark clouds gathering over the west side of Portland, obscuring some of the larger buildings downtown.

"What have I gotten myself into?" I wondered aloud.

NINE

THE KID WAS SITTING in my car when I got outside. I walked over to the passenger side and opened the door. His boom box was pounding out heavy metal.

"Get out," I said as I held the door open. Sean's head was tilted back against the headrest. He might have been sleeping but it was hard to tell since he was wearing a pair of silly assed sunglasses. There was a stretched out hanger on the dashboard. "What did you do?" I asked incredulously. "Break in?"

"Like I'd steal a piece of crap like this." Sean scoffed. He turned off the music so I could clearly hear his insults. His lip was curled in a scowl. He sat up and pulled a pack of cigarettes from the pocket of his denim jacket. "I need a ride to the store, so I thought I'd catch one from you. I'm almost out of smokes." He sniffed.

I sighed, shut the door, and walked around to the other side to get in. What the hell. I might as well take the kid to the store. But there was no such thing as a free ride in my car. He was going to have to pay up—in information.

"You don't look like my dad's type," Sean observed as I started the car and pulled away from the curb. Out of my rearview mirror I noticed a black Camaro as it crawled over the top of the hill leading to the DeOrca mansion.

"What do you mean?" I knew damn well what he meant. Little jerk.

"His other girlfriend is blonde." He sucked on his cigarette and blew the smoke in my direction. Then he sniffed again. I rolled down the window a crack. Elana had mentioned it was common knowledge her husband was cheating on her but it's pretty bad when even your own son knows.

"Your dad and I didn't date. In fact, I've never met him. He came to my office before he died and left a note. He wanted to hire me I think."

"Oh, you're the private dick, then. You don't look like one of those either."

I bit back a salty reply. "Which store do you want to go to? Is QFC's okay? It's only a few blocks away."

"Yeah, whatever." Sean took one last puff on his cigarette then tossed it out the window.

I drove past a park, then a middle school and pulled into the QFC parking lot. Piles of pumpkins were stacked in front of the store and a big sign in the window advertised a special on Halloween candy. Since I live in an apartment building I don't get trick or treaters but that doesn't stop me from stocking up anyway. There's nothing better on a rainy afternoon than lying on the couch, watching Oprah, and eating Snicker's bars until the floor is covered with little brown wrappers.

"Any chance of you buying me some beer?" Sean gave me an impish grin as he opened the door.

"Nope," I said cheerfully. I still hadn't forgotten his crack about not being his "dad's type."

"Aww." Sean got out of the car, slammed the door, and went into the store. I leaned back in the seat and turned the radio off. The black Camaro I had noticed at the DeOrca mansion pulled into the parking lot. A white guy in his early twenties with skin and short blonde hair got out. His face was dotted with zits. He was wearing a black leather jacket, black pants and boots. He tucked his hands into his jacket and strode into the store. He didn't take a cart.

I got out of my car and followed him in.

The store was crowded with shoppers. I followed the man,

watching him crane his neck as he walked past each aisle. He was looking for somebody. I turned to the check out lines and spotted Sean with his nose in a National Enquirer. The woman in front of him paid for her groceries and a courtesy clerk pushed her cart away. Sean stuffed the tabloid back in the rack and moved forward. When I reached the counter he was trying to persuade a skeptical clerk to sell him a package of Marlboros.

"He's only fourteen," I said to the clerk as I grabbed Sean's arm. "C'mon. We need to get out of here."

"What the hell!" Sean pulled his arm back, an angry look on his face.

"Someone is looking for you," I hissed. Sean's head whipped around. He caught sight of the guy in the leather jacket. He was standing in front of a huge cracker display. Their eyes met for an instant, and Sean shot past me. The guy in the leather jacket started to barrel forward but was blocked by a little old lady with a shopping cart. I followed Sean, leaving the clerk with her jaw hanging down.

I ran to the car. Sean was already inside, looking anxious. I opened the door, jumped in, and started the car just as the guy in the black leather jacket emerged from the store. I saw his hand go into his pocket as I peeled out of the parking lot.

"Omigod!" I took a right on 33rd Avenue into a sea of moving cars. "Sean! Who is he?!"

"Just a dude who is gonna kick my ass if he catches me. SHIT! Can you lose him?"

"Hang on." I gunned it through the intersection on Broadway and sailed through two signals, one green, one yellow, to Sandy Boulevard. The Camaro was two cars behind. I made a sharp right hand turn on Sandy. A Tri-Met bus was coming towards me from the other direction. I pulled in front of it and turned down a side street. I missed it by an inch but the Camaro plowed right into it as he attempted the same turn. I drove leisurely down the street, then around the corner to pull onto Sandy again. I knew the perfect hiding place. Sandy Boulevard is a commercial street lined with adult video stores and used car lots. I found a car lot advertising rent a wrecks and pulled into the middle of the row. A moment later the Camaro careened down the street. The front of it was bashed in.

"Sean, what is going on? That guy had a gun for God's sake."

Sean stared moodily out the window. "I owe him money. It's no big deal."

"Can't you ask your mom for it? You don't want a guy like that on your back."

Sean was silent. Then he sniffed. This sniffing business was driving me crazy.

"You have a cold?"

"No." His tone was defiant.

I put two and two together. He did have a cold—a cocaine cold. The guy chasing us was probably selling him drugs.

"Was he your dealer?"

Sean folded his arms. "What's it to you? Unless you want to buy something."

"Maybe I do." Right.

Sean looked at me again, sizing me up. Then he shook his head dismissing the idea. "Quit screwing with me. It's none of your business."

I looked out the window at the traffic shooting past. "Do you want me to go to the police station to report the guy in the Camaro? I'm pretty sure he didn't stop to give the bus driver his insurance information."

"Are you outta your mind?"

"Talk to me then. What's going on here?"

Sean slumped in his seat. "All right. He deals. What's it to you?"

Finally. Dialogue.

"Okay. Now let's talk about your stepfather."

"What are you? A shrink?"

"Hardly. But your stepfather was murdered in my office and I want to find out why. Do you think the guy in the Camaro had anything to do with it?"

"Nah. Nobody messes with Freddie the Whale." The boy's voice was proud.

"Well, somebody did or we wouldn't be sitting here talking."

Sean was silent.

I tried again. "Your stepfather left me a note saying that he had an urgent matter to discuss. Do you have any idea what it might have been?"

More silence.

"What about those bullet holes in the window at your house? Do you know how those got there?"

"I didn't do it."

"So, who did? And more importantly—why? Do you think your stepfather's business partner might have had something to do with it?"

"Leave him out of it. He didn't do nuthin. You wanna take my advice? Don't stick your nose where it don't belong. Otherwise you're gonna get your ass kicked."

"What?" I exploded. "If it wasn't for me, you would've gotten your ass kicked!"

He rolled his eyes. "Don't worry about me. He's history."

"Uh huh." I started the car and pulled out of the parking lot. A police car with flashing sirens was parked by the Tri-Met bus. Passengers milled about on the sidewalk. I decided to go the opposite direction and take the long way back to Sean's house. He was sullen for the rest of the trip. I pulled up to the curb and Sean grabbed his CD player and got out of the car.

"Thanks for the ride." He turned to walk away.

I rolled down the window. "Wait!"

Sean turned around.

"I have one more question. Where were you when your dad was murdered?"

"Jail."

"What?"

"I was on my way to a party with some of my buddies and the cops pulled us over. Poured out our beers. A whole case. None of us had been drinking yet but they hauled us in anyway. Mom was out at a fund-raiser so I was in a cell half the night. When she picked me up she gave me the bad news." His tone was matter of fact.

"Okay." It was no wonder Elana didn't want him driving. I pulled a business card from my pocket and handed it to him. "Give me a call if you think of anything that might help."

Sean stepped forward and grabbed the card out of my hand. I watched him slip around to the rear of the house as I pulled away from the curb. Sean was one messed up kid. Was it the drugs or his family?

My answering machine was blinking when I got home. I played the messages back. My mom had called and wanted to know about the dead man I found in my office. She also wanted to know if I was still hosting Thanksgiving. Mom is divorced. She lives in Seattle, where I grew up. She owns a bookstore on Queen Anne Hill. I get books every birthday and Christmas. Mostly hard bound classics I never read but every now and then she'll throw in a lurid romance as if to remind me that I should have one. My sister Bonnie, a cop with the Seattle PD, lives there too, with her husband Matt Polo. They have a daughter named Ginny, and a cat named Wham. Normally I spend the holidays with them but this year Thanksgiving is at my house. The thought fills me with more dread than finding a corpse in my office. I don't know how I got suckered into that one. I'm an apartment living, Lean Cuisine eating, single girl with no pots and pans. I guess I'll have to learn how to microwave a turkey.

I called mom back and relayed the story of the DeOrca murder so she could share it with her "Stitch and Bitch" sewing group. Mom is a murder mystery aficionado and watches re-runs of the show *Murder She Wrote* with Angela Lansbury. She grilled me so well she made the Portland homicide detectives look like weenies. After an hour I hung up and went to the kitchen for a Diet Coke. I cracked it open and settled into a chair with the photocopies from the library.

There were several articles about the Crombie murder, a few pictures of Elana from the society page, and two small blurbs in the business section. I looked at the ones from the murder trial first.

Everett Crombie was murdered early in the morning of February 17, 1988. The janitor found him slumped over his desk in a small office in the rear of the Starlite Lounge. He had been shot in the throat. Although there were over a hundred people in the club that night, no one remembered seeing Crombie, and no one had heard the shot that killed him. I flipped through some other articles. An anonymous tip led police to the murder weapon a week later. They found it in a restaurant dumpster in Gresham. Part of a fingerprint tied the gun to DeOrca. Police arrested him while he was attending Sunday Mass at Madeleine Church in NE Portland. To my disappointment there was no photo. Later a Multnomah County grand jury indicted him for murder. He retained a high powered lawyer from downtown to represent him.

Everything seemed to go his way after that. The judge was forced to declare a mistrial after a twenty-year-old juror named Sarah Winningham disappeared. Her friends thought she might have gone to Hollywood to audition for a movie role. The two alternate jurors were fortunate to have won round trip tickets to Paris, France. They left the country without notifying the judge of their plans. Then the murder weapon mysteriously disappeared from the police evidence

room. The DA's office declined to retry DeOrca and he was
freed. A photo showed DeOrca and his oily haired lawyer.
They were all smiles. I flipped through the other articles.
DeOrca bought a chain of Mexican restaurants six months
later. Then he acquired a trucking firm. Elana DeOrca was
featured in a few articles in the women's section. She wore a
long off the shoulder dress to a ball to benefit a drug abuse
rehabilitation clinic. In another photo she received an award
for her volunteer work for a battered woman's shelter. It
looked like the marriage of DeOrca and Elana was some kind
of sinner and saint type arrangement.

The phone rang. I eased myself out of the chair and
picked it up.

"Hello." I stretched the cramps out of my legs.

"Jane, this is Henry." His voice was cheery.

"Hi, Henry, what's up?"

"I'm in Salem right now, covering a story at the State
Capitol. I'm running a little late. I'd like to meet you somewhere around nine o'clock if that's all right with you."

"Fine." I suggested we meet at the Starlite Lounge. He
seemed a little mystified by my choice but he agreed to do it.

The Starlite Lounge is located on the edge of the downtown
area. It's a little seedy in sections despite its proximity to Waterfront Park and the city center area. The official designation
of the neighborhood is Old Town. Upscale bars and restaurants are within a few blocks of the homeless shelters and
charity missions. By day it's a thriving business district.
Families come downtown on the weekends to visit the outdoor
Saturday Market with dozens of vendors selling handmade
products and food items. Kids roller blade on the pavement
at Waterfront Park. At night, the world turns upside down and
the vampires wake. Drugs are sold in the shadows of
doorways. The strobe lights on the police cars compete with
the gaudy neon lights of porn shops. The homeless abandon

their cardboard houses and wander until daylight comes. The Starlite Lounge is located smack in the middle of Old Town. There's an adult video arcade on one corner and an art gallery on the other end of the street. Pictures of naked ladies can be found at both places.

I puttered around for the rest of the afternoon. Around eight o'clock I changed into a black stretch velvet turtleneck with a matching short wrap skirt. The turtleneck hid the purpled bruises on my neck very nicely. I rummaged around and came up with a pair of almost unsnagged black pantyhose. I finished the outfit with tiny diamond earrings, a college graduation present from my dad and stepmom, Cruella DeVille. Her real name is Camilla, but it's fun to tease her since she's short on humor. Dad married her when I was ten. She's a veterinarian, which I find hilarious, since Dad hates anything cute and furry. That's what he gets for leaving mom.

I went into the bathroom, applied makeup, then fluffed my hair. I slipped my feet into black heels and studied my reflection in the mirror. I looked good but the hookers in front of the video arcade wouldn't have anything to worry about. I called a cab and waited by the front door of the building until it arrived. The driver looked at me twice when I told him where I was going but he kept his mouth shut. I tipped him an extra dollar for his tact.

The sign on the Starlite Lounge was illuminated by bright flashing lights. It's a three story structure that has seen better days. The walls of the building were decorated with gang graffiti and peeling paint. Several of the lights on the Starlite Lounge sign had burned out so the place looked like the "tarlite lounge". I opened the door with the heavy brass handle and went in. The room was cloudy with smoke, and the ceiling was painted with faded silver stars. It was heaven for bar flies. Several red booths lined the walls. Tables filled the center space. All of them were occupied, mostly by old, overweight men. Some of them wore pinky rings, open shirts and toupees. Too bad I already had a date. In the rear of the room there was a small stage with a dirty red curtain. A sign next to the stage said "Miss Theresa LaSalle. Appearing nightly." Below the sign was an 8x10 glossy of a half naked woman adorned with strategically placed feathers. Although all the tables were taken I noticed a pair of empty seats at the bar. I walked over and sat down. The bartender, a big red headed guy, looked my way. He was filling a coffee mug with beer.

"What do you want? Besides me, I mean?" He chortled and took a belt from his mug.

"I'm fine right now. I'm waiting for someone." I tried to be nice so he wouldn't spit in my drink later. In college I had several friends in the fast food industry so I'm careful not to insult anyone that handles my food or beverages.

"Do you want some water while you wait?"

"Sure, that would be great." I smiled and tried to relax. There's no fun like waiting for a date by yourself in a bar. I could feel the eyes on me as I shrugged out of my long dark coat. It was as if I wasn't wearing a shirt for God's sake. I put my coat and purse on the stool next to me to save it. Thankfully, Henry arrived a minute later. He paused in the doorway and looked around. I waved and he made his way over. He must have come straight from work. He was wearing a suit, tie and overcoat. Very corporate. But no pinky ring.

Henry has the kind of personality that makes him a good looking man. Glancing at him you see an average fella— brown hair, brown eyes, six feet tall, more thin than muscular. But when he talks he draws you in. Even when he's on the news. He has a way about him that makes you think he's talking directly to you. I gave him a warm smile as he slid onto the bar stool next to me.

"Hi, Jane. You look great."

"Thanks." I stopped myself from pointing out the big zit on my cheek.

"What are you having?"

"I haven't ordered yet. I just got here. I think I'll have a glass of that fancy wine from a box."

"You got it," Henry said as he pulled out his wallet. The bartender drifted by, took our orders, and returned with a beer and a glass of wine. He set the wine down in front of me, giving me a wink. Henry caught it without comment. He pushed a ten towards the bartender then turned towards me. "What made you pick *this* bar?"

"I'm working on a case and I thought I'd check it out."

"It wouldn't have anything to do with the DeOrca murder, would it? I know he owned this place."

Henry would know. Mr. Reporter. "What else do you know about DeOrca?"

"Around the station he's known as the Teflon Triggerman. Rumor had it he was selling drugs out of this bar. You could order crack cocaine with your drink if you were a big tipper. Anyway his business partner complained and ended up dead over a dozen years ago. He was a suspect in a couple of other murders too but nobody could ever pin anything on him. How did you get mixed up with the man?"

"I'm not sure myself. But he was killed in my office and I'd like to know why. Let's just say I'm making a list of suspects."

"Anyone could have done it. Think about it." Henry took a pen from his pocket and started sketching an outline of the Galleria building on his cocktail napkin. "There's six exits in that building, if you count the sky bridge to the Smart Park or the underground parking lot." He quickly penned in doors. "Once you're out you hop Max to the train station or Greyhound."

"Did you do it, Henry?" I asked playfully. He had done some thinking about the case I could tell. I wasn't ready to lay my thoughts on the table yet. I might hear them repeated back to me on the five o'clock news.

"Nah. But if you want to catch a murderer, sometimes you have to think like one."

"True. But for now let's just soak up this killer atmosphere." I inhaled some of the stale smoke floating by.

Henry laughed and backed off. After we finished our drinks, I excused myself to go to the ladies room. The archway next to the stage led to a narrow hallway. The first door had a silhouette of a big breasted woman in a dress, the door across the hallway had the silhouette of a man. He was not anatomically correct. I walked past the restrooms, opening doors. The first door was locked. The second was full of extra chairs, stacks of liquor, boxes of wine, and other types of bar supplies. The window in the room was painted black. I wandered to the next door. There was a glittery homemade sign on it in the shape of a star. It said "Theresa LaSalle." A voice called out "just a minute" when I tried the door. The last door was a janitorial closet. I could hear some bumping and moaning behind that door so I left it alone and hurried back to the bar. Henry had his coat on and he was standing up. He was looking past me. I turned around to see a woman wearing either a swimsuit or a very short dress. She was making her way past some grabby drunks to the stage. She picked up the microphone to a smattering of applause.

"Are you ready?" Henry asked. He wisely dragged his eyes away from the stage to look at me.

I nodded and we went to Henry's car. It was a truck with white dog hair on the seat. I sat down gingerly, hoping to avoid making my wool coat a fur one. We drove to Papa Hayden's in my neighborhood for dessert. Over my favorite cake— "Death by Chocolate"—we played the "get to know you" game. I found out he had worked as a newscaster in the Midwest for several years, gradually working his way up to the bigger, Portland market. I mentioned I had worked as a journalist for a Seattle paper, but I didn't go into too many details. The last story I ever wrote for the paper was about a mayoral candidate. He was a principal at a local high school. I uncovered some information about his extracurricular activities with some of his students. My sources were unimpeachable. The mother of one of the students had contacted me to say that her fifteen year old daughter did not want to be silent any longer. I talked with my editor. We decided to do the interview (changing the name of the young girl to protect her identity), and talk to some other sources. If the story checked out, we would run it. It did. It was on the front page of the newspaper three weeks before the election. It created a furor. The man committed suicide a week later. I got the news at three o'clock one afternoon while I was sitting at my computer editing a candidate profile for a local school board race. My phone had been ringing off my hook all day because the Associated Press had decided to pick up the story and run it nationwide. I erased the copy I was working on, wrote my letter of resignation, and packed the contents of my desk. I tossed all the awards I had ever won in the trash. I put my letter of resignation in my editor's "in" box on my way out. Ten days later I packed my car with some of my belongings, and my sister Bonnie helped me drive a U-Hall truck with the rest of them to Portland. A few close friends know about what happened but it's not something I can talk about. Would the man have killed himself if someone else had written the story? I'll never know.

Henry and I lingered over coffee, swapped stories, and before we knew it were the only people left in the restaurant. We decided to get more dessert to go and to have it at my place.

TEN

AS LUCK WOULD HAVE IT, Stan Oscram poked his head out of his apartment as we walked to my door. He was holding a dirty magazine in his hand.

"Hi, Stan," I said in a "go home" type of voice. He didn't. Instead he walked out and joined us.

"Jane, I heard some noise coming from your place. You having a party or something?" His greedy eyes fell on the cake box in my hand.

"Without you? Of course not." I pulled my keys out my purse. Then I unlocked the door and hurried in. I ran smack into a floor lamp that wasn't supposed to be in the middle of the hallway. I flipped on the light. Someone had tossed my things into a furniture salad.

"Oh hell," I said as I stepped over some broken glass. Henry and Stan were right behind me. Pictures had been knocked off the walls, the carpet was pulled up, and the couch cushions had been slashed. My photo album was spilled over the living room floor and a picture of me from first grade had a big foot-print on it. My desk had been overturned and bills and receipts were scattered all over. I picked up a notice that said "OVERDUE" in big red letters and stuck it in my pocket. Henry moved past me and picked up the phone to call the police. When he turned around he had a funny look on his face.

"Jane—there's no dial tone."

I walked over to the phone and took it from him. "I paid my bill…" I said, confused. I looked down. The phone line had been snipped in two. "Oh, the line's been cut." I thought for a second. "Well, there's a police officer who lives upstairs. I'll go see if he's home."

"I'll come with you." Henry offered as he peeled my bank statement from his shoe. He set it down on top of the television without looking at it. I wish I had his restraint. Stan did not. He walked over and eyeballed it. I snatched it away.

"Stan, this won't interest you. It doesn't have any pictures of naked people in it." Stan had the gall not to be offended. Instead he went and sat down on what was left of my couch. He opened the bakery box I had dropped on the coffee table and peeked inside.

"Got any milk to go with this?" he asked, licking his lips.

I bit back a reply. Henry put his arm around me.

"Are you okay?"

"Yes. Stay here and keep Stan out of my underwear drawer," I whispered in a strained voice. "I'm going to go look for Detective Dermott. Maybe I can get him to arrest Stan for loitering." Henry gave me a quick hug and let go. On my way out I caught a glimpse of my bedroom. There was no need to keep Stan out of my underwear drawer as my undies had been flung all over the place. A pair of purple ones were hanging on my light fixture. My suitcase was open on my bed but no clothes were inside. I ducked in and weeded all of the Victoria Secret items and control top panty hose from the mess on the floor, dumped them into the suitcase, and shut it. Dignity is like virginity—once you lose it it's hard to restore.

I left my apartment and took the stairs to the second floor. I had seen Dermott take the stairs on a couple of occasions but I didn't know which apartment was his so I knocked on them all. Eight doors later I found him.

"Detective Dermott?" I said as I put my eye to his peephole. I heard a swear word from behind the door before it swung open. Tom Dermott stood in the doorway wearing a sweatshirt and a pair of Levi's. His dark curls were matted in a bed head style like he had been sleeping.

"What do you want?" he asked. He sounded a little cranky.

"My apartment has been ransacked! I want you to come take a look." As I was speaking my attention was drawn to a mess almost as great as the one I had left downstairs. Chinese take out containers were heaped on top of a stack of empty pizza boxes. There was a squashed beer can on the floor next to a big easy chair. A litter of dust kitties were curled up to a live one on the floor. "It looks like your place has been ransacked too," I commented.

Dermott started to shut the door. I stuck my foot in. "Really, Dermott. I'm not kidding. I would've called the police but my phone line's been cut." I heard a big sigh, then the door opened again.

"Let me get my shoes," he said wearily. "I'll call the station, then meet you downstairs. Don't touch anything."

I went back downstairs. Henry had managed to coax Stan back into the hallway. Dermott showed up a minute later. He did a double take when he saw Henry.

"Channel 7 right?" Henry nodded. Dermott looked at me. "What did you do—call the press?"

"No, Henry is a friend of mine," I said, a little irritated that I had to offer an explanation.

"Is he a friend too?" Dermott looked at Stan.

"Whatever," I said, tugging at Dermott's arm. "Come in and take a look at my place."

I followed Dermott inside while Henry and Stan waited in the hallway for the police. Two officers arrived a few minutes later. They greeted Dermott by name. He led them to the kitchen, where the burglar had entered by breaking my window. They spoke briefly, then Dermott returned to my side.

"Do you have any idea what they were looking for?" he asked as he surveyed the room.

"Not really. It might be related to the DeOrca murder though. I've never had any trouble with a break-in before. I just don't understand this."

Dermott studied me for a moment. "I think you know more than you're telling."

I remained silent. I didn't have anything solid. No sense in bringing rumors up. I was puzzled as to the reason for the break-in. Nothing seemed to be missing. Maybe the point was to scare me.

Dermott shook his head at me. "When you're ready to talk, let me know. I hope you get ready before you get killed. Three incidents in three days is too many—don't you think?" He gave me a meaningful look then returned to the kitchen area. Ten minutes later, he and the officers left together. Henry came in and started to clean up as I took inventory of the damage. The broken kitchen window was my biggest concern. I might as well put a "Free television and CD player" sign up.

"Henry, I'm going to go downstairs to the storage room and get a board. I want to nail it over the kitchen window until I can get it fixed," I said in a strangled tone. My anger was starting to surface. Dermott's lecture had come at a bad time.

Henry was re-hanging a picture. He turned around. "Do you need help?"

"No, thanks. I got it. I'll be right back." I ran downstairs, grabbed a board and when I returned I nailed the board to the window with gusto, imagining that I was using it on the person who broke in. Henry looked at me, but didn't say anything. He swept up the broken dishes in the kitchen, cleaned up the living room, and then started in on my laundry.

The only problem was that I was wearing it.

ELEVEN

When I woke up the next morning Henry was gone. I rolled out of bed, took a shower and went into the living room. It was still a wreck even though Henry and I had picked up most of the mess. Sweeping up broken glass isn't such a big deal but it's not so easy to stitch up a slashed couch or rebuild a broken table. These items would need to be replaced and they weren't cheap either—I only charge the very best. I thought of Elana DeOrca's offer. I had a lot of work to do if I was going to earn her retainer and I needed every cent of it. The furniture in my apartment was trashed, my office was blood spattered, and my car was a heap of molten metal. If the mob didn't kill me my insurance deductibles certainly would.

I grabbed a Diet Coke from the fridge and wandered back to the living room to make some calls. I grabbed the phone and yanked the shades up. The light stung my eyes momentarily. What a great day for a funeral. I set my Diet Coke down and picked up the receiver. There was no dial tone. I had forgotten that my phone line had been cut. Time for Plan B.

My green sweats weren't too stinky so I threw them on, laced up my tennis shoes, and went over to Stan's apartment. Since we're neighbors, let's be friends and all that jazz, I thought as I knocked on the door. I heard heavy footsteps, then the door opened.

I took a step back. Stan's face was puffy and stubbled. He was wearing a stained blue terry cloth bathrobe and his hair was sticking up in a waterfall of a cowlick. Worst of all—he had morning breath. He blinked at me in annoyance as if I had roused him from one of his x-rated dreams.

"Good morning!" I said in a sunshiny voice. "I need to borrow your phone for just a minute."

Stan hesitated, then he opened his door. "I guess that would be okay. It's not long distance is it?" he asked suspiciously.

"No, local." Miser. It's not as if he doesn't know where to find me when the phone bill arrives. Stan moved aside to let me in. We've been neighbors for over two years but this was my first look at his living quarters. I felt like I had stepped back twenty five years. The floor was covered with a burnt orange shag carpet that crunched a little when I walked on it. There was a bright blue bean bag chair heaped with clothes and junk next to a turntable record player. The couch was a lumpy thing on wooden legs with a lime green afghan spread over it. On the wall there was a clock shaped like a big daisy. It wasn't working but I'll bet if it could tell time it would say "1975."

Stan went into the kitchen and returned a moment later dragging a rotary phone attached to a cord that snaked around the corner. "Thanks," I said as I took it. "Do you have a phone book? I need to call the phone company and see if they can fix the line."

Stan tapped a thick finger on his chin as he pondered my request. "I think I have one around here someplace but I'll have to have a look see." He walked over to the couch, picked up a tattered cushion and peered under it. The man was nuts.

I turned my back to him and dialed my friend Maggie. I wanted to ask if I could borrow her office to type up my contract for Mrs. DeOrca. Maggie's also a private investigator and we help each other out on cases when we can—for the price of a lunch. At this point I owe Mags four hundred of them.

"Maggie, this is Jane." I spoke in a loud voice so Stan wouldn't have to eavesdrop. I could tell from the lack of noise that he had given up his search for the yellow pages.

"Hang on a minute, Jane!" Maggie's breathless voice came on the line. "I'm getting dressed. Be right back!"

I studied a nudie calendar that Stan had nailed to the wall while I waited for Maggie to return to the phone. It will always be May at Stan's place.

"Jane! How does it feel to be in the middle of a high profile case? Glad it's you and not me, although the publicity must be bringing in big bucks as far as clients go."

I smiled. Maggie had probably seen the *Oregonian* story. "Well, did you see the picture of me in the paper? I looked HUGE. You should be glad that it's me and not you." We chuckled a few minutes, then I told her about my officeless-ness. She was sympathetic and willing to let me use her office as a home base.

"I'll leave a key with the receptionist at the office next door. He's an airhead but I think he can be trusted not to lose it before you get there. Anyway, let's get together for lunch soon. We'll drink it!"

I laughed and hung up. Stan started fumbling through a stack of papers on his bookshelf when I turned around.

"Did you find the phone book?"

"Umm…not yet." Stan got down on all fours and stuck his hand under the couch. He pulled out a wad of socks that looked a little ripe. Then he shoved them back underneath the couch.

"No problem. I'll help you." I went over to a desk and opened a drawer. I didn't find a phone book but I did find part of Stan's *Hustler* library.

"I FOUND IT," Stan boomed as he handed me the phone book. I continued to poke through the desk as if I hadn't noticed the urgent tone of his voice. Kind of a payback for last night. My hand touched on a picture frame and I picked it up. It was of a young woman standing out in a field of rippling grass. Her wispy brown hair was cut shag style and she was wearing a fringed poncho, purple pants and platform shoes.

"Who's this?" I held the picture up. Stan stood very still.

"It's my wife." His customary leer slid off his face. I glanced at the picture again. It looked like it had been taken some time ago.

"I didn't know you had a wife. Where is she?" The only women I ever sighted in the vicinity of Stan's apartment were the paper kind from *Playboy* magazine.

"I don't know." Stan took the picture from me and disappeared into the kitchen. I flipped open the phone book, found the number for my insurance company and for the phone line repair. I made my calls then ducked into the kitchen to wave good bye to Stan. He was sitting at a crumb covered formica table eating a bowl of Fruit Loops. The photo of his wife was gone.

"Thanks a lot," I said. Stan nodded without looking up. I felt uneasy as if I had hurt his feelings. I just didn't know he had any. "You'll have to tell me about your wife sometime," I said on impulse. Stan looked up, his eyes sad.

"Not now." He stirred his cereal and then took a big bite.

"Okay," I agreed. "See you later."

I went back to my place. Within a few minutes I forgot about Stan.

Everyone has their own problems and mine was named Freddie DeOrca. I went into the bedroom to get dressed.

Elana DeOrca had invited me to the funeral, but I forgot to ask where it was being held. I'd have to check the obituary pages. I went to my closet to find something to wear. I found a black form fitting suit behind a never worn strapless gold silk evening dress. I used to date a musician and he got nominated for a big award. I bought a beautiful floor length Armani gown (which I couldn't afford) and then the bastard canceled on me. I watched the awards on television instead, with some of my friends. We all cheered when he lost.

I inspected the suit. The person tossing my apartment must

have been a little careless because it was still in the dry cleaning bag. I put it on and looked at my watch. It was nine thirty. Time to head to Maggie's office.

Maggie's office is located on 42nd and Fremont. It's a small brown duplex office building. She's not in it a lot—like me she's always in the "field". I stopped by the office across from Maggie's to see the receptionist that she spoke about. He was on the phone. I was treated to a secondhand account of his wild night at a gay bar before he hung up and handed me the key.

I crossed the hall to Maggie's door. A small sign read "McGuire Investigations." I unlocked the door and let myself in. It was a one room office with a window facing Fremont street. The shades were up and I was able to see the cars zoom by. I took off my coat and hung it up on the back of Maggie's chair. She has a large desk swamped with papers near the window. Maggie's area of expertise is not housekeeping but I was able to find her computer after a few minutes—it was draped with yesterday's issue of the *Oregonian*. I picked it up and thumbed through it to the obituary page. A small announcement said that DeOrca's funeral service would be held today at noon at Pioneer Cemetery on Stark Street. I jotted down the address and set the paper aside.

It only took me a few minutes to prepare a contract for Elana DeOrca. I have a standard contract I normally use, but it was in my office. I kind of doubted that the Portland PD would be willing to run one over to me. I looked the contract over. I stipulated that I was to be paid a hundred dollars an hour plus expenses. Having my office cleaned was going to be my first expense, I decided.

I checked my voice mail and returned a few calls. Vaughn, King and Sachitano wanted me to track down a missing witness to a car accident. And a local landlord needed a background check on a potential tenant. I took notes and tucked them into my purse. The smaller jobs are my bread and butter. Speaking of which, I was starving. I grabbed my coat and purse, and ran across the street to Favorite's Bakery. Dee, the manager, smiled at me when I walked in. I don't even live in the neighborhood and I'm a regular. If I went on a diet, I'd probably put half the bakery workers in town out of business. I bought a slice of "Death by Chocolate" cake for myself and an extra one to leave for Maggie. We both follow a diet with four major food groups—sugar, salt, caffeine and grease.

I "died" by chocolate, then scribbled a hasty "thank you" note to Maggie. Then I returned the key to the receptionist at the dentist's office before I left. He was on the phone in the midst of a tale involving his break up with Jerome, an exotic dancer, but he took time to waggle a goodbye to me.

I hopped in my car and headed to Southeast Portland by way of 39th street. Pioneer Cemetery is located on Stark Street. At first glance it looks like a huge park—trees tower over the fences, the lawn is lush and green. But then the lack of laughter gives the place away.

The streets surrounding the cemetery were bordered by cars; some from the mourners and some from the students who attended a nearby high school. Two limousines were parked by the front of the cemetery. I parked behind a station wagon with a "GO RAMS" bumper sticker and followed an elderly couple to the entrance of the grounds. I was greeted at the gate by a slab faced man dressed in a black suit. He handed me a program. I glanced at it long enough to figure out the service would be short.

In the distance I could see people congregating by a grave site. A priest stood between two large flower arrangements propped up on easels. The sun was beaming down through the tall fir trees and the area of the service was illuminated by a bright light. Despite the sun, there was a chill in the air and it weighed me down with a sense of dread. I hate funerals. I slowly followed the wide paved path through the cemetery to the service. Somehow, attending the service, made the murder in my office seem more real. As I approached I could see Elana at the head of the coffin. The wind was blowing back her hair, and she had one arm around Sean's shoulders. She was dressed in a long black fur coat and her eyes were hidden behind dark sunglasses. Sean was dressed in a suit and tie. I caught a glimpse of his stricken face and looked down. This wasn't going to be easy.

I joined the edge of the group as the priest began to speak. He spoke in general terms about Federico DeOrca, praising his civic record and stuff like that. It was obvious that Freddie and the priest weren't acquainted. As the priest droned on, I looked around. There were about forty people present. Good turn out for such a bad man. Rita, the woman from the Suds and Duds laundromat had made it. She was standing next to the red-faced man I had seen at the laundromat. He was wearing gold chains on his wrist and a shiny suit. She herself was wearing something tight for the occasion; a short blue dress with long sleeves and matching shoes. And no coat. Maybe her fake tan was keeping her warm.

Sam Madsen was standing near a tree next to a woman with honey blonde hair. The woman was a little tearful. Sam was watching with interest but he made no attempt to comfort her. They must be strangers, I decided. The wind gusted through the cemetery, just then, toppling over the flower arrangements. The priest stopped speaking and reached out to catch one of them. In the moment of silence a woman's voice boomed from behind me.

"ROT IN HELL, FEDERICO DEORCA!"

Everyone turned to look in my direction. I ducked their eyes and turned around myself. A woman, forty or so, stood there, like an actress making an entrance. She was small, maybe five foot three, with short auburn hair framing her angry face. She was wearing a red coat, a red dress, patent leather red high heels—and she was drunk. The smell of booze wafted toward me and I took a step back.

The woman lurched forward, moving past me to the open grave where DeOrca's coffin stood ready to lower him to the underworld. I looked at Elana. Her face was unmoved, but everyone was slack jawed. The priest even looked scared. His hands were fumbling with his rosary. Only Sean was enjoying the commotion.

The woman stood at the edge of the grave and leaned forward. "I've been waiting over ten years for this day, you miserable bastard," she hissed. "Now you're in hell where you belong. Good riddance."

She looked at Elana and stopped abruptly. "I'm sorry, Elana." Elana's face was expressionless. The woman turned around and stalked past me to the path leading out of the cemetery. For the first time I noticed that Detective Dermott was standing off to the side. He was in a leather jacket, brown sweater and chinos, with sunglasses to shield his eyes. The woman pushed past him and he followed her.

I turned around. A murmur ran over the crowd. The priest looked helplessly at Elana. The poor man looked like he was going to have a heart attack. Elana stepped forward.

"Thank you all for coming here today. I hope that you'll join me back at the house for food and coffee." Her voice was calm and cucumber cool. I was impressed by her fortitude. She gave the priest a half smile, then she took Sean's arm and walked out to the path.

The woman in front of me, a doughy faced person in her sixties, leaned in to her companion. "Who was *that?*"

Her companion, an elegant silver haired gentleman of the same age, whispered back.

"Jackie Crombie! Can you believe it! DeOrca was accused of murdering her husband. He got off—I heard he bought off half the jury!"

"I wonder who killed DeOrca?" Her voice was breathless.

"I think the private detective was put up to it."

I froze. Did people really think that?

"Or maybe the wife did it. Did DeOrca have life insurance?"

"I don't know. The man in the gray suit over there—by Lisa Norton," she pointed with a thick finger, "is DeOrca's insurance agent. I heard him say so before the service started. I think he suspects foul play."

I looked over to the man she was talking about. He was tall, and dressed in a suit that was probably off the rack from Sears. He was looking down, intent on polishing his tortoise shell glasses. I moved away and walked over to him.

"Hi, my name is Jane Lanier." I held out my hand.

He looked up, surprised. He put his glasses on and gave me a clammy handshake. "I'm Howard Kirkwood. Oregon Insurance. Glad to meet you." His brown eyes gazed at me through thick lenses. "You're the private investigator, aren't you?"

I nodded, hoping that he didn't suspect me of murder.

"Are you looking into the—ahem—incident?" His manner was diplomatic.

I hedged. "Let's just say that I'm curious about a few things. I heard someone say you were DeOrca's insurance agent."

"I'm not an insurance agent. I'm an arson investigator." His tone suggested that several pay scales separated the two occupations.

"Oh…so are you here in connection with the warehouse that burned down a few weeks ago?"

Now it was his turn to hedge the question. "Officially, that claim was closed. We paid it off a week ago. I got to know the family well during my investigation so I thought I would drop by the service."

That sounded like a lie. I let it go. "I'd like to talk to you about the fire, if you have some time this week."

He considered it. "Sure." He fumbled in his pocket and handed me a card. "Give me a call."

"Thanks." I felt a hand touch the sleeve of my coat as Kirkwood moved away. It was Detective Dermott.

"Are you a friend of the family now?" His voice was pleasant but I felt his sarcasm all the same. My cheeks felt hot. I wasn't a friend of the family—or the murderer, either, thank you very much.

"The man was killed in my office," I retorted. "This is the least I could do. Speaking of which, do you have any leads as to who might be after me?"

"No. Until you start cooperating with us, you're on your own."

"What do you mean—cooperate? I've been questioned by you guys three times. What more do you want from me?" The sun danced in my eyes. I squinted and looked up at him. My face was reflected in his mirrored police issue sunglasses. It was distorted.

"The truth for starters. A guy like DeOrca doesn't trust too many people. Why did he seek you out? I don't think that it's a coincidence that he shows up at your office the very night he was murdered. So my question is—how do you figure into all of this?"

I didn't answer. I was thinking the same thing.

TWELVE

I FOLLOWED A BLACK limousine with tinted privacy windows back to the DeOrca mansion. It swept into the driveway at the rear of the house and stopped at the guard station. I drove by. The rest of the block was lined with a variety of cars. Pintos and Pontiacs were bumper to bumper with Porsches. I parked a block away and returned to the DeOrca mansion with a copy of Elana's contract tucked in my purse.

The maid answered the door. Today she was wearing a starched white apron. She took my coat without a glimmer of recognition and admitted me into the throng of guests. The circular table in the foyer was crowded with a variety of gaudy flower arrangements. I leaned in for a sniff and caught sight of a card in an arrangement of calla lilies. It read: "With all my sympathy, Senator Caughell." Randall Caughell was a wealthy State Senator who lived in Eugene. When he wasn't presiding over legislative committees, he ran a Mercedes dealership. Rumor had it he was gearing up to run for Congress. Federico DeOrca had friends in high places.

New arrivals at the door herded me into the formal dining room. An ornate chandelier hung from the ceiling and pictures of stone faced ancestors decorated the walls. A buffet was set up with a chef at one end of the table carving a hunk of bloody meat. A bartender was doing brisk business at a makeshift bar set up in the corner of the room. I saw Sam Madsen there, wearing a black leather jacket, a black shirt and slacks and boots. No tie. He was sucking up a beer. I elbowed my way over.

"Hi, Sam." I looked over at the bartender. He glanced up at me as he poured tomato juice into a glass with a celery stalk sticking out of it. "Glass of pinot gris, please."

"How are you, Jane? Are you here on business or pleasure?"

I could see what he meant. The funeral guests seemed to be having a good time. The room was alive with laughter and party chatter. People were feasting and the wine was flowing freely. I took my glass from the bartender.

"I'm fine." I ignored his second question. "Do you know anyone here?"

Sam shrugged. "A few. Most of the people here are employees. Mrs. DeOrca gave everyone time off to attend the funeral and the party, err, reception." He stopped talking and smiled into the distance. The fake and bake blonde I bribed at the Suds and Duds Laundromat stood in the doorway. She gave him a coy smile and a little wave. He turned back to me.

"That your girlfriend?" I took a sip of wine. I wouldn't put it past Sam. I'll bet he was a real ladies man.

Sam smiled, took another swig of beer and changed the subject. "Have you seen the woman that turned up at DeOrca's funeral?"

"The drunk one?"

"Yeah. If she's here she'll blend in. Plenty of DeOrca's employees felt the same way she did. I hear that he was a mean old bastard."

"Sounds like a motive for murder doesn't it?" I turned to Sam and our eyes met. He wasn't smiling anymore. He was about to say something when the blonde sidled up to him and hugged him without using her arms. He looked down at her in surprise.

"I'll catch you later," I said as I eased away. Sam gave me an awkward grin.

I wandered over to the buffet table and took a plate. Might as well get a bite before I talked to Elana.

The door to the pantry swung open and the caterer arrived with replenishments for the buffet table. I started to fill my plate with Swedish meatballs, St. Andre cheese, bleu cheese with pears, and Carr water crackers. I even scooped a large spoonful of something I didn't recognize onto my plate.

"What's this?" I asked the caterer. He was a large Asian man with triple chins. His face was flushed from the heat.

"Mouse De Fois De Chanard Truffle!" he said grandly. The woman next to me exclaimed and put a large serving on her plate. Food snob.

"Translation, please," I said looking dubiously at my plate.

"Duck liver," he whispered with a wink.

Suddenly I wasn't hungry anymore. I looked for a place to dump my plate. I slipped around to the other side of the table and pushed the swinging pantry doors open. It was large, with ceiling high cupboards. I could hear the bustle of dishes rattling and the flurry of voices from the kitchen. I put my plate down on the counter and started to move away. The sound of a voice pulled me back.

It was coming from the ceiling.

I looked up to see an air vent. What fun! I stood still so I could hear.

The voice was low and gravelly. I could make out snatches of a one sided conversation. "Stall him…until the shipment arrives. I need more time to get the money—" The voices from the kitchen obscured the rest of the sentence. I look around for a chair so I could get my ear closer to the vent.

The door from the kitchen swung open and a skinny waiter with a crew cut pushed his way past me with a platter.

"Can I help you?" he said over his shoulder.

"I'm looking for the loo," I said hastily.

"You need to go back through the dining room to the entryway. It's at the end of the hall."

"Great, thanks."

I weaved through the clusters of guests balancing glasses and plates, to the hallway. Elana was coming down the stairs. She was wearing a knee length black wool dress with black hose and black heels and three pearl necklaces. She looked the part of the widow with her black dress, white face, and haunted eyes. What happened to the confidence I had seen yesterday?

Elana caught sight of me and came forward. "Jane. I'm glad you're here. Let's go somewhere we can talk."

I followed Elana down the hall to a door that opened into a library. The room had two ceiling to floor walls of books. A fire glowed in the grate. Two dark green leather chairs faced the fireplace. There was a desk with a gold lamp on it tucked into the corner. Elana crossed the room to a set of French doors and opened them. A gust of cold air blew in. I longed to sit by the fire but I followed Elana outside instead.

A paved walkway led into a garden area. We walked to the garden and sat down on a cold, damp bench next to a fountain choked with leaves. The white plaster cherub on the top tier of the fountain was covered with splotches of bird poop. A tall hedge afforded privacy from the street and the living room windows.

The wind blew a fresh spray of leaves down the walkway. I shivered and pulled the contract from my purse. "Elana, here's a copy of the contract. I charge a hundred dollars an hour plus expenses. This is a standard rate, you can check around if you like. I'll also need a 25 percent deposit. I'll make weekly oral reports to you, with a written report at the end of my investigation. If you decide to hire me I would appreciate it if you could take care of the other expenses I've incurred since your husband paid his visit to me. In exchange I'll look into your husband's murder if I can do it without interfering with the police investigation. I can't promise I'll find anything but I'll try my best."

"Start with Brute Mortimer." Elana's voice was dull. "I'm

sure he's guilty of something." She took my pen and read over the contract. Then she laid it down on the bench and scrawled her signature on it. I noticed her hand was shaking. The composure she had shown at the funeral was wearing thin. She handed the contract back to me. Then she reached for my hand and pressed a small key into it. "Keep this for me. I may ask for it back in a few days or a few years. Don't tell anyone that you have it. I can't tell you why right now, but it's important."

"Okay." I agreed. I slipped the key into my purse. I couldn't help wondering what it was for. It was small, like my mailbox key.

She stood up. "If you come inside I'll write you a check for the retainer. As for your expenses, I'm fully prepared to pay what your car insurance doesn't cover. Does that sound fair?"

I admitted that it did.

"Let's go inside then. It's freezing out here."

We walked toward the door. "I'm curious, Elana. Why did you want to meet outside?"

She stopped with her hand on the door handle and looked at me. Her face was full of fear. "It's safer. I think my house might be bugged by the Feds. Federico's line of work, you know. He hired Sam Madsen to come in and sweep for microphones but I want to be careful. Now that Federico's gone I suppose there isn't any need but you never know who's listening."

I froze, then exploded. "What about the conversation we had in your living room yesterday?" My stomach started to turn. "Elana, someone broke into my apartment last night and turned it upside down. I think they may have been looking for something connected to your husband's murder. If we're going to be careful, we need to be careful all of the time. There's a killer on the loose and I don't want to take any unnecessary chances."

"I understand," Elana said in a chilly voice. She turned away quickly and pulled open the door. She went inside and

I followed, pulling the French doors shut. Elana went over to the desk in the corner of the room, pulled open one of the drawers, and removed a checkbook. She scribbled out a check without entering it in her register. I wish I had that luxury.

She handed me the check and I gulped. It was for ten thousand dollars.

"Thank you." I shoved the check in my purse. The money made me feel a little guilty for being annoyed with her a minute ago. After all, she did just bury her husband.

"Let me know if you need more." Elana dropped her checkbook into the drawer and shut it.

"Thanks. You'll hear back from me in a week. I'm going to need more information to go on though. Does your husband have an office?"

"Upstairs. But I'm afraid that the police have already removed everything."

"Really? Do you remember who came by?"

"Detective Vance from Homicide. He took several boxes of papers."

I made a note to myself to catch up with Detective Vance. I doubted if he would share any details but I wanted to know what he took.

"One more thing, Elana. That woman at the funeral— Jackie Crombie. Do you consider her a threat? She seemed pretty worked up."

Elana dismissed the notion with a wave of her hand. "No, she's harmless. I can't say I blamed her for the scene. It was her way of getting even for her husband's murder. She was sure that Freddie killed him."

"What do you think?"

Elana paused. "I don't know what to think anymore. Anyway, I wouldn't worry about Jackie Crombie if I were you. For God's sake, she volunteers all of her time at a homeless shelter."

"Which one?"

"The Burnside Shelter."

Frieda, the maid, appeared in the doorway. "Mrs. DeOrca, there's someone at the back door you might want to talk to."

"Thank you," Elana replied. She moved away from the desk. "If you'll excuse me, Jane."

"Of course."

Elana left the room. I walked over to her desk and opened the drawer where she had dropped the checkbook. Might as well make sure that the check was good. I picked up a pen and eased the register open. The last recorded balance was for twelve thousand dollars. Elana was cutting it close, especially if she had to pay the mortgage on the mansion. And had she paid the caterer yet? I decided to deposit my check right away. I was about to shut the drawer when a business card caught my eye. I picked it up. The plain small print read: "Robert—, Investigations." The last name was blacked out as if someone had been doodling on the card. There was a local phone number listed but no address. I was confused. Had Elana called someone else in to investigate?

The door opened and a woman with jet black hair walked in. I shut the desk drawer and tried not to look guilty. Her eyebrows, which were painted on in thin black arches, jumped in surprise when she saw me. She was dressed in a short leopard print skirt with a bright yellow polyester blouse. Her skinny arms were loaded down with bangles and the smell of cheap dime store cologne wafted through the room. Inwardly I gasped. This woman was at least seventy years old and she dressed like a street hooker.

"Sorry, sweetie." Her voice was high and whiny. "I thought this room was empty. Do you have a light?"

I shook my head.

"That's good. The lady of the house don't allow smoking— least that's the way it used to be." She dug into the yellow vinyl purse she was carrying and pulled out a pack of cigarettes. Then she produced a book of matches. She extracted one and lit up. She looked at me and squinted her eyes as she brought the cigarette to her lips. "So who are you?" She blew a cloud of smoke my way.

I coughed. "Jane Lanier."

She sucked on her cigarette again as she squinted at me. "Ah, the private detective. I read about you in the paper. So who killed my son?"

"You're DeOrca's mother?" She was too skinny to warrant the comparison.

"I'm not a nun. Call me Violetta, sweetie." She put her hand on her hip as she surveyed the room. "Wow, what a joint!"

"Haven't you been here before?" Maybe the late DeOrca and his mother weren't close.

"I haven't seen my son for more than ten years. I live in Reno. That's where Freddie grew up. He sends me a check every month so I'll stay away. The check for this month was late so I called to find out what the deal was. That's when I found out my son was murdered. I hopped on a bus as soon as I heard the news, but I was too late for the funeral." Her voice was resentful. "I guess that's something I'll need to take up with the lady of the house. Where is she anyway?"

"She's with a guest. I'd go easy on her. She seems to be taking your son's death pretty hard."

Violetta snorted and wandered out in to the hallway.

I followed her. The crowd had thinned out somewhat and the caterers were picking up dirty plates and crumpled cocktail napkins. Elana was nowhere to be found.

"I don't see her," I said as I looked into the living room area. A couple of people were drinking wine and estimating the value of the furniture.

"Maybe she's upstairs. I'll go look." Violetta turned and walked up the staircase.

I sighed and looked for Frieda. I wanted to get my coat and get out. I found her sneaking a cigarette in the kitchen. She stubbed out her cigarette and without comment went to fetch my coat. When she returned I thanked her sweetly and got out of her way.

I was pulling on my coat in the entryway when I heard angry voices. A woman yelled. It was an old woman. A door slammed and Violetta appeared a few seconds later at the top of the stairs. A beefy looking man in a dark suit was leading her forcefully down. She was furious and sputtering a few choice obscenities.

"Get your hands off me you, little hooligan!" she cried. Frieda appeared again at the front door. She was holding a suitcase banded in beige duct tape. She dropped it with a thud and ambled away.

"Did you find Elana?" I looked at the bouncer's placid face as he picked up the suitcase and handed it to Violetta.

"Yes," she said huffily as she swatted the bouncer's hand off her arm. He released it and folded his arms. "She was talkin' to someone. I walked in on them and Mr. Tough Guy here got his panties in a bunch." She scowled at him. He grabbed her elbow again, opened the door, and gave her a little shove. Was this a hint the party was over? I stepped outside. The door slammed behind us.

"Who was she meeting with?"

Violetta's face was dark. For a moment I didn't think she was going to answer, but when she spoke her voice was cold.

"Brute Mortimer."

THIRTEEN

"BRUTE MORTIMER KILLED my son. I'm sure of it."

We were sitting in a pea green vinyl booth at Denny's restaurant. I offered to give Violetta a ride to her hotel but then discovered she didn't have a room yet. The woman had taken a liking to me and I found myself to be her new best friend. We had stopped at Denny's so Violetta could use the restroom and pick up the Grand Slam special.

"What makes you think that?" I set down my coffee cup.

"I don't think—I know." She corrected me. "This has happened before." She paused as the waitress set down a plate of eggs, bacon, hash browns and toast. The food looked like it was floating in a puddle of grease. It was too bad she was thrown out of the DeOrca household before she had a chance to eat.

"What do you mean that it's happened before? Do you have another son?"

"No…" Violetta shook salt over her eggs. "Brute Mortimer has killed before. He's an evil son of a bitch."

I didn't doubt that. "Who did he kill?"

Violetta leaned forward. "Ever heard of the Lucky Lady Casino?"

I shook my head.

"It's a little hotel in Reno. Slots, crap games, poker, keno, blackjack. It was owned by a man named Charlie Sharkey. Freddie worked there as a pit boss. Musta been oh, twenty years ago. One day Brute—he was known as Bruce in those days—came in and sat down at one of the poker tables. He threw the first coupla games, then he started to win. He kept on winning for seven straight hours. He cleared nearly two hundred thousand dollars in the time it takes an honest man to earn a day's pay. The next afternoon he came in and did it again. Freddie was working that day too and he let the win ride. When Sharkey found out he was furious. He fired Freddie on the spot, accusing him in front of everybody of rigging the game. Two days later Sharkey turns up at the bottom of the hotel swimming pool with a bullet in his head. Brute Mortimer used his winnings to buy the Lucky Lady from Sharkey's widow. Then he hired Freddie back as his partner."

"Was Brute ever accused of the crime?"

Violetta stabbed her eggs with a fork. "Hell no," she said as she took a bite. "Everyone was too afraid of ending up like poor old Sharkey." Her voice was suddenly soft.

A vision of Freddie sprawled on my desk flickered through my mind. Did Mortimer kill DeOrca over the missing money? The Sharkey story troubled me.

"Violetta, do you think Brute Mortimer might try to harm Elana or your grandson?"

Violetta set her fork down. "If there's money involved he might. That's why he's got to be stopped."

"I'll need some kind of proof before I can go to the police."

"No police. They won't do anything. Mortimer has probably bought them off. I need a hit man."

"A hit man?" I couldn't believe that I was sitting in Denny's discussing hit men with an old lady. I gripped the table to make sure that I wasn't dreaming. I wasn't—my fingers found a piece of old gum.

"Yeah, have him whacked. It's the only way," she said as she spread some grape jelly on her toast.

"Forget it. This is Portland, not Sin City. We don't do that here—it's considered rude."

"Well, that animal is gonna have to pay for what he did to my son!"

"Just don't kill him," I warned. "We put little old ladies in jail for that in Oregon."

Violetta just smiled.

"Tell me about Elana," I said as I changed the subject. "What do you know about her?"

"She's a stuck up hoity toity." Violetta sniffed derisively. "Thinks she's better than anyone else. She grew up in a fancy house, went to private school, she even had her own pony. Her dad owned a bank but he pissed away all of his money and everybody else's by gambling. Elana had to drop out of school and go to work. Freddie met her when she was waiting on tables at the Lucky Lady. Guess he left her a big tip, cause she married him. A gold digger is what she is."

I didn't comment, but I had gained some insight as to how mother-in-law myths get started.

After Violetta finished eating I paid the check and drove her downtown. I expected she would want to stay at an economy priced motel, but she surprised me by asking to be dropped off at the Hotel Vintage Plaza. It's a ritzy place with ten dollar valet fees and suites where they drop rose petals on the sheets at turn down time.

"Are you sure you want to stay here?" I got out of the car and handed the valet my keys. "It's expensive."

"Don't you worry about it, dearie." She winked at me. "Money won't be a problem."

Whatever, I thought as I followed her in. A red cheeked bellboy in a brass buttoned uniform took Violetta's bag from me. She checked in while I checked out the menu posted for the restaurant adjoining the hotel. I've eaten there a few times. Best bread basket in town. I'm a girl who likes her starch.

The bellboy picked up Violetta's bag and we took the elevator to the third floor to her room. She tipped him a quarter and he gave her a strained smile in return. I made sure that Violetta was settled in, then left as she busied herself with stealing the soap. I walked back to the elevator and pushed the down button. While I waited I walked over to the railing and looked down to the lobby three floors below.

I was just in time to see the bruiser (Mr. Panties in a bunch) who had bounced Violetta from the DeOrca mansion. He was carrying two suitcases. The dark haired man with him was clad in a long dark overcoat, black leather gloves and sunglasses to protect himself from the glare of the indoor lighting. He walked out of my view to the elevator. Even though I wasn't able to see his face I had a feeling I had been looking at the man called Brute Mortimer.

I looked at the row of buttons over the elevator. The first floor button lit up, then the second, and the third. I moved away behind a post as the doors slid open. Then I peeked out in time to see both men disappear into Room 333.

FOURTEEN

I DROVE HOME AND PACKED a bag with the essentials; clean underwear, toothbrush and picklocks. I changed into black jeans, a black turtleneck and a leather jacket, before I left. Cat burglar garb. I made a quick stop at a convenience store and bought a bag of M&M's and a six pack of Diet Coke. If I was going to be in for a long stakeout I needed to be well prepared.

The lobby of the Vintage was quiet except for a well dressed woman sitting on the couch by the fireplace with the fake flames. I checked in, requested my favorite room, number 334, and paid with my Visa. Then I took the stairs to the third floor and cautiously looked into the hall. No hit men in sight. I sprinted down to my room, unlocked the door and darted inside. I closed it quietly and looked around.

I was booked in the "Nights in White Satin Suite." For 240 dollars a night I had the run of a townhouse. It boasted a two person jetted Fuji soak tub, a chilled bottle of champagne, a white satin nightgown and a free shoe shine. Given the location of our rooms it was probable Brute Mortimer had the same deal. I wondered if his free nightie fit him.

The drapes were open revealing a view of traffic on Broadway street. Beyond that I could see the lights twinkling on the West Hills. I closed the curtains, kicked off my shoes and stationed myself over by the wall adjoining Brute's suite. The only sounds I could hear were garbled. I ran upstairs, grabbed a water glass from the bathroom and returned to my position. With the glass pressed against the wall I could hear snatches of their conversation.

"Any news of the kid yet?" The deep voice sounded like Mortimer's.

"We're working on it, boss."

"Little bastard. If we don't have the money, the deal falls through. Cut the cards."

It was quiet for a while. It seemed like I was spying on a poker game. I dragged my treat bag over to the wall and ate some candy while Mortimer won 500 dollars.

Surveillance is boring work. After a while my ear hurt so I put the glass down and leaned against the wall. I had determined from the number of voices there were four men in that room. Mortimer's was the only one that consistently I recognized. I gathered from the conversation and from the overall results of the game that he was the big boss. He won every time.

The big boss of what was the question. I thought of the businesses that comprised the DeOrca-Mortimer empire. A dumpy bar, a trucking company, a dry cleaners with dirty windows, and a chain of crappy Mexican restaurants. El Mesa del Rey restaurants are everywhere in Oregon and Washington. The first one opened at a shopping mall. They distinguish themselves from Taco Bell cuisine by their "build your own burrito bar" and watery margaritas in big bowls. I went there once when my mom was in town. When we went to pay the bill they tried to keep her credit card. Since then I haven't been back but that hasn't stopped them from building sixteen more restaurants. Unless they own Pepto-Bismol stock I really can't explain their success.

After a while I could hear noise from the other side of the wall. The boys were going downstairs to the restaurant to take a dinner break. I checked my watch. It was 7:30. I stood up and went to the peephole by the door. The peephole did not allow a great view but I could see all four men go down the hallway towards the elevator. I sprang into action.

I grabbed a flashlight, a camera and picklocks then I crammed my feet into my shoes and left the room. Pazzo's, the restaurant downstairs, is normally very crowded and the service, though friendly, can be a little slow. Even if the boys ate fast and skipped dessert it was going to take them at least an hour before they were back. At McDonald's I can get in and out of the drive thru in three minutes.

When I was sure I had the hallway to myself, I went to work. I pulled out my picklocks and inserted the pick in the keyhole. I used the tension wrench directly below it to hold the pins in an open position while I manipulated them. I had to stop once when I heard the elevator rumble by. I breathed a sigh of relief when it didn't stop on my floor. Eighty five seconds later, with the theme of Mission Impossible pounding in my head, I heard the distinctive click. I was in.

The set up of Mortimer's room was like mine except that theirs had been fashioned into a mini poker parlor. Room service had thoughtfully provided a card table. It was covered with empty glasses, overflowing ashtrays and poker chips. I didn't see any cards. Maybe Mortimer had a special deck.

I hurried through the place. I knew from my own room that the front door was the only way out. The windows are bolted shut and there's not a good place to hide unless you have a fourteen-inch waist. Which I don't.

Luckily for me, the fellas had left the lights on and the drapes shut. I started upstairs. A suitcase had been tossed on the bed. I opened it and pawed through a bunch of starched white shirts and silk boxer shorts. Mortimer's, I guessed. Three Armani suits hung in the closet. I checked the pockets and came up with a package of cigarettes, a pair of Ray Bans and a book of matches from the Hotel Vintage Plaza which had the name "Natalie" scrawled on the inside of the cover. A phone number was underneath it. I memorized it and put the items back. It could be a clue or it could be the name of a hooker.

A leather toiletry bag was out next to the sink in the bathroom. I went through it and learned that Mortimer practiced good dental hygiene and safe sex.

I went downstairs and opened a closet. There were a couple of coats inside. I slid my hand into one pocket and touched dirty Kleenex. I recoiled and then I heard footsteps by the door and the jingle of keys.

Damn.

If I had thought to insert toothpicks in the lock I could have bought myself some time, but I would've given myself away. Instead I slipped into the closet and closed the door just as the front door opened. I held my breath as I burrowed behind the coats. They smelled like smoke. I crouched down next to a briefcase that had been tucked in the back of the closet.

Footsteps thumped by my hiding place and stopped near the window. A man picked up the phone and made a call. After a moment he spoke.

"Freddie the Whale is out of the picture now. Brute's running the show." There was a silence then I heard him say: "She's gonna try to raise the dough but she has to get a hold of her lawyer, who's in Hawaii on vacation. We're looking for him now." It was quiet, then the man said: "Everything is in place even if we don't find the kid by Friday. But we still need to find him…uh huh….do it."

What kid? I thought. This didn't seem like a good time to ask.

There was some movement in the room then the man walked to the door and let himself out. I didn't move or breathe for the next minute, then I eased the door open. My armpits were damp and I could feel sweat trickle down my back. I brought the briefcase into the living room to get a better look at it.

It was an expensive looking black leather Coach briefcase

with a combination lock on it. I could take a knife or a screw-driver and break the lock off but that's a sure sign that someone has been screwing around with your briefcase. I flipped the case upside down to look at the bottom of it. I noticed a white powder residue of some kind had dusted the bottom of it. I returned the briefcase to the closet and took one last look around to make sure I hadn't missed anything.

Then I got the hell out.

FIFTEEN

IT WAS MISERABLY COLD OUT, but no rain. The moon hung in the clear sky like a giant block of ice, freezing the world below. I zipped my jacket up to my throat and stuffed my hands in my pockets as I hurried back to my car. Instead of spending the night at the hotel I had opted to take my free nightie and check out. I needed more than a wall between me and a killer.

I put my bag in the trunk and got in the car. I drove around for a while just for the bliss of having the heat blast on my face and my feet. Then I thought about Brute Mortimer. What was he up to?

I thought about the story Violetta told me about the casino owner in Reno. Charlie Sharkey. I shuddered as I envisioned his bloody body in the pool. I had a private eye friend in Nevada who could check out the story for me. I'd call him tomorrow.

I started to head home but I found myself driving by the Starlite Lounge instead. A silver Porsche was parked out front. It looked like Sam Madsen's car. What was Sam doing at the Starlite? I decided to find out. I pulled in behind his car and got out.

The door to the lounge opened and a drunk stumbled out. He was in his forties and he wore a business suit and a loosened tie. He looked as if he had come straight from work. I moved past him and stepped inside. A cloud of cigarette smoke hung in the air, obscuring the silver stars painted on the ceiling. The place was crowded but there were a few seats left near the empty stage. The red curtains were closed however, a big sign advertised the talents of Theresa LaSalle, SINGER in an eight by ten glossy. I looked for Sam in the red vinyl booths that lined the walls. No luck. He was probably in the men's room. I walked over to the bar.

There was a woman in her early thirties sitting on a stool who caught my attention. She had honey blonde hair and she was dressed in a tight silver dress with her breasts popping out of the top. She looked familiar. A man with a receding hairline was standing next to her. He was big, with a belly that hung over his wrinkled chino pants. His sport coat was a little too short and an unlit cigar was stuck in his mouth. It bobbed up and down as he talked. The woman was staring straight ahead into the mirror behind the bar as if she was trying to feign deafness.

I remembered her now. She was the tearful one at DeOrca's funeral.

I moved over to the bar and slid onto one of the stools. The man looked me over, then went back at the blonde.

"So, doll," he said in an oily voice, "what are you doing after your number? Wanna come back to my place later? I'll show you my instrument." He chuckled and laid his meaty paw on her back. She stiffened.

"Go away, please," she said in a dull voice.

The man took his hand off her back and his face turned ugly. "Jeez, okay. You don't have to be such a bitch." He turned and decided to take his chances with me. "Buy you a drink?"

The smell of alcohol of his breath nearly knocked me down.

"No, thanks." I turned away. What a pig.

"Your loss." He picked up his drink and swaggered off.

I looked at the blonde sitting next to me. "What a creep!"

"Yeah." She agreed. "There's a lot of them here." Her voice was husky as if she had a barbecued larynx from all of the smoke drifting through. She picked up her drink, drained it and signaled the bartender. He nodded and came over.

"Jamisons. With a beer back," she said. The bartender looked at me.

"I'll take one too." I was out of my league, liquor wise. A beer back?

"Okay," he said as he moved away. The woman's eyes returned to the mirror behind the bar. Instead of looking at her reflection, she was using it to survey the scene behind her.

"I'm Jane Lanier," I said in an effort to break the ice. "I've seen you before."

She turned to me. "I'm Theresa LaSalle. I sing here five nights a week."

The bartender returned with a quartet of drinks. He slapped cocktail napkins down and placed the drinks on top of them. I pushed a twenty dollar bill at him.

"For both of us. Keep the change."

"Thanks," Theresa said carelessly as she picked up her glass. "I've seen you here before too. In fact, you were here last night with the news reporter."

"You have a good memory."

"Too good a memory is what they tell me." She knocked her drink back with a single gulp and set the glass down. "So, are you doing a story?"

"No, we were just thirsty."

"Don't tell me then. Doesn't matter." She mumbled.

"Actually, I am here on business of sorts—but I'm not a reporter. I'm looking into the DeOrca murder. I hoped you might be able to answer a couple of questions. He owned this place, didn't he?" I reached into my pocket for a business card and passed it to her.

She glanced at the card and her face registered fear. "I don't know anything. What do you want from me?"

"Well…" I remembered her tears at the funeral. She was

the only person to cry. I took a stab in the dark. "I've heard that you and DeOrca were close. I thought you might know why he came to see me on the night he died."

"I didn't kill him," she whispered.

"I wasn't accusing you," I said carefully. "But I need your help to find out who did."

Theresa sat up straight. "We do need to talk. I don't have much time tonight—I go on in ten minutes—but we can talk until then. Let's go to my dressing room. We'll have more privacy there."

I followed Theresa through the crowd to a door by the stage area. Several of the more drunk patrons tried to get her attention by grabbing at her rear but she waved them off. I planned to smack anyone who tried that stuff with me but no one did. Theresa opened a door with a large "KEEP OUT" sign and we walked into the sour smelling hallway. A mop was propped against a wall by an emergency exit but I doubted if it had ever been used. The hallway was dingy and the concrete walls were bare. The restroom door opened and a woman in tight jeans with high hair came out. We walked past her to the dressing room.

Theresa opened the door and I followed her in. The room was about the size of a large closet. A dressing table cluttered with cosmetics and jewelry was pushed up against the wall. A rack of glittery costumes, limp with age and wear, crowded the remaining space. Theresa shut the door. I wondered if we would both be able to breathe at the same time.

"Have a seat," she said as she pulled a metal folding chair out from behind a rack of clothes. She opened it for me, then sat down on her bench in front of her dressing table. She picked up a powder puff and proceeded to pat down her face. "We can talk while I get ready. Weren't you at Freddie's funeral?" Her voice was suddenly timid.

"Yeah," I said as I wedged myself into the small space by

the rack of clothes. A feather boa slid off the rack and floated to my shoulders. I took it off and held it. "Elana wants me to find out who killed her husband."

Theresa bit her lip. "I'm surprised that she would care. She didn't care about Freddie. She only cared about his money."

"It sounds like you knew him well," I said softly.

"We were going to be married." She picked up a lipstick and applied a thick coat of red over her lips.

"Oh," I said. "Did Elana know about your plans?" Bigamy was illegal in the State of Oregon as far as I knew.

"No. Freddie wanted to wait. He was going to talk to her just as soon as he wrapped up a big business deal. He said that if she knew how much money was involved she would never agree to a divorce."

"But something went wrong."

"I can't really go into that now. It's a long story," Theresa said, her eyes darting around.

"Okay. Let's go back to the night of the murder. Federico DeOrca came to see me the night he was killed in my office. Do you have any idea why DeOrca came to see me?"

"Yes…" Theresa's face looked miserable. "He was looking for one of his employees. A young guy named Joe Arnim."

"Why?"

"Joe stole a lot of money from Freddie's business."

"So this Joe kid stole some money and skipped town. And DeOrca wanted me to track him down and recover the cash."

"Right. Actually it was my idea. I saw you on the news. You were being interviewed about your work tracking down runaways. I told Freddie about the show and suggested he hire a private eye like you. He seemed to think it was a good idea." Theresa's eyes widened. "The guy you were with last night interviewed you. I remember now. I thought you guys looked familiar."

"You remembered me from that interview with Henry

Sullivan?" I said in surprise. That was several weeks ago. And the interview was short.

"I ran away from home when I was young. Nobody ever came looking for me." She picked up her brush and gave her hair a couple of whacks. Then she picked up some pins, twisted her hair into a French roll and poked them in. "So, I just remembered you—that's all." I caught her eye in the mirror. Her expression was pained and she looked away. She picked up a bottle of hair spray and whizzed it around her honey blonde head. I swallowed a lung full of chemicals and coughed. Somebody knocked on the door with two sharp raps.

"Two minutes!" A male voice on the other side of the door called.

"I've got to go." Theresa stood up.

"One more thing. Where were you the night that Freddie DeOrca was killed?"

"I was here. In fact he came by to see me. He wanted to get something he had left at my apartment."

I took a wild guess. "Was it a fancy silver briefcase?"

"Yes. How did you know that?"

"Did you know what was inside?"

Theresa shook her head. "I didn't look."

I shrugged. "Let's talk later."

We agreed to meet at two o'clock the next day at the Virginia Cafe. I had wanted to meet earlier but Theresa said something about a private audition. I left her to finish getting ready for her act. I found my way back to the main bar area and discovered Sam sitting at a table near the front of the stage. He glanced up at me as I went by but I made a beeline for the door. I had a pretty good idea of why he was at the Starlite Lounge. The fella must like blondes. As I walked outside I heard the roar of catcalls. It was show time for Miss LaSalle.

SIXTEEN

NO ONE WAS HIDING in my apartment when I walked in about ten. I checked the closets, the bathroom, the boarded up window and underneath the bed. I even opened the oven door. When I was satisfied I was alone, I went to take a shower and wash the smoke out of my hair. I opened the linen closet. There was no killer crouched inside, nor were there any fresh towels. It was laundry time.

I gathered my dirty clothes, scrounged for quarters, and lugged my laundry basket down to the basement.

A stranger coming to the building would know by their nose how to find the laundry room. It smells like a stew of bleach, mildew, and dirty gym socks. I walked in to the laundry room and crammed four washers full of my stuff. I had just finished plugging the machines when Tom Dermott walked in. He was dressed in Levi's and a faded sweatshirt that said "PORTLAND POLICE BUREAU." He carried a large laundry bag which he put down on the washer next to mine. He looked exhausted.

"Hi," I said as I hoisted myself on top of the washing machine. It rocked me back and forth like one of those motorized beds you find in the really nice motels.

"How's it going?" Dermott asked as he emptied his bag into a washer.

"Well, no one has broken into my apartment tonight as far as I can tell." I watched as he poured a liberal amount of detergent from the box into the machine. If he wasn't careful the room would turn into one giant bubble bath.

"That's good." He inserted three quarters into the slot and started the machine. Then he moved to the next one.

"Have you had any breaks in the DeOrca case?"

"I should ask you that." Dermott loaded another machine and shut the lid. "You seem to be pretty tight with the DeOrca clan now."

"Not really." I thought about mentioning the Joe Arnim lead but I wanted to check it out first. I also wanted the credit for solving the case.

"Did you go to the reception at the DeOrca house after the funeral?"

"Yeah, Mrs. DeOrca invited me." I caught myself just in time from calling her Elana. "While I was there she mentioned that Detective Vance had emptied out the drawers and file cabinets in DeOrca's home office. Did he find anything?"

Dermott folded his arms. "Hard to say. Did anyone interesting attend the reception?"

I got it. Dermott wasn't going to tell me a damn thing. Fine. Maybe he could do some of my leg work.

"Now that you mention it, I got to meet DeOrca's mother. Her name is Violetta. She's quite a character."

"Oh?"

"Yeah. She told me a story about DeOrca's business partner, Brute Mortimer." I told Dermott the story about the alleged murder of Charlie Sharkey, the casino owner.

"I've heard that story before," Dermott commented.

"Any truth to it?"

"Could be but it would be hard to prove. Sharkey was cremated before an autopsy could be done. The medical examiner there said it was an oversight but it's more probable there was a payoff. I'd stay clear of Brute Mortimer."

"Yeah, I will. But if that story is true, then I'm worried about Elana DeOrca." I shifted on the washing machine. "Have you every heard of an organization called Widows Inc.?"

"No, why?" Dermott looked up with interest.

"No reason." I didn't want to spill out any of the information that Elana had confided in me. Violetta's Sharkey story was another thing all together. She wasn't a paying client.

"We'll keep an eye on Mrs. DeOrca, but that's about all we can do. If you think she's in any immediate danger then we need to talk."

"I'll let you know." Another thing came to mind. The crime scene. "Say, are you guys about through with my office?"

"Yeah, but the criminalists left a lot of powder shit all over when they swabbed the place for prints."

"I'll bring Pine-sol. Anything unusual turn up?"

Dermott gave me a half smile. "You'll have to read the papers when we wrap up our investigation."

Smartass. "Can you tell me how the security guard is doing? If that's not proprietary information."

"He'll be okay. But he seems to have contracted a severe case of amnesia." Dermott looked at me. "So, don't get any bright ideas about talking to him. I want you to leave him alone."

"Absolutely." I could probably sneak to the hospital to visit him before my meeting with Theresa LaSalle.

Dermott picked up his detergent. "Well, I'll see you later. I think I'll put my stuff in the dryer in the morning."

"Bye." I watched him go. I stayed in the laundry room until the clothes were out of the dryer. Maybe no one wants to steal a load of sweats and jeans, but my underwear was too expensive to leave unattended.

I went upstairs and folded my laundry in front of the television. When I was done I remembered the key Elana had given me. I retrieved it from my purse. What was it for? She was hiding something—of course. But why would she trust me with the key to her secret? I wouldn't trust her. I walked through my apartment looking for good hiding places. Places that hadn't been disturbed in the course of the recent break in. Finally I taped it to a mousetrap in the kitchen under the sink.

I took a quick shower, dried my hair, then went to bed. I dreamt of DeOrca again during the night. This time the hole in his throat had a metal lock in the middle of it.

SEVENTEEN

I WOKE UP TO THE SOUND of someone banging on my door. I opened one eye and squinted at the clock; it was a little after eight. It couldn't be a friend, I thought as I rolled out of bed and grabbed a robe. They'd know better than to come this early.

I glanced at the bedroom mirror before I went to open the door. I had a serious case of bedhead and my face was bloated from nighttime water retention. The banging on the door continued.

"Coming!" I hollered as I walked over to the door. I opened it and peeked outside. I hoped to hell it wasn't the man of my dreams.

But it was—almost.

The man who stood in front of my door was middle aged with a bulbous nose protruding from his face. His stomach strained against the buttons on his grease stained shirt. But he was gorgeous to me. His name badge read: Warren, US WEST. It was the phone repairman!

"Come on in!" I urged as I flung open the door. He sniffed, hitched up his pants, and walked past me. I showed him where the phone jacks were then I went to the kitchen for something to eat. I wanted to take a shower but I was afraid that he would try to look at me while I was naked. I popped some toast in the toaster, cracked open a Diet Coke, and wandered over to the window. The trees were waving in the wind and rain sprayed the windows. A man in sweats jogged by, his face miserable. I went back to the kitchen, feasted on toast with strawberry jam, washed a few dishes, and generally puttered around until the phone guy called out.

"Okay, looks like I'm finished here."

I put my pop can on the counter and went to the living room. Tools were scattered all over the carpet. The phone guy was kneeling down on the floor with his back to me. I caught a glimpse of the moon as he started to gather his equipment.

"What was the problem?" I asked as I averted my eyes.

"The wiring." He answered shortly. He collected his tools and put them in his tool box. "Don't screw with it anymore. Leave it to the professionals."

"All right." I agreed. I didn't bother to explain that it wasn't my fault. "Thanks for coming out so soon." I showed him out. What unbelievable luck having the phone repair folks come out so fast. Maybe things were starting to go my way again.

I went to the bathroom and hopped into the shower. By the time I finished blow-drying my hair my face had deflated to a somewhat normal size. I dressed quickly in a sweater, jeans, and a navy blue Armani pea coat. I bought the coat at the Nordstrom Rack for 90 percent off. It was the shopping coup of the century. I picked up my set of keys, ready to roll. On impulse I went to the kitchen and retrieved Elana's key from the bottom of the mousetrap. It was too obvious of a hiding place. Much better to hide it with my apartment, mail, car and office keys.

The wind was blowing hard when I got outside. I circled my car and checked for visible explosives. Then I got in and headed to the Oregon Health Sciences University Hospital (OHSU) to see Peter, the security guard. He didn't talk to the police but he might be willing to talk to me—he knows that I can hit pretty hard.

OHSU is located at the top of a steep hill in Southwest Portland, a few minutes from downtown. It's known as "pill hill." The hospitals there have a commanding view of the

Willamette River and the entire city. I drove up the winding curves of Sam Jackson Park Road, past Shriner's Children Hospital and into the construction zone. The landscape was dotted with big cranes. I pulled into the parking lot as a brigade of cement mixers moved slowly past. I got out of my car and looked around. There were several hospitals on the campus and I wasn't sure where to go. An attractive woman with shoulder length blonde hair wearing a white physician's coat hurried past me on the sidewalk. Her name tag read "Laura Pomerenke, MD". I stopped her.

"I'm here to visit a patient and I have no clue where to find him. He just came out of a coma…"

She gave me a sympathetic look. "He's probably at University South. The Intensive Care Unit is located there." She pointed to the main entrance across the street. "By the sky walk." I looked up at the glass enclosed sky walk. It was connected to another building.

"Thanks."

I walked over to the hospital. The doors slid open and a man in a wheelchair whizzed past me. I moved to the front desk, dodging a man in a stretcher pushed by two orderlies with shower caps on their heads.

The front desk was manned by a sweet little old lady with white hair piled high on her head and cat eye glasses. Her volunteer name tag had little stickers over it. She was on the phone. She gave me a pleasant smile and held up her finger to indicate she would be just a minute.

I looked over to the crowded waiting room. A television was on but the sound was turned down low. Several people with trance like expressions on their faces, were staring at it.

"How can I help you?"

I looked at the volunteer. "I'm looking for Peter Sundstrom—my fiancée." I improvised lamely. "I've been out of town and I just heard he was hurt very badly. I need to see him right away."

"Of course, dear." She turned to her computer monitor and tapped on a few keys. She frowned at the machine as she scrolled down a list of patients. "Good news! It looks like he's been released."

"That is good news. When did it happen?" The man was in intensive care three days ago. Something strange was going on.

"Yesterday morning."

"Thanks a lot," I said. She nodded at me with a sunny smile and I walked out into the lobby area to a pay phone. I opened the telephone book and looked up the name "Sundstrom". There were two Peter Sundstroms. One lived in southeast Portland, the other near Gresham. I could try the address in Southeast Portland without too much trouble. I ripped out the page and traced my steps back to the parking lot.

I drove back down the hill and threaded through downtown and across the Morrison Bridge to the Southeast section of town. The address listed was located on Belmont. I drove past a commercial area to an older neighborhood characterized mostly by Victorian houses with Volkswagen vans parked in front. I pulled up in front of an apartment complex unimaginatively named Belmont Court. It was an old brick building, maybe six stories, and it was in a state of disrepair. The concrete steps leading to the building were chipped and the outside of the building was weathered with peeling paint. There were faded curtains hanging in several windows and a few were covered with newspapers. I got out of the car and walked past a pair of movers loading a mattress wrapped in plastic into a new truck. Someone was moving out and up into the world. I mounted two sets of steps to the front door. The apartment had an old fashioned security system with a grimy phone to buzz visitors in. I looked at the names on the board. Each one had an apartment number listed next to their buzzer. Sundstrom lived on the fourth floor.

The front door opened and a young man with a bandage

wrapped around his head stepped out. His face was black and purple with bruises and his nose was taped up. He was dressed in jeans, a sweatshirt, and a jacket. He carried a duffel bag in one hand and a soft sided suitcase in the other. There were splints on his pinky fingers. It had to be Peter, although it was difficult to recognize him.

"Excuse me," he muttered as he brushed me aside. I stopped and watched as he hobbled down the stairs to the new truck and opened the passenger door. The truck was so new I could even see the Buyer's Guide still stuck to the window. He tossed the suitcase in and turned to speak to one of the movers. I walked back down the stairs and went over.

"Excuse me." The men stopped talking to look me over. I turned to the man with the bandages. "Are you Peter Sundstrom?"

"Who wants to know?" he asked, scowling at me. His voice sounded a little feeble despite the bravado of his words.

I held out my hand. "I'm Jane Lanier." I looked in his eyes for a flicker of recognition, but his eyes were blank. He ignored my hand, which angered me. Punk. "I'm surprised you don't remember me," I said a little spitefully. "You attacked me in my office and I beat the crap out of you. I came over to see if you were okay, that's all. I went to the hospital and they said you had been released."

The movers snickered and Sundstrom turned around and glared at them. Then he looked back at me. "I'm gonna live. Thanks for caring. Now if you'll excuse me, I've got stuff to do."

I looked at the truck. The mattress was tied down with a rope and there were several boxes packed around it. "It looks like you're leaving town."

"Yeah, and you're in my way." He started to shoulder me aside but I held my ground.

"Could you hang on a minute? It's important that we talk." I dug into my purse for a twenty. "I'll even pay you."

Peter Sundstrom looked at the bill, wavering. He made up his mind quickly. "Okay." He plucked the twenty from my hand. "But only for a few minutes. Follow me upstairs, I've got a few more things to pick up."

I followed Sundstrom back into the apartment building. It smelled like cooked cabbage. We got into a rat trap of an elevator and Peter pulled the metal grate closed. Then we lurched to the fourth floor. We got out and I followed him down a rancid smelling hallway with shabby wallpaper to an apartment with an open door. We walked in. The room was in disarray with stacks of newspaper against the wall and an overflowing garbage can full of beer bottles by the door. A Murphy bed sans mattress was the only piece of furniture left in the room. I could see an open closet with a couple of empty wire hangers but that was it.

"Looks like you're pretty much finished," I said.

"Yeah," Sundstrom said shortly. He went to the mattress and lifted it up. He extracted a brown paper sack. I hoped it wasn't his lunch.

"Look, I know we didn't meet under the best of circumstances, but I need your help. I need to know what happened the night of the murder."

Sundstrom sat down on the bed. "I don't remember anything."

"Can you try? Any little detail would be a big help."

"Well…I was on my rounds, checking to see that all the doors were locked. Theft is a big problem in the downtown area. There was a light on in your office." He stopped. "At least I think it was your office…"

"It was," I interrupted.

"…and I heard a loud thump, so I ran over to see if anyone was hurt. I knocked on the door but nobody answered so I unlocked it and went inside. The last thing I remember is getting my head bashed in." He gave me a baleful look with his bloodshot eyes. "Did you do that?"

"No, the nose." I patted mine sheepishly. "I showed up around ten o'clock. I unlocked the office, then you rushed me—so I had to defend myself. I guess I knocked you out. Federico DeOrca was dead by then. I found him on my desk. What time did you make your rounds?"

Sundstrom hesitated. "Little after nine o'clock. I always do a walk through before I lock the doors on the main floor."

"So the killer must have already been in the office."

Sundstrom shrugged. "To tell you the truth, I don't remember a damn thing. He must have heard me knocking cause the minute I walked in the door—BAM! Right on my head. I was beat up pretty bad. That's how come you were able to knock me out," he said defensively.

"Oh, absolutely," I agreed. A little ego massage. "Why were you working last Friday night?" I asked curiously. "I expected to see Artie Harris, the regular guard."

"Art was off that night. Called in sick, lucky bastard. We work for the same company. I work the night shift cause I go to school. I was taking classes at PCC until I could save enough to go back to Oregon State. Friday was just my second week on the job."

He must have been hit on the head pretty hard. He had already told me he was saving up to go back to school.

"That's too bad. So where are you headed now?"

"I'm going back to Oregon State."

"But you just said you didn't have enough money." I thought about the new truck parked downstairs.

"Umm…I got some money from a scholarship." Sundstrom stood up. "Look, I've got to get going."

"No problem. I'll show myself out."

Sundstrom walked me to the door and shut it behind me. I could hear the snap of the lock. What was the deal with him? And where did the money come from? I didn't believe his scholarship story. I took the stairs down to the lobby and walked out. The moving guys were gone but the truck was loaded up. I walked over to the window and looked at the price sticker on the Buyer's Guide. It was purchased at Broadway Toyota for 24,999 dollars with all the options.

I got in my car and headed back downtown. I stopped at the Safeway on Tenth Avenue to pick up some cleaning supplies before I headed back to the office. Dermott had said they were through with my office, but call me fussy, I can't work with blood on my desk.

My parking angel was with me and I was able to find a space near the Galleria. I parked, plugged the meter, and grabbed a souvlaki and Diet Coke from a food cart on the corner. Afterwards, I went inside the Galleria, took the elevator to the fifth floor and walked to my office.

The sign outside my door was sticky with some kind of tape. I rubbed at it a little with my sleeve. It was probably from the yellow tape that the police place over crime scenes. I unlocked the door and pushed it all the way open before going in. This time there weren't any bodies on my desk.

Instead the office was covered with a film of black powder on white objects, white powder on dark objects. The desk was fairly clean. I interviewed a homicide detective in Seattle once, and he told me that you can't lift prints off a wooden surface because fingerprints are basically oils. I looked around the room. The criminalists had been at work. Pieces of my carpet were cut out by my desk but the rest of the carpet was freshly vacuumed. I went over to the window and opened it to get rid of the stale smell in the room. Then I sat down at my desk. The blotter was bloodstained. It looked like the rest of the year was shot. I rolled it up and threw it in the trash. I remembered Elana's key and took it off the ring. After a moment I took it off and taped it to the underside of the desk. Inspired, I grabbed a piece of gum from my purse, chewed it, and stuck it on top of the key. Now that was a hiding place!

My amusement subsided as I thought back to the murder. A lot had happened since last Friday night and most of it didn't make sense. What went on here? I closed my eyes and imagined the killer crouched in the shadows with a gun in his hands, lying in wait for me to open the door. How did he or she know that DeOrca would be visiting me at that particular time? How did DeOrca get in? I know my office door was locked. The killer must have broken in.

DeOrca went into the building at ten o'clock. A few minutes later he was dead. But Sundstrom was spared—why?

I opened my eyes and pulled open a drawer. Maybe it would help if I had all my facts on paper. I rooted around in the drawer and came up with my nameplate and business cards. Normally I keep them on my desk but maybe the cops cleared them off. I picked up a card and inspected it. I didn't want to hand it out if it was splattered with guts. But it was clean.

How could that be?

EIGHTEEN

"YOO HOO! IS ANYONE HOME?"

Someone was speaking to me through the opening in my mailbox. It sounded like Linda Driscoll, my neighbor. I was tempted to hide underneath my desk, but instead I walked over to the door and answered it.

"I thought you were here, darling," she said triumphantly. "I saw the light on."

"Come in, Linda." I forced a smile.

Linda marched by me. She's in her late forties with hair dyed a vivid red color and sprayed crisp. Normally she wears flowing clothes draped over her ample figure. Today she was wearing a vivid blue suit with a cat pin on the lapel and blue high heels.

"You look nice today. Did you have a meeting?" Linda and her husband Rob run a construction management company. Linda takes care of the little office down the hall from mine and her husband goes out to visit construction sites to drum up business.

"No! I had to go down to the police station to give a statement."

"Oh? I wonder why they didn't interview you while they were here. Did they make all of the tenants go in?"

"No siree. Just me." She paused and widened her eyes. "Because I was in the building at the time of the murder!"

"Sit down." I grabbed a chair and dragged it over. I sat down on the reception desk. "Tell me everything!"

"Well, I was working late that night trying to get a bid

together that was due on Monday. I heard a loud noise a little after ten o'clock coming from your office. It sounded like a fight. I ran back to my office and called the police."

"Did you hear the gunfire?"

Linda looked crestfallen. "No... I missed that. You see I had stopped to visit the little girls room. I was walking by your office on the way back to mine."

"Wow."

"Did you get hurt, Jane?"

"Not really. Just some bruises. But someone blew up my car the next day."

Linda shook her head. "Whatever possessed you to get mixed up with that DeOrca character? It's a wonder you weren't killed."

"He found me. I didn't ask for his business. What do you know about him?"

"He's crooked as hell. He has a trucking company and we've bid against him on a couple of jobs."

"So how is he crooked?"

Linda scrunched her nose. "Where do I start? The trucking business was a front, I think. The trucks were legit, but none of the drivers were licensed. They would do a job here and there but their big money came from contraband cargo if you know what I mean."

I did.

"Anyway, there's something you should know." Linda paused and clasped her hands on her lap. She looked concerned.

"What's that?"

"The police asked me a lot of questions about you. One of the detectives," She paused, scrunching up her forehead "—his name sounded like 'dammit', wanted to know if I thought you were capable of murder."

Must have been Dermott, I thought. "So what did you tell them?"

"Of course you are! We all are—especially during that

time of the month." She laughed heartily. "I once knocked a man out with my handbag because he broke into my car. No telling what I'd do if someone snuck into my office."

I groaned inwardly. My only hope was that the police had figured out Linda was half crazy. "Thanks for standing up for me. I hope you'll visit while I'm in the slammer."

Linda got up. "Now, don't you worry. My cousin Ed is a lawyer if you need one. He specializes in personal injury law, but I think he might be able to help you. Never known him to turn down a client. Let me know if you'd like his phone number. In fact, he's single, if you're interested."

"Thanks, Linda." Get out of my office please!

She seemed to heed my silent plea. I showed her to the door, then I shut and locked it. I placed a call to the management office of the Galleria to request help from maintenance. They weren't all that happy to hear from me. Murder makes people a little anxious, I guess.

Ten minutes later a maintenance guy brought me by a bucket. I saw him peer into my office as he handed it to me. I should charge for tours, kind of like the Jack the Ripper walks in London. I thanked him before walking down the hall to the restroom to fill a bucket with water and swipe a roll of paper towels. Then I returned to the office and scrubbed the place down. When I was done, I rinsed out the bucket and left it by the Galleria maintenance closet. Then I went back to my office and stowed my cleaning supplies in a file cabinet. Who knows, I might want to clean again next year.

I sat down at my desk to rest. My mind kept returning to the night of the murder. What did I have? A man was murdered in my office and I still didn't know how or why. It didn't make sense; I had seen him walk by just minutes before he was killed. How could I have missed the killer?

I stood up and turned to the window. Clouds were gathering over the West hills again. Across the street I could see a steady stream of cars circling through the parking structure. Suddenly I remembered that a pair of headlights had flashed at me right after I had discovered Federico DeOrca's body. Could it have been the killer?

Only an Olympic track star could've accomplished it.

The killer would've had to shoot DeOrca, run down five flights of stairs, run across the street, go up five flights of stairs, drive down the ramp, and pay the eagle-eyed parking attendant, who could later identify him and his vehicle.

Too risky.

So, how did it happen? I mentally sketched the sequence of events. The killer broke into my office to wait for DeOrca. He probably picked the lock to get in. Possibly he made noise and Peter, the security guard, went to investigate. Then Peter was assaulted. I shuddered. It could have been me. Since the doors were unlocked and the elevators were still running, it must have been about nine thirty p.m.

Ten o'clock. DeOrca gets out of the cab, goes into the Galleria. I follow a minute or two behind. Wait for the Max train to pass by. I go into the building and take the elevator to the fifth floor. Takes me two or three minutes—tops.

In that time, DeOrca was shot, his suitcase was stolen, and a killer escaped.

Did he see me?

The day after the murder, my car was blown up. A warning, perhaps? Then after that my apartment was tossed. What was he looking for? I felt like I had a puzzle in front of me but all the pieces had legs.

Everett Crombie was a big piece of the puzzle. According to the story in the *Oregonian* he had died in a nearly identical fashion as DeOrca. The men were partners. What linked them together besides their business?

Brute Mortimer. The third partner, now the only partner left alive.

I reached for the phone directory. I needed to get in touch with Jackie Crombie—even if she did seem a little unbalanced. Maybe she could clue me into the history of the "business."

I left a message on her home phone, then I remembered Elana had said she volunteered at the Burnside Shelter. It's a homeless shelter located in downtown Portland in the heart of Old Town. I called the number and was transferred to Jackie Crombie. I could hear the din of voices in the background.

"Jackie Crombie?" I said politely.

"Yes, what is it?" Her voice was impatient but she sounded sober—unlike the day of the funeral.

"My name is Jane Lanier. I'm a private investigator and I'm looking into the death of Federico DeOrca. I was hoping I could come by to talk to you."

"Why? Do you think that I did it?" Her tone was sarcastic.

"Did you?" I asked for the heck of it.

Jackie Crombie laughed. "No, somebody beat me to it. Yes, you can ask me some questions. Shoot."

"Actually, I wanted to come down and talk to you." I'm better at reading faces than reading voices over the phone. I looked at my watch. It was nearly time to meet Theresa LaSalle. "Look, I have a meeting at two o'clock. Maybe I could come see you after that. My meeting shouldn't take more than an hour or two."

Jackie hesitated. "I'm working, and that's our busiest time, you know, the dinner hour. Things quiet down here around eight o'clock. Can you come by then?"

"Sure."

We hung up. I put on my coat and picked up my purse. Before I left the office I took one last look around in case the murderer still lurked in the shadows. Everything appeared normal except for the missing chunks of carpet, and my memory of a dead man on my desk.

NINETEEN

THE VIRGINIA CAFE IS a bar and restaurant that caters to the Generation X crowd. I've been there a few times after work for happy hour. The drinks are cheap and so is the decor. The word "bordello" comes to mind. It's located across the street from Nordstrom, an upscale department store. V.C. customers can watch the store detectives collar shoplifters from the comfort of their bar stools. A tally is kept on a small chalkboard on the wall. It was up to 26 for the year when I walked in around 2:00 p.m.

I scanned the room for Theresa. A scruffy man at the bar looked at me with interest. I averted my gaze. The bartender was intent on watching a soap opera that was playing on a television suspended by cables from the ceiling. The tables by the bar were occupied by a scattering of folks catching a late lunch of burgers and fries. I didn't see her. I walked around the partition separating the booth area from the tables and spotted Theresa's dark haired twin. She waved at me. I slid into the booth.

"Theresa, is that you?" The change was remarkable. Her hair had been dyed a dark brown and pulled back into a ponytail. Instead of a silver, shimmery dress, she was wearing a denim jacket with a sweatshirt underneath. Her face was scrubbed clean of makeup and she looked rather haggard.

She put a finger to her lips. "Hi. Keep your voice down. I don't want to call attention to myself."

"Sure," I said under my breath. I sounded silly to myself so I spoke up a bit. "Is everything okay?"

Theresa shook her head as a waiter approached. I shut my mouth. We both ordered coffee and he returned in a few moments with two steaming cups. As soon as he left, Theresa looked up at me.

"I don't have much time."

"All right. Do you want to tell me about the new look?" I suspected it was a disguise. No one would make herself look that bad without a good reason.

Theresa picked up a packet of sugar, ripped it open and dumped it in her coffee. "I'm getting out of town. I want to start a whole new life where nobody knows me. I want to be left alone. You don't get left alone when you have big boobs and big hair."

So that explained my active social life.

"Did you quit your job at the Starlite Lounge?"

"They'll figure it out when I don't show up tonight."

"What are you going to do now?" I picked up my coffee and took a sip. It scalded my tongue.

"I've got a few bucks saved. Doesn't matter what I do as long as I get far away from here." She dropped her voice. "It's not safe."

"Because of what happened to DeOrca?"

Theresa bit her lip. "Maybe…" Her voice wavered a bit. "Somebody broke in my place last night while I was at work. They slashed my bed apart and emptied all my drawers. I packed a few things and got the hell out. I can't go back now."

"The same thing happened to me! Do you have any idea who might have done it?"

Theresa picked up her coffee. The cup clinked on the saucer a bit and I realized she was shaking.

"Might have been the kid."

"Which kid?" Sean?

"The one that Federico was looking for…"

"Joe Arnim?"

"Yeah." Her eyes started to tear. "I'm afraid that Freddie's murder might have been my fault."

"How?"

"Joe came to see me after work one night. He was worried about Freddie. The news had traveled about the missing money—and Joe wanted to know what Freddie was thinking."

"What did you tell him?"

"That his ass was grassed if he didn't give the money back. Joe tried to tell me he didn't have it, but I didn't believe it for a second. Joe is a liar. I told him that his best chance of reaching old age was to give the money to me to pass along to Freddie."

"Did he take your advice?"

"No. He said that Freddie would never find him if he didn't want to be found." Theresa made a face. "Dumb ass. I told him that Freddie was going to hire you and if he knew what was good for him he'd give up the money."

"Why didn't you just tell Freddie that Joe was in town? Then he wouldn't have to go to the trouble of hiring a private detective."

"I should have. But I wanted to buy Joe some time to make things right. I didn't know that Joe was going to kill him!" Her mouth twisted down in despair. "Now I'm afraid that Joe's after me. I know about the money and I'm the one who told him that DeOrca would be at your office on Friday night. I've got to get away before I'm next."

"You need to go the police with this."

"I can't." Theresa gave me a pitiful look.

"Then I will."

"Do what you have to do. But wait until I'm out of town. I want Joe behind bars so I don't have to look over my shoulder for the rest of my life."

"You'll need to testify."

"I can't."

"Why not?"

Theresa gazed past my shoulder to the window. "There are a lot of things you don't know, things I've done that I'm not proud of. I can't afford to go to the police. You'll have to take care of this yourself. I'm sorry." She reached into her tote bag and pulled out a scarred leather wallet. She extracted two wrinkled dollar bills, laid them by her coffee cup, and slid out of the booth. "I've got to go. Do what you can."

I sighed. "Okay. I understand. One more thing—have you ever heard of an organization called Widow's Inc.?"

"No." She looked puzzled. I didn't feel like offering an explanation.

"All right. Thank you for meeting me, Theresa. And good luck."

Theresa picked up her tote bag and looked me in the eye. "My name is Sarah," she said quietly. "Theresa was my stage name. Good-bye, Jane."

She walked past me to the door. She was gone before I realized that I had just been speaking with Sarah Winningham.

The missing juror.

TWENTY

THE LIGHT CHANGED. The sea of traffic parted and the pedestrians waded as a group across the street. I nearly knocked down an old lady hobbling by on a cane as I ran down the block looking for Sarah. I caught a glimpse of her denim jacket as she rounded a corner by the Nordstrom store, but when I got there she was gone.

Vanished.

And I had so many questions. The trial, her relationship with DeOrca, and all the years since. Had she helped a murderer go free? What kind of hold did he have on her? Why did she do it? And why did she want to help Joe?

I spent the rest of the afternoon searching for her to no avail. I drove up and down the streets of Portland, talked to parking attendants, shopkeepers, panhandlers. The clerk at the Greyhound bus station told me that half of the passengers fit the description of Theresa/Sarah. A glance around the terminal told me the clerk was either a blind man or a liar. The folks at the train station were equally helpful.

It was five o'clock by the time I got home. I made a quick call to Tim King, a private eye located in Reno. He owes me one since I bailed out his college aged daughter from jail one night after a rowdy party. She's a college student at the University of Portland and I think her major is in "fun".

Tim wasn't in so I left a message requesting more information about the Sharkey murder. I turned on the evening news while I went into the kitchen for something to eat. I was nuking a Lean Cuisine when I heard Henry's voice over the hum of the microwave. I dashed into the living room to watch his report. Normally, Henry does pre-taped human interest type stories but tonight he was reporting live from a marina. He was standing by a dock speaking into a microphone. Despite his heavy coat he was shivering and the wind was brushing his hair away from his face. I could see a flurry of activity as policemen and medical personnel moved in the background.

"Hello, this is Henry Sullivan reporting live from McCormick Pier. The Coast Guard pulled a body from the Willamette River about twenty minutes ago. At this point we know that the deceased is a Caucasian male, in his mid to late fifties. He was discovered this afternoon by a fishing vessel." Henry stopped speaking as two ambulance attendants walked in front of the camera. They were carrying a sheet-covered body on a stretcher. I could see Detective Dermott walking grimly behind them. Henry reached over and stuck the microphone in front of his face.

"Detective, can you give us any more information on the cause of death? Eyewitnesses have reported that the dead man had been shot. Can you confirm this?"

"No comment," Dermott said in a terse voice. His shoulders sagged as if the weight of the dead man was on him alone. "We'll issue a statement after we've notified the family." He trudged off leaving Henry standing alone. Henry looked startled but recovered quickly.

"There you have it," he said in a serious tone to the camera. "Back to you, Shelley."

Henry's face was replaced by a woman with a helmet head hairdo. I turned off the television and went to the kitchen to eat my diet lasagna. The cheese was a bit gluey but I ate every bite of it. For dessert I pulled out a carton of chocolate chip cookie dough ice cream that was nearly empty. With surgical precision I dissected the box open and scraped the sides with a spoon. While I ate I reminded myself that Henry hadn't called me since he spent the night. Maybe my phone line had been cut but I still didn't consider that a good excuse.

To put myself in a better mood I went to my desk to sort my bills. I opened the stacks of envelopes, including sweepstakes entries and book club notices, and made little piles. Some of the bills were several months old so I threw away the duplicates. I hadn't had time to deposit the check from Elana, but I entered it into my checking account anyway, and watched as the number slowly dwindled after each check I wrote. When I was done, I sat back with a sigh of relief and put a stamp on each envelope. The only bill left to settle with was VISA. Guiltily I remembered my upstairs neighbor's VISA bill. If I waited much longer to give it to him his credit would be as bad as mine. I grabbed the bill and ran upstairs to his apartment.

I was shoving the bill underneath the door when it opened. An African American man, probably in his late twenties, stood in front of me. He was wearing a pale blue shirt with the sleeves rolled up and his red silk tie was loosened. His pants were rumpled as if he had been sitting in them all day. The wire glass frames on his nose completed his corporate uniform. I stood up hastily and handed the bill to him. He gave me a questioning look.

"I'm Jane Lanier. I live downstairs," I said sheepishly. I pointed to the Visa bill in his hand. "I got your VISA bill by mistake." We both looked at the envelope. The edge was ragged from where I had torn it open.

"I'm Jim Lerner. As you've guessed." He extended his hand and I shook it. "Come in. I think I've got your bill in here somewhere."

I followed him into his apartment. It was sparsely furnished with sleek modern furniture and a huge big screen television set which was turned on to a Blazer game. In the rear of the room a telescope was positioned behind a black leather couch. An open box of Hot Lips pizza was laid out on the glass coffee table, next to a grease-stained napkin and an open bottle of beer. The smell of the pepperoni teased my nostrils and it took a great deal of restraint to keep from grabbing a slice and running out the door.

Jim disappeared into his bedroom and came out again with my bill. "Here you go," he said in a cheery voice as he handed it to me. I grinned at him. He had opened my bill too.

"Thanks. Next time this happens, why don't you just pay my bill and I'll pay yours."

He shook his head decisively. "No way! I've seen…" He broke off as he glanced toward the window.

"What's the matter?" I said, following his gaze. Through his window I could see the apartment building next door, beyond that, lights twinkled in the hills. It was dark already.

"Someone is watching us," he said, tilting his head toward the window. "What the hell for, I don't know, but they've been at it almost constantly since last Saturday."

I froze. That's when my trouble started. "Turn out the lights and let me see," I whispered. Jim nodded, hit the lights, then we moved toward the window. Jim pulled the telescope down a bit for me to look into.

Several scenes were being played out in front of the illuminated windows. The brick building across the street was about twelve floors high with ivy climbing the walls. It reminds me of a college library somehow. On the second floor, a heavyset woman in an apron set down a casserole dish. A man in an undershirt and suspenders put aside his paper and reached for a spoon. Dinner, boring. I tilted the telescope to the floor above, where a couple was locked in an embrace. I smiled, then scanned the rest of the building. Most of the windows were cloaked in curtains and shades. On the very top floor I could see the figure of a man hunched over a telescope. His lens was angled in my direction!

"I see him!" I said excitedly. "He's been at it since Saturday?" I moved away from the telescope.

"Yup," Jim said, taking a look for himself. "Pretty strange if you ask me. Probably a pervert. Keep your curtains closed."

No more streaking out of the bathroom, I decided. "Thanks, I will." I wanted to stare out the window at the peeping Tom some more, but I remembered my appointment with Jackie Crombie. "I've got to go now. I'm meeting somebody. Would you mind keeping me posted about the freak across the street? I sure don't like being watched."

"Me either," Jim said as he drew the drapes shut. He reached over and snapped the light on. I saw him look at his pizza. It had cooled and the cheese was starting to congeal. Time for me to go. We said goodbye and he showed me to the door. I went downstairs to get my coat and keys to keep my appointment with Jackie Crombie. Before I left, I shut my curtains and peeked outside. The window from where the man had stood was dark.

Was he still watching?

TWENTY-ONE

JACKIE CROMBIE'S second floor office was crammed full of empty barrels stacked in threes. Paper signs that read "FOOD DRIVE, BURNSIDE SHELTER", were glued to the front of each barrel. Her wall was covered with civic awards, including a photo of her with the governor. A desk, swamped with papers, faced Burnside Street. A cracked shade was pulled down over the window. Outside I could hear the swish of traffic and the voices of the men lined up downstairs, waiting to get in.

"Thanks for taking the time to meet with me," I said as Jackie showed me in. "I appreciate it."

Jackie had met me in front of the building, then she took me on a quick tour of the place. There was a dormitory room set up with rows of cots covered with gray blankets. The dining room was also furnished in a Spartan style with long tables and benches. Several men were seated at the tables, eating and talking. The kitchen area was a hub of activity as several sweaty faced volunteers plopped mashed potatoes and meatloaf on plates in assembly line fashion. One of the volunteers passed Jackie a paper bag and a cup of coffee before we left.

Back at her desk, she pulled a meatloaf sandwich with ketchup oozing out the sides from the bag. After offering me half, which I refused, she took a bite.

"Do you mind if I eat while we talk?" she said after swallowing. "If I don't have dinner now, I might not get a chance tonight. Things can get a little crazy around here. We have fifty beds and twice as many bodies to fill them."

"That's really something." I looked at Jackie as she gulped down some coffee. The hand wrapped around her cup sported a large diamond wedding ring. Her hair was freshly cut and the tint and style showed that it had been in the hands of a professional. She was dressed simply: in slacks, a sweater, and Cole Haan loafers. She looked more like the president of the Junior League than the director of a homeless shelter. I told her so.

"The Junior League kicked me out after I showed up drunk at one of their fund-raisers." She laughed. "So, I ended up here. But I'm not that much different from the guys standing outside. A lot of us are alcoholics. I just happen to have money. In fact, working here is the only thing that keeps me sober. But enough about that. Don't you have some questions to ask me?"

"I do." I was a little startled by her bluntness. I was also surprised that the composed woman sitting in front of me was the drunken woman who had ranted over DeOrca's grave.

"I was going through some old newspaper stories having to do with your husband's murder. I noticed that Federico DeOrca had been charged—"

"—with my husband's murder," Jackie finished. "Yeah, he was charged all right. He would've been convicted if he hadn't paid off everyone in sight."

"Do you know for sure if he bribed members of the jury or the police department?"

"Of course, I do, but I can't prove it—no one can. Just like I can't prove he was a drug dealer. But everyone knows he is—or was, I guess."

"Why would DeOrca kill your husband?"

"My husband was a real estate developer. He bought the Starlite Lounge twenty years ago as an investment. Thought the property might be worth something down the road. That didn't happen. The plan was to bulldoze the building but the funding fell through. By that time Everett was spending more and more time there—drinking his profits." She looked at me ruefully. "We had a lot in common. Anyway, he met DeOrca and his shady pal Mortimer through the bar. They were regulars. Somehow they persuaded him to let them buy into the place as silent partners. I was all for it. I didn't like having Everett hang out at the bar, night after night, while I was drinking by myself at home. So he sold them each a third. Soon after they started to use the bar to launder their drug money. Everett threatened to go to the police. A few days later he was dead." Her face clouded over.

"Jackie, where did the drugs come from?"

"Back then, I'm not sure. It's been over ten years since my husband was murdered. But I've heard they had a drug lab set up in a warehouse by the river. There was a fire there a few weeks ago. Maybe the police were finally on to them and they were destroying the evidence." Her eyes gleamed and I wondered if the police had been tipped off.

"Why didn't the police close the place down?"

"Oh, I think that DeOrca and Mortimer were too slippery—and ruthless. The two of them had the nerve to come to my house the day after they killed my husband, to try to buy out his share in the bar."

"Did you sell?"

"Yes." She picked up her coffee cup and took a sip. "I didn't want any part of their operation. I took the money, the payoff, I guess you could call it, and started volunteering here." A bitter look crossed her face.

"Do you mind telling me where you were the night DeOrca was shot?"

Jackie set her cup down. "I was at a fund-raiser for a drug and alcohol treatment center. I saw Elana there in fact." She opened a drawer, pulled out an invitation on heavy card stock, and handed it to me. I glanced at it. It was for the New Beginnings Adolescent Treatment Center for drug and alcohol addictions. I opened the invitation. Jackie Crombie had been a special guest of honor.

"Mind if I keep this?"

"Go ahead. After the banquet I came down to the office to finish a grant application. The deadline was Monday."

"So you didn't swing by my office and knock DeOrca off."

"No. But believe me I've fantasized about it a million times in a million different ways. Yes, I wanted to kill him. But sitting in a jail cell the rest of my life wouldn't bring my husband back. It took me years of therapy to realize that."

"Speaking of Elana, how well do you know her? Do you think she could have done it?"

"And get her hands dirty? Get real. Elana is a princess. Shows up for photo opportunities, waves to the masses and then leaves the grunt work for the little people. Like the fund-raiser last Friday night for the treatment center. It took months of planning. She showed up at the initial meeting, wrote a check, and was never seen again until banquet night." Jackie stopped. "Granted, it was a big check, but that doesn't really change anything. Nor does it make up for the fact that her late husband was a big contributor to the problem."

"One more thing. Have you ever heard of an organization called Widows Inc.?"

Her eyes narrowed. "No."

The phone rang and Jackie picked it up. "Okay, I'll bring a mop," she said in a weary voice, then she hung up.

"I've got to go," she said as she stood up. "I'm the Executive Director of this place but I'm also the Chief of Vomit Patrol."

"I understand. Thanks for your time." I stood up to leave.

"No problem. If you ever have a free afternoon, we could always use some help around here," Jackie said as I inched towards the door. Downstairs I could hear the throes of a fight breaking out.

I flinched at the thought of being second in command of the Vomit Patrol. "Would you take a post dated check instead?"

"You bet," Jackie said with a satisfied smile. "We accept cash too."

I dug in my purse for my checkbook. Admission to the Burnside Shelter was free but it cost me fifty bucks to get out.

It was worth it.

TWENTY-TWO

THE PHONE RANG JUST as I was sinking into sleep. No good things happen with the middle of the night calls. Perverts pant in your ear, people die…I wish all of the horrors of the world could just wait until morning. I hate being awakened. With my eyes closed, I reached over to my nightstand and smacked my hand around until I found the receiver.

"Hello?" I mumbled into it.

"Jane? It's Henry." He sounded excited. A booty call. Too bad. There was no way he was coming over now. I opened one eye. The luminous glow of my clock read 12:03 a.m.

"Hi, Henry. Where are you?"

"I'm still at work. I'm sorry to wake you, but it's important." He didn't sound sorry. "Did you see my report tonight?"

"I did—you were great. Who's the floater?"

"Thanks. Roger Vance, a homicide detective from the Portland Police Department. Didn't you say he interviewed you the night DeOrca was killed?"

I was wide awake now. I sat up in bed and turned the light on.

"He did. I can't believe he's dead! Are you sure it's him?"

"We just received confirmation from the Portland Police Department. The medical examiner said he's been dead for two days, maybe more."

"That's interesting. After my car was blown up I went back to the station on Saturday to talk to Detective Dermott. I thought maybe the explosion might be connected to the DeOrca case. Anyway, Vance wasn't there. I wonder if—"

I stopped mid-sentence. Wait a minute. I hadn't told Henry that Vance had interviewed me the night of the murder. Wherever he got that information it wasn't from me. I changed the subject. "So, how did he die?"

"He was shot in the neck."

Just like Federico DeOrca and Everett Crombie. I took a deep breath. "Stay where you are. I'm coming down to the station. We need to talk."

When I arrived at the station, a security guard buzzed me in. I walked past a set of glass doors into the newsroom area. It was quiet except for the whir of a fax machine spitting out a press release. The news never stops, I guess. The last time I was by the station was during the day for my interview with Henry, it was a hub of activity. The show was about to go on and reporters and producers were putting last minute touches on the night's stories. Henry had given me a quick tour of the station. I went up to the studio and watched the broadcast from the "God box", a window walled room where the producer cues the anchors and directs the show.

I looked at my watch. The eleven o'clock news had been over for over an hour and almost everyone had gone home. I glanced at the in/out board near the door. Only Henry Sullivan, Steve Shibaura and Anne Kern remained. Steve and Anne were the co-anchors of the eleven o'clock news. I looked around at the maze of cubicles. Which one was Henry's? I couldn't remember. I started to wander, taking a private delight in being alone in an office. What sort of things do people keep in their drawers? I would've loved to find out. Instead I kept to the main aisle, glancing in the different work spaces. The assignment board over the story editor's desk showed that Henry Sullivan had been assigned to the "Vance" story. As I studied the board, I could hear a low conversation behind the walls of one of the cubicles. The voices sounded like Anne's and Steve's. I started over to ask where Henry was, but I stopped when I heard Anne complain that the "bastard was trying to steal my job." I hung back to listen, wondering if the "bastard" was Henry. Could be. Steve made some consoling noises, then said, "let's call it a night." Anne Kern emerged from the cubicle as I tried to sneak past. Her crisp suit, stiff blonde hair and heavy camera make up made me self conscious of my own outfit—a raincoat thrown over a sweatshirt, jeans and tennis shoes. She was lugging a tote bag that bulged with papers. Steve was right behind her.

"Oh." She paused in front of me, startled.

"I'm looking for Henry," I said by way of explanation.

"He's at his desk. On the other side of the room," she said, flinging her free arm in the direction of the hallway. As she swept past I heard her mutter something that sounded like "the asshole." Steve gave me an apologetic look as he went by.

I followed Anne's direction and found Henry at his desk with a phone attached to his ear. His cubicle looked like a pig sty. His "in" box was stacked precariously high with file folders. Piles of newspapers, magazines, and press releases littered the floor. There was a blizzard of papers on his desk and four jammed rolodexes. I don't know anyone else that popular. The rest of the office wasn't decorated. Not a single family photo, picture or paperweight. It was as if he didn't expect to stay long.

Henry said good-bye, hung up the phone and stood to greet me. He was rumpled, with his shirt sleeves rolled up and his tie loosened. The look he gave me reminded me that we were more than colleagues, and I wished I had taken the time to comb my hair.

"Hi, Henry."

"Jane. Let's go grab a cup of coffee so we can talk in private." There was a steaming cup of coffee in a Channel 7 mug already on his desk. If I had any caffeine I would be up all damn night.

"Relax." I perched on the edge of his desk. "Your co-workers just left. They were talking about you. Besides, I don't like to drink coffee this late."

Henry frowned. "What did they say?"

"Just flattering things."

He brightened up. "That's a change. Anne was—oh, never mind." He dropped back into his chair. "I'm glad you came over. I have two days to find out everything there is to know about Roger Vance."

"Well, I can't prove it, but I think the Vance murder might be connected to DeOrca's."

Henry leaned forward. "How so?"

"On February 17, over a dozen years ago, Everett Crombie was murdered. You remember—he was DeOrca's business partner. Fast forward to now. Federico DeOrca is murdered. The next day Roger Vance gets it." I left out the Sharkey murder. I still wanted to get some kind of confirmation from my colleague in Nevada.

"Where are you going with all this?"

"They were all murdered by a single gunshot wound to the throat."

"Wow." Henry gave me a look of admiration. "So, how do we link them together?"

"At this point, I'm still investigating." I thought about the picture from DeOrca's arrest after the Crombie murder. Vance was in the background. I was about to mention it when Henry spoke.

"Have you shared your observations with the police?"

"No. I didn't know Vance was dead until you called me. I probably need to talk to Detective Dermott."

Henry cleared his throat. "Actually, that's why I called you tonight. I was thinking maybe we could visit the detective together. He seems to like you—maybe you could smooth things over for me. He was pretty upset earlier today when I tried to put him on camera. Later on he refused to take any of my phone calls."

"I can see why. Vance was his partner after all. But I don't know if I would be of much help. I seem to make him mad too. I think he only tolerates me because I might be useful in the DeOrca murder investigation, but I'll see what I can do."

"Thanks." Henry absentmindedly took a sip of his coffee. I could tell that his wheels of thought were spinning.

"Do you have any ideas on why a cop might be linked to the murder of an alleged drug dealer?" I seemed to be doing all the thinking here.

"What?" There was a blank expression on his face.

I repeated my question.

"Uh, no…I don't have any idea. Look it's late. We should get out of here."

Henry was lying to me. I was sure of it. I didn't know why but I was going to find out. I looked at him and he avoided my gaze as he piled some pages in a folder. He tucked them in his briefcase under his desk. I scooted close to him and he looked up in surprise. He caught his breath like something kinky was going to happen.

"All right, Henry, let's get out of here," I purred. I reached over to grab his tie and knocked a cup of hot coffee into his lap with my hip. He jumped up.

"Whoops!" I cried. "I'm sorry! Let me help you clean it up." I grabbed a press release from the "in" box on his desk and started to lean towards him with it.

"No, ouch, that's okay." Henry grabbed the press release from me and looked down at his wet pants in dismay. "I'll go get some paper towels from the men's room."

I felt a little bad as I watched Henry run out. But I got over it. I went around to the other side of his desk and pulled the papers out that he had slipped into the pocket of his briefcase.

It was difficult to read Henry's crabbed handwriting, but

it looked like he had an informant at the Portland Police
Bureau. I guessed that was how he found out Vance had
been one of the detectives to interview me last Friday night.
According to the notes, Detective Vance had recently been
the subject of an internal investigation for a large bank
deposit to his account. He was cleared later. However,
Henry's informant had noticed Vance had recently purchased a home for his grown daughter and he had bought a
luxury car for his wife. The source of the income was suspicious since Vance earned in the neighborhood of fifty-five
grand a year. He claimed he won 250,000 dollars in Reno
last October at a casino. I returned the notes to Henry's
briefcase and opened his desk drawer. I was stunned by
what I saw.

It was an article that I had written for the *Seattle Times*
about a mayoral candidate. I flushed as I spied my byline
above the story that had caused a man to take his own life. I
peeked underneath the first piece of paper. There were other
articles I had written during my four years at the paper. A
follow-up article from a rival paper noted I had resigned my
position at the *Times* after the man committed suicide. I felt
sick inside. I shut the drawer and stood up.

Footsteps came from the direction of the hallway. Henry
appeared in the doorway and I stood up from behind his desk.
He looked at his desk drawer, then at me. He knew. I didn't care.

I eyed his pants. A dark stain had spread over his crotch
area. "Sorry," I whispered. I was sorry about his pants but not
sorry about snooping through his file. What an idiot I was to
think that Mr. Ambition was interested in me, not my case.

"I think I better go now. I'm tired." The anger was
starting to brew.

"All right," Henry said slowly. He looked troubled. "I'll
walk you to your car."

"I'm fine," I said in a curt voice. I left the office without looking back or responding to the guard's friendly wave as I went out the front doors.

Bastard! Anne Kern was right. I stewed all the way home. Once inside my apartment, I fixed a stiff drink and pulled out the articles that I had copied at the library. I tried to read into the photo of DeOrca with Vance, but all I could see was a cop and a criminal. I scanned the articles one more time, looking for a link. Only one thing caught my eye. The DeOrca warehouse burned down last October. DeOrca later won a big insurance settlement. Funny enough, it was the same month Vance won big in Reno.

TWENTY-THREE

HE WAS A FUNNY LOOKING MAN. His head was shaped like a potato. His coloring was also spud like; brown hair with a wide, shiny section of scalp, small brown eyes hidden behind wire frames, and a tight mouth. His body was small and spare under the weight of his enormous Mr. Potato head. He was dressed in a black suit with a bright red bow tie knotted at his neck. And he had a gun in his hand. He pointed it with jerky motions, toward his head and pulled the trigger. I watched in horror as his face broke, like a big piece of china, and the pieces crashed to the floor.

"NO! NO! NO!"

I woke up to the sound of my own voice. My nightgown was damp with sweat and my heart was thumping furiously. I opened my eyes, trying to reassure myself it was a dream, only a dream. But it wasn't. A man was still dead.

No matter where I go, he still follows me. Mr. Downey was his name. Vincent Downey. Principal of Harding High School, divorced father of three, dog owner. Dead man. Until I opened Henry's drawer—the Pandora's Box—I hadn't seen the Downey article for quite some time. But I knew his story by heart. He was forty-five years old, a candidate for mayor. Polls were heavily weighted in his favor. He graduated from Stanford University, married his college sweetheart, and had taught for several years in the Seattle area while raising a family. He had served two terms on the City Council in the late eighties and early nineties. He'd made his mark by organizing a rally to fight proposed budget cuts to school funding. Five thousand school kids marched outside the Capitol building in Olympia. Hand lettered signs pleaded legislators to "SAVE OUR SCHOOLS!" And they did. A unanimous vote for children it was called. The school budget was protected. Mr. Downey was a hero.

Until October 19, 1997. My article was published that day. I told the world the story of Karla, a fifteen-year-old student at Harding High. Pregnant by her principal, the candidate for mayor. The public outcry rained bricks on Mr. Downey's political aspirations. His ex-wife filed a petition to gain sole custody of their children. His political colleagues roasted him. The religious right and the radical left sent out press releases endorsing Downey's opponent in the mayoral race. An outraged PTA demanded Downey's resignation from Harding High. He ended his life the next week and changed mine forever.

I left my job, my family, and my friends in Seattle. And I started over because I couldn't bear the daily battlefield of my conscience. You did the right thing I would tell myself. You killed him! A voice would answer.

I had found some peace with my new life in Portland. Henry had no right to take that away.

I turned on my side and looked at the clock. It was three a.m. I sat up, pulled off my sweaty nightgown, then flopped back down on my pillows. A movement from upstairs told me my nightmare had awakened my neighbor too. A wave of nausea flooded through my body. A tumbler full of whisky is not always a good substitute for milk and cookies at bedtime. I closed my eyes again.

The first light of dawn crawled into my apartment after seven a.m. but I had been awake since six. Moving about restlessly in my ratty bathrobe. Thinking of Roger Vance, the warehouse fire and of Joe Arnim. Sometime during the night

I had come up with a lengthy "to do" list. My number one priority was to find Joe Arnim. He was my top murder suspect for the moment—if I could believe what Theresa/Sarah had told me… Number two, I wanted to see if there was some kind of connection between the warehouse fire and the DeOrca and Vance murders. Howard Kirkwood from Oregon Insurance Co. might be able to help me with some of the details. At DeOrca's funeral he had mentioned that he had worked on some kind of claim DeOrca had filed before his death. I dug Howard's business card out of my purse. The corporate headquarters for Oregon Insurance were located downtown.

I dialed the phone number on the card. An early bird receptionist answered and told me Howard Kirkwood would be out until the afternoon. At her urging I left a message on his voice mail. After I hung up I dialed into my office voice mail. I had two messages; one was from an attorney wanting me to interview a witness to an accident, and the other from Eddie Dickerson, Private Eye.

He wanted a favor. It was urgent.

He could wait. I haven't forgiven him for trying to cop a feel at the convention for Northwest Private Investigators in Seattle. When I confronted him, the ass told everyone that I wore falsies. Maggie McGuire and I broke into his hotel room and cleaned the toilet bowl with his toothbrush, but I still don't feel as if we're even yet.

I took a shower and got dressed. Then I called the law firm and got the details from the harried attorney in charge of the case. She was a little snippy at first because I hadn't returned her earlier call but I explained about the murder in my office. She interrupted my excuse to tell me that my assignment was to track down a Burger King worker and get a statement. I sighed and took notes.

The accident took place in Southeast Portland by the Hawthorne bridge. There was a Burger King located nearby. The worker left his name with the driver but he hurried off before the police arrived. This was one job that I'd like to turn down, but the attorneys keep me fed year round. I'd have to find the time.

A quick call to Burger King revealed that the teenage fry cook that I was looking for would report to work at ten o'clock. I decided to stop by for lunch on the law firm. Next I grabbed the phone book and tried to look up Joe Arnim's address. There were two listings under the name Arnim. The first one was in the Clackamas area, the second in Northeast Portland. I dialed the Clackamas number and woke up someone surly. She informed me that she was not related to Joe Arnim and hung up in my ear. There was no answer at the other number. The address was nearby—I could drive over after breakfast.

A timid knock at the door interrupted my thoughts. I hesitated a moment—bad guys don't tap on the doors, they bang on them, I think—and went over to look out the peep hole. It was Stan Oscram. I'd rather it was a bad guy.

I opened the door. "Hi, Stan. I was just on my way out…"

Stan shuffled his feet and wiped his fingers on his sweat pants. They were coated with orange Cheetos dust. As a habitual snacker, I'm familiar with the syndrome.

"It will only take a minute and there might be a little money in it for you. Do you have time to grab a cup of coffee?"

I sighed heavily, just like I used to when my mom would ask me to mow the lawn. "Okay, but you're buying. We can walk over to Jamie's. I haven't had breakfast yet—have you?"

"Nope," Stan said, sticking his hands into his pockets. "I'll go get my coat."

The walk to Jamie's was the longest of my life. It's only eight blocks but I was scared to death I'd see someone I knew. It was the adult equivalent of going to the prom with your brother. I should have suggested a bowl of cereal at my apartment. Stan was looking dashing with holes in his tennies and unwashed hair. His belly was poking out from under his sweatshirt in a particularly attractive manner. When we got to the restaurant I told Minnie I wanted a booth in the rear.

She looked at Stan and grinned. "Something private?" she teased. Her freckled nose wrinkled at the joke as she led us to the back of the restaurant.

Stan looked nonplused. "I gotta take a leak," he said as he took his coat off and wadded it into a ball. He left it on the booth seat. "Order me some pigs in a blanket with a fried egg on top. I'll take a cup of joe too."

I sat down. Minnie stood there in amusement. "You won't have anything to do with my Uncle Eddie but you'll date him?"

I rolled my eyes. "This is business."

She laughed. "By the way I saw Uncle Eddie last night at a family dinner. He's in town to work on a missing person's case. I didn't say anything about knowing you."

"I'm grateful. But he did call me. I wonder what he wants."

Minnie shrugged. "Who knows. The usual today?"

I nodded and she went back to the counter and called out the orders to the cook. Eddie's case must have been important for him to come to Portland. He lives in Medford, close to the California border. It's a five hour drive.

Stan returned to the table and wedged himself into the booth. "Good music," he commented. Elvis was blaring from the jukebox.

"Yeah," I said shortly. "So what is it you want?" I wasn't going to spend all morning with Stan—even if I was getting free food.

"I want you to find Patty."

"Who's that?" I asked as Minnie brought our beverages to the table.

"My wife."

Minnie raised her eyebrow as she set my coffee cup in front of me. Stan dumped half a cup of sugar into his coffee and took a sip.

"You mean that woman in the picture I saw in your apartment?"

"Uh huh. Ever since you came by I've been thinking about her. It's been nearly twenty years. The last time we were together was at a Grateful Dead concert in Eugene. She stayed to follow the Dead and I went home. I had to work."

"You haven't seen her for nearly twenty years? You guys can't still be married—"

"Never got a divorce. What for? I'll never find anyone like Patty. I told her I would wait for her to come home. I've been in the same apartment ever since, in case she wanted to come back. She followed the Dead for several years, selling beaded jewelry to pay her way. I offered her money but she refused it. She sent me a postcard or two but neither one of us was any good at keeping in touch. Last I heard she was living in a commune in California."

"When was that?"

"Long time ago. I guess eighteen years or so." He pulled out his wallet from his pants pocket and extracted the photo of Patty I had seen. Given the Carol Brady type shag haircut and platform shoes, I guessed the photo was taken in the late seventies.

"I hate to break it to you, Stan, but she's probably married or something. Eighteen years is a long time to be out of touch."

Stan looked at the picture. "I'd settle for just knowing that she's okay."

He was breaking my heart. "All right, all right. I'll look for her. But I need something more to go on—like a last name, addresses of relatives, stuff like that. And I charge a hundred bucks an hour, with extra for expenses."

"I'll pay it," he said softly. He was still looking at the picture.

After breakfast Stan and I went our separate ways. I told him I was in the middle of a case and it might be some time before I started looking for Patty Oscram. He said he had waited eighteen years and he could wait a little longer. I went back to the apartment and picked up my rent-a-couch car and drove to the address for Bo and Reeva Arnim. The neighborhood was in the Parkrose area. The houses were modest with small yards. A few of the yards had cars parked on them. It was difficult to tell what the Arnim household looked like.

It had burned down.

The front of the house was black with charred lumber. A yellow tape that said "CRIME SCENE DO NOT CROSS." was draped across what was left of the railing. A shriveled pumpkin with evil eyes and no teeth lay rotting on the front porch. The windows of the house had been broken out on the second story and the front door looked like it had been chopped down. As I got out of my car I caught a whiff of damp campfire. I walked up to the front window and peered in. The lacy curtains were a sooty brown color and the edges were scalloped by flames. Beyond that I could see the remains of a broiled couch and a vinyl recliner, both positioned toward a melted television set.

"Hey! Whatcha doing over there?"

I turned around in the direction of the garrulous old voice. A white woman in a housecoat with a bandana around her head to hide her curlers was yelling at me. She was probably in her eighties but it didn't affect her agility at all. She had a broom in her hand and she was swinging it in my direction as if to shoo me away.

I flashed a smile. "Well, I'm here to visit the Arnims. What happened here? Looks like there was a fire."

"Damn right there was a fire! The Fire Marshall wants everyone to stay away until they're done with their investigation."

"Investigation?"

"ARSON," she said dramatically.

"Wow. Where did the Arnim family go?"

"I dunno. She's got a sister in Woodburn, I think. Maybe they went to stay there. I don't know where the darn kid is."

"You mean Joe."

"Yeah, him," she said turning to go into her house. "I'm going inside now. It's cold out here. Don't let me catch you poking around here again or I'll call the police."

"Wait. Can I ask you a few questions?"

The old woman sized me up. "Oh, I guess. But I'm in the middle of watching Regis and that new gal. We can talk during the commercials."

I followed the woman into her house. It was filled with doilies and pictures of Jesus. It smelled like she had fried something in the kitchen recently. The living room was crammed with oversized furniture. An ironing board was set up by the window with a full laundry basket next to it. We sat down in front of an enormous television on a couch that had butt depressions on each of the cushions. A calico cat was busy chewing the side of the couch. There was a picture of a rosy cheeked toddler on top of the television.

"What a cute baby," I cooed, so as to break the ice. "Is that your—"

"SHH!" She held a crooked finger to her mouth. "I can't hear Regis."

I sat captive in front of the television until a commercial for feminine protection came on.

"Mrs…"

"I'm Mrs. Nielsen. My husband's been dead for thirteen years. Not that that's any of your business. Who did you say you are?"

I told her and handed her a card.

She put on her cat eye glasses to read it. "You're a private investigator?" she said in surprise. I had her attention now.

"Yes. I was hoping you could give me more information about the Arnim family and the fire. I'm trying to find Joe."

"His mother hired you?"

I gave her a little smile that lied for me.

Mrs. Nielsen grunted. "If the woman had any sense she'd let that kid stay lost. He was always up to no good—stayed out late, and came home drunk. I know, I saw him from my window. Once when his parents went camping for a week he stayed home and had big parties every night. I about wore my fingers out dialing the police until I figured out that speed dial button. They'd come by and the party would calm down long enough for the police car to pull out of the driveway. One morning I even found used syringes on my lawn. He was a bad kid, I tell you."

"What about the fire?"

Regis and a bubbly blonde lady appeared on the set again. Mrs. Nielsen was on a roll and didn't seem to notice. "It happened a few weeks ago. I woke up when I smelled something burning. I got out of bed and went to the window. There was smoke pouring out of the house and flames jumping out of the roof. I was scared to death. I called the fire department then I threw a coat on over my nightgown and went outside. Didn't take them long to get here, I'll say that for them. I had to stand across the street in my housecoat and slippers while they put the fire out. There wasn't anyone in the house but I heard one of the firemen say later he thought the fire might have been started by a coffeepot."

"Have you seen Joe since the fire?"

No, his parents were here to look at the damage. Reeva Arnim was very upset. They lost everything. Luckily for them they had just taken out an insurance policy. They're not rich people." She looked at me with suspicion. "I'm surprised that she can afford you."

"Oh, well…that's confidential," I said in a crisp tone.

"Hmmph." Mrs. Nielsen's eyes strayed back to the television. Regis was roller skating across the set while his co-host clapped her hands.

I stood up. "I guess I'll be going now. Please call me if you remember anything that will help me find Joe."

Mrs. Nielsen reluctantly left Regis long enough to show me out. Maybe she was afraid I might steal one of her Jesus pictures. She stood on the porch until I drove away. As I left I could see her looking at what remained of the Arnim house. She was shaking her head.

TWENTY-FOUR

THE BURGER KING fry cook agreed to talk but I had to wait until his break. The manager, a middle aged Asian man wearing a soiled white dress shirt with an ugly tie, glowered at my fry cook until he returned to the grill. The burgers were burning. I ordered a Diet Coke and sat down at a plastic booth to wait. I had an hour or so to kill before Howard Kirkwood would be in his office and I wanted to get my report for the attorney out of the way.

After I interviewed the kid I stopped at a phone booth to look up the address for Roger Vance. He lived in the Westmoreland neighborhood in Southeast Portland. I got in my car and headed over. Once I approached his house I passed several well tended homes. There were little kids playing out in front of them on their trikes and Big Wheels while their parents raked leaves. It looked like a nice, safe area. So why was Roger Vance dead?

I parked across the street from a tidy yellow colonial style house and checked the address. This was Vance's house. There were several cars parked in front of the driveway and on the street. I could see some movement in front of the windows. I sat in my car and debated my course of action. Dare I knock on the door? I wanted to speak to Mrs. Vance—it was the only way I could think of to determine the extent of Detective Vance's involvement with the DeOrca family. I sure as hell wouldn't be getting any information from Dermott. Still, it was a little awkward to ring the doorbell and say "Hi! My name is Jane Lanier. I think your husband was killed because he was mixed up with some bad ass drug dealers." That wouldn't work.

While I plotted my next move, a maroon colored sedan pulled up in front of Vance's house. A older woman with hair too dark to be natural, emerged. She was dressed in a black coat buttoned to her chin. She leaned in and picked up a casserole dish. Then she shut the car door with her hip. She walked up to the front door, transferred the dish to one hand and knocked on the door with the other. A young girl with yellow braided hair answered it. Probably a grandkid, I thought. She took the casserole, then a woman appeared behind the girl. She also had gray hair and she was wearing a black sweater set with pearls and a mid length skirt. She was crying.

The woman with the casserole stepped inside and the door shut. I started the car. There was no way I'd knock on the door now. I'd wait.

I headed back downtown, stopping at the bank to deposit the check from Elana and at the post office to mail my bills. Once I got to my office I whipped out the report on the Burger King witness and faxed it to the attorney. Then I called Howard Kirkland. Not only was he willing to meet with me, but his afternoon calendar was clear. I locked up my office and walked the ten blocks separating our buildings.

The corporate headquarters for Oregon Insurance are located in downtown Portland near City Hall. It's housed in a steel skyscraper with forty-eight floors. It took me about ten minutes to walk there from my office and another five to take the elevator up to Howard's office on the 32nd floor. I was glad the elevators were in working order.

A receptionist with a frizzy perm greeted me when I walked through the glass doors of the Oregon Insurance Company. Her face was gray under the fluorescent lights. She pointed me in the direction of Howard Kirkwood's office.

It turned out to be a cubicle. I'm glad I don't have one anymore. Somehow they remind me of cages. Howard was seated at his computer typing away. His office was furnished in the manner that suggested he was there for life—tons of knickknacks and clutter. An award on the wall announced he was employee of the month in February of 1986. I could see pictures of his family displayed on top of a small bookshelf that held binders and other corporate Bibles.

"Howard?"

He greeted me with a smile and stood up with his hand extended. He was wearing a shirt with the corporate logo on it and tan slacks. "Nice to see you again, Jane. Are you still working on the DeOrca murder?"

I shook his hand. It was a little clammy. "I am. I wonder if you might be able to help me."

"Sit down." Howard pulled out a guest chair for me, then he sat down at his desk. "What can I do for you?"

"I'm curious about the fire at the DeOrca warehouse. For starters, I was wondering if you suspected arson."

Howard leaned back in his chair and banged into the wall. "Ouch," he said sitting up. "Well, we settled up with Mr. DeOrca shortly before he died. The terms are confidential, but I can tell you off the record—" Howard stopped and winked, "that it was in the neighborhood of two million dollars."

"That's a lot of money."

"Well, they lost the building and two semi trailer rigs. They also lost a lot of the inventory for their Mesa Del Rey restaurants. I've never seen so much melted Cheez Whiz in my life."

"Where's the warehouse located?"

"Are you familiar with the industrial section in Northwest Portland?"

"You mean near the shipyards?" That was riverfront property.

"Yeah. DeOrca's warehouse was in that area. I heard he was trying to get the property rezoned so he could put up some condos. The fire was a lucky 'accident' or it would have been if he hadn't been murdered. I could show you if you're interested. It would be kind of nice to get out of the office."

"I'd appreciate that."

Howard put on his coat and I followed him down the hall to the check out board. He marked himself out for the remainder of the day. We took the elevator down to the parking garage in the basement. Howard led me to a Ford Taurus with an Oregon Insurance sign emblazoned on each door. We got in and headed for Naito Parkway. The day was chilly and bright. Perfect for curling up in front of a fire with hot tea and a good book or even joy riding with an insurance arson investigator. I was so busy looking at the ships moored at the river's edge that I didn't notice Howard had pulled into a parking lot.

"Are we here already?" I asked looking at my second burned out building of the day. In the Northeast corner of the lot I could see a charred shell of a two story warehouse. It adjoined a large dock area. The parking lot was empty except for our car.

"Yeah. What's left of the place—which isn't much."

Howard and I stepped out of the car. Our feet crunched the gravel as we walked toward the darkened warehouse. The outside of the building was scorched in a "V" shape which seemed to point to a broken window on the first floor. We walked around to the opening of the building which faced the river. I looked inside the mouth of one of the truck bays which was cordoned off with yellow "DANGER, DO NOT ENTER" tape. The skeleton of a truck was parked in the shadows. The place smelled of damp wood and cinders. The beams of the ceiling were scarred black and a makeshift skylight had been hacked into the roof. Underneath, a big pile of soot and rubbish was heaped next to a door with a sign that said "EMPLOYEES ONLY."

"Is it safe to go inside?" I asked as the wind whipped up a pile of damp ashes to blow through my hair.

"Nah," Howard said. "The roof is liable to cave. The fire fighters had to cut part of it out to hose down the fire. I can show you around outside but it's too dangerous to go in."

"Hmm. Were you able to figure out what started the fire?"

"Near as we can tell the point of origin was the break room." He pointed to the "EMPLOYEES ONLY" door. "Electrical short of some kind with one of the appliances. Somebody forgot to turn off the coffeepot I guess."

The coffeepot again. I thought of the fire at the Arnim's house. "How do you determine the point of origin?"

"Well, a number of factors come into play but basically, the fire will burn longer at the point of origin then at any other place to which the fire has spread. The Fire Marshall uses that information to determine the cause," Howard explained. "For a fire to start you've got to have three elements: a fuel source, an oxygen source, and an ignition source of some kind. Then you've got to have a reaction among all three."

"Howard, is there any chance that this place had been used as a drug lab or distribution center?"

Howard turned to look at me. His forehead was wavy with wrinkles as he frowned. "If you've got any information like that, there could be a big reward in it for you—if we can prove that it started the fire."

"I don't have anything that I can prove—just rumors." A barge chugged by and we both turned to watch.

"That's all we have—besides a two million dollar loss." Howard put his hands in his pockets and shivered. "C'mon, it's cold, let's get out of here."

TWENTY-FIVE

HOWARD DROPPED ME OFF at my office building. Instead of going upstairs I bought a huge sandwich and a Diet Coke from a street vendor and walked over to Pioneer Square to eat it.

Pioneer Square, also known as Portland's living room, is a brick paved courtyard covering a city block. The upper level of the West side of the square is bordered by a Starbucks coffee shop. There's a fountain next to the coffee shop. Powell's travel bookstore is located on the opposite end of the square. The center area is used for festivals, concerts, and rallies. It's a prime people watching place. Today a street preacher was roaring on the corner about Satan. I sat down on the cold brick ledge facing the square and unwrapped my roast beef sandwich. After a sloppy bite, I was suddenly aware that I was being watched.

A white boy, in his late teens was leaning against the wall smoking a cigarette. He was dressed in a leather jacket, torn jeans and heavy Doc Marten boots. His head was shaved and decorated with tattoos. His eyebrow was pierced and a hoop earring jutted from it. When he saw me look at him he tossed his cigarette away and walked towards me. I wiped mustard off my fingers.

"Jane Lanier?" His ice blue eyes bored into mine.

"Who are you?" He looked like he had been vandalized by his tattoo artist. There was a skull and crossbones etched on his scalp and a dragon tattoo was crawling out of his sleeve.

He sat down next to me. I smelled cigarette smoke.

"Joe wants to talk to you."

Adrenaline started to rush through me. Finally! A break. Or was it a trap?

"What for?" I tried to feign disinterest.

"You know. About that guy who was murdered. Joe thinks he might be next."

Theresa had said the same thing. The wind blew then, spraying leaves into the air. The street preacher stopped his ranting and headed to Starbucks.

"Why doesn't he talk to the police?"

"He can't. He knows that they're looking for him."

I took another bite of my sandwich and considered the information. Joe was up to something—but what?

"Okay. I'll talk to him. Where is he?"

"He'll find you."

How freaky. What if I didn't want to be "found"?

The man stood up abruptly and walked in the direction of a nearby department store. A moment later he disappeared into a throng of shoppers. I looked around to see if anyone else was watching me. The people I saw just looked cold as they hurried back to work clutching bags of take out food. I was the only lunatic dining al fresco today. I finished my sandwich and beverage, tossed the wrappers in a trash can and walked back to the office.

I took the elevator to the fifth floor without incident but when I approached my office I saw Violetta DeOrca was waiting for me. She was wearing a fuzzy faux leopard coat, Jackie O glasses, and a flimsy lime green dress. Her pumps were worn down at the heels and her nylons sagged a bit at the ankles.

"FINALLY," she said when she saw me. "Hurry up. I've got news."

"Hi, Violetta," I said half heartedly. Shouldn't be too hard for Joe Arnim to find me if DeOrca's mother could. I unlocked the door with Violetta breathing impatiently down my neck. She faltered a bit as she stepped into my office.

"Is this where my son was murdered?" Her heavily mascaraed eyes surveyed the room and stopped on my desk. I felt a stab of sympathy for her.

"I'm afraid so," I said gently. "Would you like to sit down?"

"No," she said decisively." We don't have time. I'm on the trail of the murderer and I need your help."

"What?" This woman was nuts.

She opened her vinyl purse and pulled out a matchbook. I sighed. There was no way that I was going to let her smoke in my office. I glanced around for the fire extinguisher.

"Here." She thrust the matches at me. "I broke into Brute Mortimer's hotel room and found these."

Great. Now everyone had broken into Brute Mortimer's room. I looked at the matches. They were the ones that I had pulled out of his pocket. I flipped open the cover. The name "Natalie" was written on the inside flap. A local phone number was scribbled beneath it. Mentally I slapped my forehead. I had meant to call the number. But I didn't.

"Should this mean something to me?" I wasn't going to admit I had seen these before.

"Of course! Natalie must be the name of the assassin Brute Mortimer hired to kill my son. Only a woman could have gotten close enough to Freddie to kill him. I know my son. He didn't trust no man."

"I'll look into it," I said to calm her down.

"I'm going to help you. We're getting close now. We'll get those sons of bitches." Her eyes flashed.

Bad idea. I didn't want or need a sidekick. This cowgirl rides alone.

"But, Violetta, I need to have you keep tabs on Mortimer— see who he hangs out with, where he goes. You're the perfect person to do it. You're already staying at the hotel."

Violetta thought about it. "I guess you're right," she said, reluctant to be taken out of the action. Her eyes brightened. "I can bug his room!"

"Yeah, do that." Where did this woman come from? Of course, I had listened in on Mortimer using a water glass, but that was business.

I walked Violetta to the elevators and followed the trail of her acrid cologne back to my office. The number on the match-book had a local Northeast Portland prefix. I sat down at my desk and dialed. After two rings a man picked up the phone. I hung up quickly. I knew the voice, and I knew the man.

It was Sam Madsen.

TWENTY-SIX

IT WAS DARK. And I had to pee. I took a final swallow of the cold coffee I had bought at the McDonald's drive thru two hours earlier and crumpled the cup into a ball. Surveillance is really hard on the bladder although my male colleagues brag about the benefits of pop can port-a-potties. I crossed my legs and looked at the clock on the dashboard. It was ten thirty. From my parking spot across the street I could see that the lights were still on in Sam's store. The dry cleaners had closed promptly at ten. A red pick up had idled in front of the cleaners until Rita, the fake and bake blonde, emerged. She locked the front doors then got in the passenger side of the pick up. She and her boyfriend drove off. Sam's dime colored Porsche was the only car left in the lot. Now where was Sam and what was he up to? I intended to find out.

As soon as I could break in that is.

Ten minutes later the lights went off. Sam walked out the front door, locked it and jiggled the handle. He walked to his car, got in, and tore out of the parking lot in a squeal of flashing silver.

I waited five minutes before I got out of my car. I could hear traffic on Sandy Boulevard, a block away, but this street was quiet and not very well lit. My hair was hidden in a baseball cap, and I was wearing my cat burglar uniform—everything black, including my gloves. I stole around to the rear parking lot by the dry cleaners and the store. There was a big dumpster out back heaped with boxes and smelly trash. A cat was foraging through it for dinner. She hissed at me then turned her attention to some rotten delicacy in a Kentucky Fried Chicken bucket. I moved to the door and tried the handle. It was locked. Of course. I pulled the picklocks out of my pocket and went to work. In less than a minute I was in. It was easy. Too easy.

For a security business, Sam's store was very vulnerable. Instead of selling surveillance equipment he should think about using some of it. I opened the door and paused for a second to listen for the telltale beep of an alarm. I heard nothing. I stepped inside and closed the door.

It was pitch black. I felt in my pocket for the flashlight I had brought and turned it on. The beam illuminated the room showing me a tired couch and a round table with scattered newspapers and empty donut boxes on top of it. Sam's desk was facing the hallway leading to the front of the shop. There was a second short hallway at the rear of the office. A door labeled "MEN'S ROOM" was at the end of the hall. It was closed. I walked over to the door and opened it. I beamed my light inside long enough to find out the room was empty and the sink and toilet were dirty. The paper towels were also low. I shut the door and crossed the room to the hallway separating the store from the office. I doused the flashlight and looked around. The counter with a cash register was to my right, the rest of the room was lined with display cases full of debugging devices. Across the street I could see shoppers milling about in the Rite Aid store. The parking lot in front of Sam's store was empty.

I returned to the back room and turned my flashlight on. I moved to the desk and played the beam of the light over the surface. The blotter was coffee stained with figures etched into the margins. I moved the light to the wall so I could get a better look at the sailing calendar. No dates were marked. There was a framed photo on the wall. A friendly looking Sam smiled at me from a yacht. He was wearing shorts, a polo shirt, and deck shoes. And he was holding a fish. The sky overhead was a brilliant blue that seemed to blend in with the water. The green lettering across the bow of the boat read: THE NATALIE.

So the Natalie was a boat, not a woman. Why would Brute Mortimer have Sam's number? Neither man seemed the least bit gay. Scratch romance. Was the yacht for rent? I went behind the desk and yanked the top drawer open. Maybe there was a brochure or an invoice book to tell me more. I rifled through the contents—several take out menus and a few back issues of sailing magazines. I pulled open a few more drawers to find stationary supplies but no invoices, payroll records or any other items associated with the business. I looked around the room. Where was the inventory for this place? Under the couch cushions?

I turned around and hit the "on" button for the computer. Maybe Sam was in the paperless mode. The screen flickered and hummed. A prompt popped up demanding my pass code. I punched in "SEX". I had heard somewhere that was the most popular password next to "GOD". Sex didn't work. I sighed and turned the machine off. I didn't have the time or expertise to crack the code. I was stumped.

Outside I could hear a pair of car doors slam in unison. I stood up and went to the small entry hall connected to the storefront area. A police car with flashing lights was outside. Two officers had gotten out of the car and were moving towards the shop.

Damn! I fell back into the shadows of the office and looked for a place to stash my 5 foot 4 inch frame. I'd be spending the night in the slammer unless I could hide in a hurry. I looked up at the ceiling. There was a vent. Worth a try.

I scrambled onto the desk and stood up. I reached up and popped off the vent in the ceiling. I could hear the cops coming around to the back door. Sheer panic helped me hoist myself up. I shimmied inside the vent and replaced the vent as the back door opened.

Heavy footsteps fell on the floor. I held my breath; partly to avoid detection and partly because the vent smelled like dust and rat droppings. The space was also very cramped. I assumed my "deer in the headlights" pose and waited.

The officers toured the shop for what seemed like a very l-o-n-g time. After an eternity of ten minutes I heard a male voice say: "All clear. Must have been a false alarm."

A female voice answered. She sounded irritated. "No way. The call from the phone booth said someone was breaking in. And the door here was unlocked. I wonder why there's no alarm?"

"Well, do you see anyone here?" The voice was sarcastic. "C'mon, we've got better things to do. The idiot must have left his door unlocked."

"All right. Maybe it was a prank call."

The thud of footsteps moved to the door and I heard it open and close. After a few minutes I eased out of my hiding place and jumped down to the desk. I replaced the vent cover, got off the desk and sat down to catch my breath. My heart was thudding in my ears and my legs were wobbly. I chanted my favorite swear word over and over again until I was certain I had full bladder control.

As soon as I was able, I slipped out of the store and ran back to my car like I had a rocket stuck in my pants.

TWENTY-SEVEN

TRAFFIC WAS LIGHT. I sped down Sandy Boulevard practicing my Lamaze breathing. Jesus, that was a close call! If I had been caught it would be difficult to come up with a good reason as to why I was hanging out in the vent above Sam's desk. I'm pretty good at coming up with fabulous excuses but that would be a stretch even for me.

I looked over to the donut shop on the corner and thought about a maple bar. There was a police car in the rear of the store but they weren't there for a snack. A female police officer with short dark hair was snapping cuffs on a teenage boy in a starter jacket and baggy pants. Another kid sat in the back seat of the police car. He looked scared. A second female police officer was holding the leash of a dog that was sniffing the ground by the bushes. I shook my head. Powdered sugar donuts are sold inside the store, powdered drugs are sold in back.

Out of habit, I braked to slow down as I drove by the police cars. Not that I was likely to get a ticket. Tonight was my lucky night. I tapped my fingers on the steering wheel and thought about Sam's store. His cupboards were bare, inventory wise, yet he owned a Porsche and a yacht named Natalie. Where was the money coming from? And a bully like Brute Mortimer had his phone number. Was Sam involved in the DeOrca/Mortimer business somehow?

An ambulance shrieked behind me, its strobe lights flashing in my rearview mirror. I pulled over to let it pass. After it went by I found myself turning right at the Shell station. I drove past a shadowy Grant park, and several bungalow style houses, toward Fremont street. And the DeOrca mansion.

I took a right on the street before Fremont and drove up the hill. The DeOrca's house loomed above me, giant pillars propping up a third floor balcony, massive trees with bare branches flailing in the wind. The ground was shrouded in dead leaves. I pulled up in front of the house and stopped. The first two floors of the house were ablaze with light. Flood-lights illuminated the property.

"What's the matter, Elana? Are you afraid of the dark?" I whispered the words in the protective darkness of my car.

A security guard emerged from the rear of the house on foot and trained his flashlight in my direction. Exposed, I blinked and drove off. It was after eleven; too late to stop by for a visit, social or otherwise.

Elana puzzled me. If she was afraid for her life, as she claimed to be, then what was keeping her in Portland? No job, no husband, no family except for her son. And he was close to eighteen I would guess. I didn't understand the woman. She could sell her house and spend the rest of her life sunning on the shores of a tropical island. Warm breezes, drinks with um-brellas, muscular men on surfboards. My lottery ticket fantasy. I should share it with Elana, give her some ideas.

I headed home. The dark figure in the window across the street was at his peeping pervert post as I parked my car. I went inside the building, stopping first at the mailbox to collect some bills and catalogs. As I walked down the hallway to my apartment I was conscious of the dim lights, the peeling paint and the well worn carpet with faded roses. Charming in the daytime, just plain old at night. The sound of Stan's tele-vision blared into the hall. Probably a Baywatch re-run.

An image of the DeOrca mansion crept into my mind. Pillars, a circular drive, marble statues, uniformed maids.

What did I have besides a lot of clothes, a torn couch and a drawer full of bills? It seemed okay for now. Plenty of time before getting a mortgage, a husband, a sensible job and 2.5 kids. I just couldn't make myself want those things. I unlocked the door and flipped on the lights. The old furniture was cozy and inviting. Pictures of family and friends smiled at me from their perches on my desk. Strategically placed pillows hid the worst of the damage to my couch. I tossed my mail on a table by the door and shrugged out of my coat. I hung it up and went into the kitchen for a bowl of Captain Crunch. I sat on the counter and ate it dry, since I was out of milk. Somehow, this lifestyle seemed rich.

I ate cereal until the roof of my mouth was raw. Then I checked messages. Kelly had called, wanting to go out for drinks later in the week. Henry called. I erased the message, angrily. Jerk. Big snoop! The last message was from Tim King, the private investigator from Nevada. I copied down his phone number and dialed. He's a night owl. His normal 8-5 starts at 8 p.m.

"King here." The voice was deep. I could hear slot machines in the background.

"This is Jane Lanier. Thanks for getting back to me. Are you on your cell phone?"

"Yeah, I'm in Reno for tonight. Tomorrow I head to Salt Lake City. Right now I'm trailing some poor slob. His wife wants to know what he's up to. Looks like an affair with the Lucky Lady Casino. He just lost six thousand bucks on the roulette table."

"The same Lucky Lady Casino that Brute Mortimer owns?"

"Yes. Formerly owned by Charlie Sharkey. I did some digging. I have a friend on the police force who worked on the case."

Of course. King had friends everywhere, including me. I met him several years ago when I was still a reporter. I was doing some fact finding on a political figure who had grown up in Nevada. A colleague had referred me to him.

"It's been over ten years, the guy's retired now. Said that Charlie Sharkey was found face down in the hotel pool. He had been shot in the throat."

"What?" Had I heard right? The same MO as the Crombie, DeOrca and Vance murders. "Tim, is there any way you can get this cop to talk to me?"

"Shouldn't be too hard. He has his own bar stool at the Flamingo. Spends a lot of time drinking beer, playing video poker, and telling stories about the good old days on the police force. I'm sure he would be willing to meet with you if you bought a round."

"Done. I'm on my way out tonight." We sorted out details. King agreed to contact his friend to try to set something up. His name was John Drysdale. He started collecting his pension checks from the Reno P.D. eight years ago. King promised to leave a message for me at the Flamingo Hilton before he left town on his next case. In turn I promised to do a background check of his daughter's latest boyfriend at the University of Portland.

I called United Airlines and booked a flight. There was one leaving after midnight, full fare. I recklessly recited my Visa number over the phone. I would expense it to Elana.

I packed a small suitcase and made reservations at the Flamingo Hilton in Reno. Another expense for Elana. Thank God she was rich. I called a cab to take me to the airport.

The Rip City cab arrived twenty minutes later. I looked out my window as a lanky young man got out from the driver's side. He was probably eighteen at the most, and he wore a black sweat suit with gold medallions around his neck. He went around to the back of the car and opened the trunk. I picked up my suitcase, put on my coat and turned out the lights. I locked the door and went outside to meet him.

"Hey! You Jane Lanier?" He extended his hand. "I'm Fresh D."

I shook his hand. "Fresh D?" My eyes fell to his Adidas running shoes shell tops. They were in good condition, but they had to be as old as he was.

"Yeah. Let me put your suitcase in the trunk." He grabbed the suitcase, put it in the trunk and shut it. I looked up at the building next door. I didn't see the pervert at his normal station. Maybe he was watching dirty movies or something.

"Fresh D, I'm heading to the airport." I got in the back of the car and sat down.

"Cool." Fresh D got in the car and fired it up. My head snapped back as Fresh D hit the gas and we jumped from the curb.

"I have plenty of time," I said in a pleasant voice as the speedometer climbed to fifty.

"You the man," Fresh D said as he eased up a little. "So where you going?"

"Reno, Nevada."

"C'mon BIG MONEY! I've always wanted to go there. You taking a vacation?"

"Nah. It's business."

"What kind?"

"I'm a private investigator."

"No way! My mom's a mystery writer. She'd love to talk to you. You have a card?"

I looked at Fresh D. He seemed like a nice enough kid. Kid being the operative word. Now that I thought about it, he couldn't be a day over fifteen.

"Sure, why not." I pulled a business card from my purse and handed it to him. He glanced at it and stuck it in the visor.

"I hope you don't mind me saying so, but you look kinda young to be driving a cab."

Fresh D laughed. "I'm just filling in tonight. One of the

other cabbies called in sick. Guess he had an accident. I'm a full time student."

"High school?" I guessed.

"Yeah," Fresh D. admitted. "Lincoln. But I do have a license to drive."

That was a relief. Somehow Fresh D managed to get us to the airport in one piece. He dropped me off on the upper deck by the Departure section. I paid him, got my suitcase, and hustled in. According to the flight monitor I had forty-five minutes to kill before my flight. I checked in at the counter and got my seat assignment. I hung out in the gift shop reading magazines and looking at the "I LOVE OREGON" type souvenirs. I bought a paperback book and stuffed it in my suitcase. I never check my luggage if I can help it. A trip to London with no clean underwear for three days taught me that lesson.

At 1:40 a.m. I went to the gate to catch the plane. A fellow lagged behind me. He was in his early forties, white, clean cut, with brown hair and a mustache. About six feet tall, and thin. He wore a suede jacket, a polo shirt, brown slacks and loafers. He carried a copy of the *Oregonian*. I had noticed him in the gift shop, hovering close by, but I thought he was security. I boarded the plane. The fellow was a few steps behind. Was he following me? I'd lose him later. He was kinda cute, otherwise I would do it now.

First class was empty except for an Elvis look-alike enjoying a cocktail. I walked past into the steerage section and looked for my seat. It was a window seat near the front of the plane. The rest of the plane was fairly empty; probably 80 percent of the seats were unfilled. The seat next to me was vacant. I heaved my bag into the overhead compartment, sat down and buckled up. My shadow walked by without looking at me, and took an aisle seat four rows back.

The flight attendant readied the plane for take off. The din of chatter could be heard over the safety instructions. As soon as the plane got off the ground I pressed my nose to the window to watch the City of Portland fall away into a glittering sea of lights.

I fell asleep almost immediately. I woke up to the announcement that we would be landing in Reno shortly. I shifted in my seat, and tried to rouse myself. I had a crick in my neck. I rolled my head from side to side to loosen up. The snack fairy had been by while I was asleep. There were two packets of dry roasted peanuts on the seat next to me. I put them in my purse. When the plane landed, the flight attendant asked the passengers to remain in their seats until the plane came to a full stop. The minute it paused, everyone jumped out into the aisle to collect luggage. I found my "shadow" guy right behind me.

We were herded off the plane. I went to the luggage carousel area and moved outside. I asked around and found that the Hilton hotel had a shuttle service. After twenty minutes it pulled to the curb. I hopped on. My shadow got on too. We sat across from one another. He buried his face in his newspaper.

The trip to downtown Reno took twenty minutes. I smiled at the godawful gaudiness of it all. The fluorescent lights, the neon signs—all clamoring for attention. Pawn shops next to casinos. Despite the early morning hour I could see people straggling in and out of the different hotels. There were signs advertising potential prizes of cars, money, and $2.99 buffets. The Eldorado had a prime rib dinner special for $5.99. So even if you lost all of your money you wouldn't starve. That was good to know.

The shuttle pulled into the parking lot of the Flamingo Hilton. A neon pink Flamingo sign greeted us. I picked up my suitcase, got off the bus and shuffled in to the reservation desk. I was welcomed by the scream of slot machines and the music of money tumbling out. There were rows and rows of one armed bandits. A brand new black Mercedes Benz was roped off by one special slot machine. A new car for a quarter. Dreams for sale! I'd have to get some nickels later.

I went up to the reservations desk. The hotel clerk, a bottle blonde with big swipes of robin's eggshell blue on her eyelids, looked up.

"I have a reservation," I said. I dug in my purse for my credit card and handed it over. I turned around as she looked me up on her computer. My stalker had vanished. I had expected him to check into a room. Maybe I was getting paranoid.

I signed a slip, accepted room keys, then took the elevator to my room on the Fifteenth floor. I walked down a carpeted hallway, past some kind of bachelor's party, to room 1526. I unlocked the door and went inside. After putting up the safety chain and the double lock, I surveyed the room. The normal set up. Two queen sized beds, a nightstand with a telephone on it, a table with two chairs, and a bureau. A television was suspended from the ceiling. I walked over to the nightstand, picked up the remote, and flipped it on. There was a special channel with gambling instructions. I left it on and quickly peeked underneath the bed, mindful of the urban myth about the dead hooker. I washed my face, brushed my teeth and stripped down to my undies. I crept inside the sheets and promptly fell asleep.

TWENTY-EIGHT

"BLACKJACK! TO WIN get closer to 21 than the dealer, without going over. Aces count as one or 11, numbered cards equal their value and picture cards are 10. Ties break even."

I opened one eye and stared up at the television screen. The blackjack dealer, a Hispanic man in a black vest, white shirt, and black slacks, was demonstrating the game. I fumbled for the remote and turned the television off. The clock on the nightstand said it was a little before nine.

The curtains in the room were open. I got out of bed and went to the grimy window. A valley of hotels, liquor stores and parking lots were spread out below me. Cars moved by on the road like little ants. The giant neon clown on the Circus Circus hotel stared at me as I stretched my arms. I went to the bathroom, took a shower and dried my hair. I wrapped myself in a towel sarong style and applied my make up. After I made myself beautiful, I sat at the little table by the window and ate the peanuts I took off the plane.

It looked cloudy outside, or maybe it was the dirty windows. There was a complimentary pen in the drawer and some hotel stationary. I sat down again and started an action plan. My first order of business was to get some real food. Next I wanted to drop by the Lucky Lady Casino to check it out and to get a handle on Brute Mortimer. It was also worth a visit to the local public library to see if there were any pertinent articles in the *Reno Gazette*. Of course, there was the visit with the cop. If time permitted I wanted to check out Violetta DeOrca, maybe chat up her neighbors.

I moved to the nightstand and pulled out the phone book. There was a Gideon Bible underneath it. I flipped through the pages of the phone book and traced my finger down a list of names in the "D" section. No DeOrcas. Hmm.

The red message light on my telephone was on. I called down to the front desk and found that Tim King had left a message without waking me up. Nice guy. I had an appointment with John Drysdale at eight o'clock in the hotel bar. Good.

I put on a navy turtleneck sweater, jeans and tennis shoes and topped it off with my Armani pea coat. The look was cute though slightly nautical. I shoved the hotel stationary into my purse along with the pen, grabbed my keys and left the room.

The buffet on the second floor was a caloric paradise. It was also possible to gamble while you ate lunch. Keno runners went from table to table collecting tickets and money. I sat down at the counter and ordered a vegetable omelet with home fries instead. I vowed to eat lightly but found myself mopping up the grease on my plate with a second slice of toast. Oh well.

By the time I paid the bill and left a tip, business in the coffee shop had swelled. There was a cloud of smoke hovering over the restaurant. The escalator took me down to the main floor. I moved purposefully through the casino, avoiding cocktail waitresses, tourists in loud clothes, and the siren song of the slot machines.

A bellboy was able to direct me down the street to the Lucky Lady Casino. The hotels I passed in the chilly morning air were indistinguishable from each other. The doors were always open, three hundred and sixty five days a year. It had been several years since I had last visited Reno. I was twenty one and I had taken a road trip with a bunch of friends from Seattle. It was a twelve hour drive, even with Randy driving

90 miles an hour. We weren't stopped by any cops but we did hit a porcupine in Katy's new car. We arrived at 1:00 in the morning and started gambling right away. By six a.m. we were drunk on free cocktails and nickel winnings. Later in the day we visited Harrah's car museum, then it was back to the casinos to try our hand at poker, roulette and 21. I was frugal and had sixty dollars in dimes to show for the trip. My friend Lori needed to ask her dad for more tuition money.

The Lucky Lady Casino was decorated like a garish whore. Red velvet adorned the walls. Neon slot machines flashed intermittently. There was a long bar tucked in the side by the machines. Three fellas sat there drinking their breakfasts. The cocktail waitresses had short skirts, fishnet stockings, their breasts nearly popped out of their skimpy blouses. The casino, small in relation to the other big hotels, was busy. Didn't anyone have a job? People were crowded around the craps tables, cheering the dice, and watching their money being raked away by bored looking dealers. I went over to one of the change cages and bought some chips. A couple of women in their late twenties with big butts and high hair, were sitting at a gaming table playing 21. I walked over to the table and hopped up on a stool. I put my chips on the table and started to play. I won six games in a row and my women friends left. The dealer, a woman in her late fifties, was white and skinny with stick like arms and heavy make up. Her hair was dyed an unnatural shade of blonde. She wore black pants, a white shirt and a vest like the other dealers. She shuffled the cards expertly, then dealt them with machine gun speed.

"Have you worked here a long time?"

She smacked her gum. "Uh huh. Honey, I've seen it all. Been working here since they opened the place in the sixties."

"Oh, back in the Charlie Sharkey days."

She set the cards down. "Did you know Charlie?"

"No, I've heard of him though. Didn't he get shot?"

"Poor guy. Ended up in the hotel pool with a bullet in him. I remember that day well. The place was crawling with cops by the time I reported for my shift. I was waitressing then." She dealt me two cards. A Jack and a four of clubs. Damn.

"Did they ever catch the killer?"

"No—" We both looked up as a siren went off. Twenty feet away an elderly man was whooping as money rained out of his machine. The dealer smiled and dealt herself a shoe of cards. The face card was a queen.

"Must have been awful for his wife."

"Vi? Yeah. She sold the place and retired. I was surprised. Despite her age, the gal liked the night life. She was a showgirl when she was younger."

"Where's she living now?"

"She has a little place near the University. Although I don't see her around much. She travels a lot to keep busy. Spends a lot of time on the Greyhound."

"Who owns the Lucky Lady now?" I scraped my card on the table and she flipped me another.

The dealer's face went blank and her eyes flicked up to the ceiling. "I don't know."

I looked at my card. It was the King of Spades. Busted. I was out five bucks.

The dealer scooped my chips up. I slid off the stool as two tourists sidled up to the table. "Thanks."

The dealer nodded and started shuffling the cards. I toured the rest of the casino. The gaming areas were on three floors, including the lower level. There was a poker den on the second floor along with a restaurant. The other ten floors were hotel rooms. I got on the escalator and took it back down to the first floor. The reservations desk was tucked into a corner. An old bald man in a loud red shirt stood by a sign that said: BIG WINNER. His shirt was open, exposing his gray chest hair. His trousers were held up by a belt with an enormous silver dollar belt buckle. Cowboy boots peeked beneath the hem of his pants. It was the man who had won big earlier while I played 21. He was getting his picture taken by a casino employee with a Polaroid camera. His gnarled hands held a tray of silver dollars. He looked happy as hell.

After the employee took the picture she congratulated him then went over to a board marked "Lady Luck Winners". She tacked the picture up on the end of a long row of pictures. I walked over and looked at the board.

Curtis Mayberry of Houston, Texas had just won a thousand dollars. Jill Miller, an attractive red head from Sacramento had won ten thousand two days ago. I glanced at the row of smiling winners. Roger Vance from Portland, Oregon won 250 grand on October 14.

A chill went through me as I moved in for a closer look. Roger Vance looked uncomfortable in a yellow polo shirt one size too small and beige slacks. He was holding a big fake cardboard check for two hundred and fifty thousand dollars in his hand.

Now he was dead.

Everything seemed to point to Brute Mortimer. Joe Arnim was probably just a muscle man. First Sharkey, then Crombie. Finally DeOrca. All business partners with Brute Mortimer. Was Roger Vance a partner too? I had a motive, now all I needed was some proof.

TWENTY-NINE

THE PUBLIC LIBRARY in Reno did not yield any local photos or articles on Brute Mortimer. I thought back to the articles I had retrieved from the Multnomah County library at home. Brute Mortimer had been mentioned only as a partner in the Starlite Lounge. No photos, no other personal information. It was almost as if the man wasn't real.

I had talked to three more Lucky Lady employees before I left the casino. Not one of them was able to identify the owner of the place. Pinning anything down on Mortimer was beginning to be like nailing pudding to the wall.

I went to the library database and entered the name "DeOrca." There was only one listing. September 12, 1984. "DeOrca assumes the role of general manager at the Lucky Lady hotel". No mention of the owner or of Brute Mortimer.

Next I typed in Sharkey, Charlie. There were numerous hits dating back to 1969. All of them were on microfiche. I went over to the librarian and she helped me locate the dates. Then I sat down and loaded the microfiche spools onto the reader. I looked at the most recent first. He was murdered on August 24, 1984. A sweltering day, with temperatures in the high nineties. His body was discovered in the hotel pool by one of the maids. He had been shot two times. The police were unable to find the killer. I scrolled back to the obituary. He was survived by his wife, Vi, and a stepson. There were six other articles relating to the murder, all with similar information. The earlier articles related to local civic events and charity functions. I looked at the one from 1969. It was a wedding announcement. I looked at the pair of smiling faces. I recognized one of them. It was Violetta.

I looked at the article in surprise. Charlie Sharkey and Violetta DeOrca, had married in the Chapel of Love in downtown Reno. It was a second marriage for both. Charlie Sharkey was mentioned as the owner of the Lucky Lady Casino in downtown Reno. Violetta was given away by her son, Federico.

Why didn't Violetta tell me she had been married to Charlie Sharkey for God's sake? No wonder she was out for Brute Mortimer. First her husband, now her son. Things were getting crazier by the minute. I got a quarter from my purse, inserted it in the slot at the top of the microfiche machine and pressed "print". A fuzzy copy of the article slowly churned from the machine. I folded it and stuffed it in my purse.

The telephone book in the library did not have a listing for V. Sharkey or V. DeOrca. At the present moment she was ensconced in her suite at the Vintage. Or she was breaking into someone's hotel room. Or maybe planning an assassination. I sighed and looked at my watch. It was nearly two o'clock.

I left the library and stopped for a Big Mac and fries at McDonalds. On the way back to the hotel I stopped to admire a display of diamond wedding rings in the window of a pawn shop. The rings looked very sad and tacky next to the used televisions and watches. I tried to imagine how they had ended up there. A good night at the roulette table, a quick trip to the jewelry store, and later a midnight rendezvous at a drive thru wedding chapel. Then morning comes, with a hangover and a new husband. I laughed to myself. As I looked up I caught sight of the man from the airport in the reflection of the glass. When I turned around, he had disappeared into the throng of tourists on the sidewalk.

He was creeping me out. What in the hell did he want? Was

he one of Mortimer's guys? He didn't look tough enough to be the type. I shivered and hurried back to the Flamingo. I took a nap in the room, and woke up in time for Oprah. I checked my offices for messages while Oprah interviewed a celebrity guest. Henry had called twice. The other message was from an attorney at Vaughn, King and Sachitano.

I called the attorney and left a message. Then I cradled the phone in my hand and thought about Henry. Why did he check me out? I had been stupid to get involved with him, especially since he was obviously using me to find out about more about the DeOrca murder. Two could play at that game. I wondered who his informant was at the Portland Police Bureau. I dialed Henry's work number. He answered on the second ring.

"Sullivan."

I almost hung up, then he spoke. "Jane?"

"How did you know it was me?"

"I don't get many heavy breathers."

I laughed, starting to remember what I liked about Henry. "Well, I'm returning your call. What do you want?"

"I think we need to talk."

"I don't know." I looked at the television. The local news was on. I picked up the remote control and flicked the television off.

"Please?"

I'm a sucker for a groveling man. "All right. You can pick me up at the airport tomorrow morning."

"Where are you?"

I ignored him. "My flight arrives at eleven-thirty. I'll be waiting outside by the United Airlines sign. And I'll be hungry." A free ride and a free meal. That was the least he owed me.

"I'll be there."

I hung up the phone and got ready to go out. I was meeting John Drysdale at eight, but that still left the early evening available for earning a new car. I put on a red turtleneck sweater, a black wool skirt, tights and black boots. The skirt was very short, but it was granny length compared to what the cocktail waitresses were wearing. I tucked some cash, a lipstick, and my keys into my pocket and went downstairs.

The symphony of the slot machines was ringing as I stepped into the casino area. I flagged a casino employee down and traded ten bucks for five rolls of nickels. I plugged the machine for the next two hours, until my hands were dirty and my money was gone. No triple sevens for me tonight.

At ten to eight I left the machines. The little old lady next to me climbed on my stool, poised to win all of the money I put into the sucker. I stopped in the ladies room, then went to meet John Drysdale at the bar.

The Flamingo bar is tucked behind a wall of slot machines. I located it and took a look around. There was a giant mirror behind the polished bar which shelved a veritable liquor store. Three bartenders were pouring drinks. A cocktail waitress was loading up her tray. There were several booths: most of them occupied by couples. Three college age boys guzzled beers in front of a television. At the very end of the bar there was a man in his early sixties with a fat cigar tucked in the corner of his mouth. It was unlit. He had gray hair, combed back, and he wore a casual shirt and a jacket. He looked down at the bar, intent on the video poker game he was playing. I made my way over.

"John Drysdale?"

"You must be Jane Lanier." The man looked up from his game and put out a big paw for me to shake.

"Have a seat then."

I settled on the stool next to him. He nodded at the bartender who came right over.

"What do you drink?" John looked at me.

"A glass of wine would be great. White, please." I'm a sissy drinker.

"I'll have another Henry's."

"Coming right up." The bartender withdrew to get the drinks.

John looked down at the machine. "If you don't mind, I'm in the middle of the game. But I can talk and play at the same time."

"No problem. Tim King said you worked on the Sharkey murder case."

The bartender arrived with the drinks. I picked mine up for a sip while John chomped on his cigar and pushed the buttons on his video poker. "Yeah, that was back in '84. I made Detective that year. Remember it was a really hot day. A scorcher. Lot of people at the hotel were mad that afternoon because there was a body in the pool and they wanted to go swimming." He guffawed.

I winced. "Was there any indication as to who might have done it?"

John cocked his head. "A drifter maybe. Charlie was always a hothead, getting into fights."

"So, you knew him then?"

"Yep. I remember when he opened the Lucky Lady. It was a nice casino then. Now it's gone to hell."

"Do you know who owns it now?"

"Why are you opening up that can of worms?"

"A man was murdered in Portland. Gunshot wound to the throat. A couple of days later a cop was killed that way."

I had John's attention now. His weary cop eyes were alert.

"So it makes sense to wonder if the Lucky Lady is somehow connected to all of this—and to Brute Mortimer."

"Girl, you are in way over your head." John took a slug of his beer. "We didn't have this conversation."

"Why not?"

"Because I don't want to end up dead." He got off his stool and pulled out his wallet.

I held up my hand. "Hey, I'm buying."

"Thanks, lady. Have a good life, if you can." He moved swiftly away, through the bar and into the casino.

I sat and stared at my glum face in the mirror as I finished my wine. Lady Luck had spit on me tonight.

THIRTY

MORNING CAME ABOUT five hours too early. The phone jangled at six a.m. I picked it up and the recorded voice of a robot told me "THIS IS YOUR WAKE UP CALL." A wave of nausea reminded me that you always pay for the free drinks dispensed while you gamble at the slot machines.

Somehow I managed to shower, dress, pack, and check out by seven. I was amazed to see people were already positioned at the gaming tables and slot machines despite the early hour. Then again, maybe they hadn't made it to bed yet. On my way out of the hotel to the shuttle bus, I noticed something gleaming on the carpet by a poker machine. I picked it up. It was a silver dollar. My luck was changing.

I shared the shuttle bus with a glum couple from Nashville who lost their mortgage payment playing roulette. They moaned all the way to the airport, trying to figure out how to juggle bills so they could buy groceries that week. I refrained from offering advice, but I do know that the power companies are very forgiving for at least two months.

The monitor at the airport advised me of the gate and time that my flight departed. I was a little early so I bought a cup of coffee, then wandered over to the slot machines to wait. The change in the bottom of my purse was heavy. What was the harm in putting it into the machines? After ten minutes I was about four dollars lighter.

A glimpse of the man who had been following me for two days made me forget my loss. He was half hidden by a phone booth but I could see him looking in my direction. I shrugged. If he wanted to "get" me, he had plenty of opportunities. He could've clubbed me on the head in the casino—no one would have heard me over the noise of the slots. Or he could have slipped poison into one of the many drinks I had last night. I shoved my hands into my pockets and turned away. Someone was obviously interested in what I was up to. Either that or the world is made up of amazing coincidences.

It was time to catch my flight. The silver dollar I found at the casino seemed to find my fingers. A businesswoman in a suit and heels vacated a slot machine offering a zillion dollar prize. A maintenance man shuffled by with a rolling garbage can. He was a big guy with a ruddy face. He stopped in front of me and reached into his can. I got up, moved to the vacant slot machine, slipped the dollar in and pushed a button. The man in the phone booth hung up the receiver and picked up a duffel bag. That was new, I thought. The other night he carried just a paper.

Sirens went off. I jumped in my skin and looked at the slot machine. There were two sevens and a joker aligned on the screen.

"OH MY GOD!" I screamed, pumping my fists in the air. Passersby stopped to point and stare. A crowd started to collect.

An attendant appeared by the machine. He was dressed in a vest and slacks and he had a change belt strapped on. "I'm getting the manager," he said. "It looks like you won five thousand dollars."

"OH MY GOD!" I cried again. "You're kidding."

"No," he said with a smile, "you're the big winner!"

"I'M THE BIG WINNER!" I yelled to everyone in the airport. Now I knew what it felt like to be on a game show.

A manager ushered me back to the office and I was presented with a cashier's check for 5,000 dollars. I also had to fill out a slew of forms for the IRS. I was giddy before I realized I missed my flight. I called Henry and told his voice mail about my good news. I also said I would be on the flight that arrived at two.

Once on the plane, my head was swirling with thoughts of how to spend the money. A new car? A down payment on a house? A trip to Europe? Someone told me once that money you win is not like money you earn. It's meant to be blown, in the same way you acquired it. It didn't seem appropriate to pay bills with it.

I ordered champagne and pushed away the plastic covered meal served by a flight attendant. I took a few sips, grinning to myself before reality set in. What the hell was I doing? I wasn't flying back to a new life as Ivana Trump, I was coming home to a world of problems. DeOrca and Vance were dead and someone was trying to kill me. The cheap champagne I ordered seemed acidic in my mouth. I pushed it away and swilled a Diet Coke instead. My head needed to be clear so I could think.

By the time the plane thundered to a stop on the runway, I had sketched a game plan. Joe Arnim was the key to solving the DeOrca murders. He had the opportunity—Theresa had told him about the meeting in my office that night. And he had the motive. DeOrca wanted to find him and the missing money. It was possible Joe hadn't acted on his own. Maybe Mortimer had ordered the hit. Two of his former business partners were dead, what was one more?

Now I just needed to get to him before Violetta did.

Henry was in the waiting area as I deplaned. He was in his work clothes—blue jacket, navy tie, neatly pressed khaki pants. He clutched a paper wrapped bouquet of red roses in his hand. All the ice in my heart melted. How could I have ever been mad at him?

The Cheshire Cat grin crawled onto my face again. Five grand in slot machine winnings and roses from a fella. I'd hit the jackpot twice today.

"Hi, Henry." I beamed at him, then looked at the roses. "Are those for me?"

"Of course. Now that you're a rich woman, I need to work twice as hard to woo you," he said with a laugh as he handed them to me. I accepted them and Henry picked up the suitcase I rolled off the plane. What is it with guys that they won't use the wheels? "It's good to see you, Jane." He smiled down at me as we walked toward the exit.

I told him all about my big moment in the airport and showed him the check. We walked outside. The day was crisp, cold and windless. Henry was parked at a meter near the airport entrance. We walked over and climbed in his truck.

"Do you have time for lunch?" Henry asked as he started the car.

"I always have time for lunch. Hey, I'm rich, I'll even buy."

"Not today," Henry said, as he backed up into the path of a taxi. "My treat."

"Where are we going?"

"It's a surprise."

We took Columbia Boulevard, and headed west toward the 33rd Street exit. We drove along DeOrca territory with neither of us mentioning the mansion was close by. Henry crossed the Broadway intersection and took I-84 to downtown. Soon we were pulling up in front of the Heathman Hotel. I looked over at Henry. The fellow doesn't make that much money. The Heathman is one of the nicest hotels in Portland with a fantastic bar and restaurant. Theater aficionados stop in the bar after shows to soak up the champagne at ten bucks a glass and the piano music.

"Here we are," he said, smiling at me. We got out of the car and he handed his keys to a valet. A uniformed doorman pulled open the heavy swinging door. We went inside.

"Reservations for Sullivan," Henry said to a starchy *maitre'd*. He led us to a table by an etched glass window facing

Broadway street. I set the roses down on the chair next to me. The waiter handed us menus and returned a few moments later with water and bread. I wasn't hungry but I ordered anyway, knowing that it wouldn't matter. The nouvelle cuisine of the Heathman features doll sized portions with dramatic sauces.

After the waiter withdrew, Henry leaned forward, a cloud of seriousness passing over his face. "I've been wanting to talk."

The words hung in the air and I tried to bat them away. "It's okay, Henry. Don't worry about it. Look, herb bread." I plucked a big piece out of the bread basket and started to butter it.

"No, really Jane. I want to explain."

The bread seemed to stick in my throat as I tried to swallow. "Okay," I said miserably.

Henry also looked uncomfortable. "When we first met, you mentioned you worked as a reporter once, but you were very vague about it. I didn't push it. I figured you would tell me about it when you were ready."

I sat there, stunned. I did not want to hear this.

"But you never did. Then DeOrca was murdered in your office. I had to ask myself 'why you?' You hadn't been in the business more than a few years, why would he pick you out of all the investigators in Portland?"

I had asked myself the same thing. I knew the answer now, thanks to Theresa, but still I didn't speak.

"So, I got curious. I have friends in the Seattle news business and they were familiar with your work. They told me what happened to—" he paused delicately "the principal, and the young student. One of them faxed a copy of the article to me. I guess you found it."

"I did." It was all I could say.

"Do you want to talk about it?"

I shook my head. "I can't," I whispered. Guilt flooded through me just thinking about Mr. Downey. If I hadn't written the article he might still be alive today. But then other lives might be ruined. It was all so complicated.

Henry looked disappointed. "Okay. I understand."

The waiter appeared then with our meals. We had both ordered chicken. The plate was decorated with swirls of sauce. I couldn't take a bite. Instead I gulped my wine and tried to regain my composure.

"Any leads on the Vance case?" I asked.

Henry swallowed a bite of chicken. "Got a couple. Like you, he also won big in Reno a couple of weeks ago. A quarter mil. Funny thing, nobody saw him win." He looked at me. "Was that what you were checking out in Reno?"

"I did find out a little bit about that, yes. There's a photo of him with a big cardboard check posted in the Lucky Lady casino."

"Did you find out anything else?"

I smiled coyly and started eating my chicken. "Is that the reason for the lovely meal and flowers?" Cheaper than an airline ticket and a hotel room in Reno.

Henry reached across the table and touched my hand. "No. Sorry."

I moved my hand and picked up my wineglass again, forgetting my resolve to keep my head clear. We finished the meal and the bottle of wine, without touching on any subject more intimate than the weather. When the check arrived I set my napkin down.

"I need to get back to the office. Can I get my suitcase from you later?"

"Yes," Henry said, reaching for his wallet. "I'll bring it by your place tonight if you want."

"That would be great." I stood up and grabbed my roses. "Thanks for the lunch and the flowers."

"My pleasure," he said looking at me. I looked away and started to move towards the door.

"Jane…"

I turned around. Henry hesitated, then spoke.

"Karla is okay. She's in college now. A journalism major."

Karla was the student who Mr. Downey had victimized. I could feel tears flooding my eyes. Henry got up, walked over and wrapped his arms around me. I buried my face in his jacket.

"It's all right," he said.

THIRTY-ONE

HENRY DROPPED ME BACK at the office, with a promise to call later. Once in my office, I set the roses on my desk, walked to the window and looked down, hypnotized by the steady stream of traffic outside. I was relieved to hear Karla was okay. In a way I finally had some of the closure I never knew I needed. I also felt emotionally exposed, like someone had been traipsing through my mind and unlocking all of the places where I keep my deepest darkest fears.

The phone rang, jarring me from my trance. I picked it up. "Lanier."

"It's me."

"What?" The voice was unfamiliar.

"We met in Pioneer Square. You were, you know—looking for someone."

That got my attention. It was the young fella with the shaved head and pierced face. "Yeah, I remember. Do you know where I can find him?"

"Yeah, for two hundred bucks."

A shakedown. Of course. An address would be too easy. Oh, well. I'd have to make a trip to the bank to deposit my Reno check anyhow.

"I can get it. Where can we meet?" The kid named a teen nightclub. I groaned. I was too old for this. "All right," I said as I copied down the address. It was located by Ankeny Square, not far from Waterfront Park. "What time?"

"Ten o'clock—and come alone or no deal." The phone

clicked abruptly. I hung up, feeling hopeful. This was the break I needed. Joe could be the link to the missing money and the murders. But to go alone? I shuddered. I'd rather run naked through a graveyard at midnight. I needed my gun.

Which was still under lock and key in the evidence room at the Portland Police Department. Even if I said "pretty please" I wouldn't be getting it until they were damned good and ready to release it.

Thinking of the gun made my thoughts drift to the bullet holes in Elana's window. Was Joe responsible? Theresa seemed to think he could be violent—or he could just be scared. His house had burned down and a heavy like DeOrca was after him…

The file folder with notes and articles on the DeOrca case was tucked in my desk drawer. I pulled it out and browsed through the clippings. The photo of DeOrca's arrest in the Everett Crombie murder made me stop. Vance was standing behind DeOrca, grim faced. That was in 1988. Ahead of him then was a two hundred and fifty thousand dollar jackpot in Reno and finally a swim in the Willamette with a bullet lodged in his throat. I tucked the photo in my purse, grabbed my coat and left the office.

The afternoon edition of the *Oregonian* had Roger Vance's photo on the front page. HOMICIDE DETECTIVE MURDERED! the title read. I stopped, plugged some change in the machine and grabbed a paper. Scanning the story, I learned Roger Vance was a highly regarded officer who had been with the Portland Police Department for his entire adult career. There were very few details about the actual murder. Most of the article focused on the community outrage over his death. I tucked the paper under my arm and hustled to the bank to deposit my own Reno winnings and to get bribery money. Was I somehow on the same collision course as Vance?

The thought stuck with me for the rest of the afternoon.

Around six o'clock I walked home, changed clothes, and ate dinner in front of the television. A picture of Roger Vance popped on the screen as I bit into a peanut butter and jelly sandwich. I choked. I finally decided to pay a visit to the Vance household. There wasn't going to be a good time to ask questions so I might as well get it over with. I put the peanut butter, jelly and potato chips away, put my coat on and got in the car. It was night already and the world seemed a little swallowed in early darkness. The drive to the Vance's residence in southeast Portland took about twenty minutes. The house was brightly lit and the curtains were drawn. There was a station wagon parked in the driveway and a new model Lexus parked out front. I pulled in behind it, got out of my car, and walked to the front door. I rang the doorbell. After a moment the door opened. A woman stood there. She was probably in her early thirties with curly blonde hair grazing her shoulders. She was dressed in a denim shirt with tight jeans and tennis shoes. Beyond her I could see a living room area to the left. There was a big gold framed mirror and several flower arrangements on the mantle. There was also a framed photo of Detective Vance in his uniform.

"Hi," she said tentatively looking at me. "Are you a friend of mom's?"

"No," I admitted. "But I'm working on a case that might be related to Detective Vance's murder."

"Are you a cop?"

"No, a private investigator."

"I'm sorry." She started to close the door. "Mom can't be bothered now. She's not feeling well."

"Diane! Who is it?" Through the narrow crack of the door I could see a woman in the hallway. She was in her mid fifties and she had gray hair and puffy eyes. She was dressed in black pants and a baggy gray sweater. A single strand of pearls hung from her neck. She looked like the woman I had seen yesterday. She came to the door and Diane moved aside.

"I'm Dorothy Vance," she said, peering out the door. Her face was pale. "Who are you?"

"My name is Jane Lanier. I'm a private investigator. I'm looking into the DeOrca murder and I think that it might be related to your husband's murder."

She gave me a hard look then surprised me by holding open the door. "Come in."

"Thanks." I stepped inside the entryway. A staircase led to the second floor. The smell of garlic came from the kitchen and the windows were steamed up from the food cooking in there. To the right I could see a dining room, the table piled with cards and flower baskets. A little girl with curly blonde hair was sitting at the table eating a cookie. When she saw me look at her she got up and ran into the kitchen.

Mrs. Vance led me into the living room. Diane followed. The room was painted a light blue and furnished with a white couch, two high backed chairs in light blue, and two small walnut tables. There were several bookshelves built into the wall that displayed knickknacks and photos in gold frames. The fireplace was empty and the room was cold. The photo of Roger Vance stared at me from the mantle.

"Please sit down." Mrs. Vance indicated one of the chairs. Both she and Diane sat down on the couch. "What do you know about my husband's murder?"

The question took me a bit off guard. I shifted in my seat. "A few days ago a man named Federico DeOrca was killed in my office downtown. He died before I could talk to him but I was under the impression that he was looking for someone who had stolen a lot of money from him. Detective Vance and Detective Dermott—"

"Tom," Diane murmured, nodding.

"—interviewed me about the murder. Unfortunately, I wasn't

able to provide very many details. What strikes me about your husband's murder…" I paused delicately, "is that he was killed by a shot to the throat. Mr. DeOrca died the same way."

"How did you know that my husband was shot in the throat?" Dorothy Vance asked in a steely tone. "The police are withholding that information."

"I found out from a reporter."

The answer seemed to satisfy Mrs. Vance. Diane piped up. "Must have been the reporter from Channel 7. He's been calling here all day."

"Anyway," I skipped over the remark because I was dating that reporter, "I wanted to ask you about a picture that I found when I was doing some research into DeOrca's past." I pulled the copy of the photo from my purse which was taken after DeOrca's arrest for the murder of Edward Crombie. DeOrca was in handcuffs and Detective Vance stood behind him. I handed the photo to Mrs. Vance. Diane looked over her shoulder.

"This was taken years ago." Mrs. Vance commented in a soft voice. "Roger has aged since then."

"The article said your husband made the initial arrest. Mr. DeOrca was charged with the murder of Everett Crombie, his business partner. The case later ended up as a mistrial—"

"Because the murder weapon disappeared. And then one of the jurors." Mrs. Vance finished as a frown wrinkled her forehead. She turned to her daughter. "Will you please call Mary Anne and Rochelle? They said they would be coming over tomorrow. I want to know what time."

Diane got up. "Okay." She gave me a strange look as she left the room.

Mrs. Vance's face sagged. "I'm lucky. I have three daughters and eight grandkids. They keep me very busy and I need them at a time like this." She leaned forward and spoke in a low voice. "About the missing gun."

I leaned forward too.

"My granddaughter disappeared several years ago in broad daylight. Right after Federico DeOrca's trial started. She was only four at the time. It happened at the day care center. Her mother went there after work to pick her up and she was missing. We were all frantic. I called Roger at work and he came right home. It was a terrible day. At nine o'clock that night a car squealed by our house. We went to the window in time to see Susie get out of the car. She ran up the steps and the car drove away. It didn't have any license plates on it but it didn't matter. We found out later that the car was stolen. She was unhurt, thank God, but we've been afraid ever since. It seems that a woman calling herself Susie's aunt picked our Susie up from day care. Susie didn't even know that she had been kidnapped. She was very trusting then. Not anymore. We learned the hard way that our family was not safe." Mrs. Vance looked me in the eye. "And yes, the gun that killed Mr. Crombie disappeared." She stood up. "My husband was a good cop. He spent his entire career on the police force and earned many commendations. And that is all I have to say on the matter. I know you have a job to do but I need you to leave us out of it. Nothing we do now will bring my husband back."

I stood up too. "Thank you, Mrs. Vance."

She led me to the door. "My daughters don't know about any of this…" Her voice trailed. "Things are hard enough right now."

"They are," I agreed. "Don't worry about it. Just take care of yourself."

Mrs. Vance watched me go to my car. She was still standing in the doorway when I drove off.

I mulled over what Mrs. Vance told me as I drove back downtown. Mrs. DeOrca was right—her husband was too mean to die. Especially if he would hold a kid hostage to manipulate a member of the police force. But he had to have had help if he were behind bars. Did he get it from Joe Arnim?

I was a bit early to meet the little extortionist but I went to the club anyway, finding it by the thunder of the music. Once I was there I realized my mistake. The bouncer checked my purse for contraband then informed me that I was entering an underage nightclub. Inside I endured a snicker or two as I made my way to the counter for a Diet Coke. At 32, I was the oldest person in the room by about fifteen years. And my outfit, a shiny silver raincoat over a black turtleneck and black pants, was totally wrong. Everybody else was wearing their shiny silver in little earrings on their eyebrows. A young man with a dog collar around his neck walked by and gave me an inquiring bark. I ignored him and carried my soft drink to a table. As soon as I could, I was going to get out of here and go to a real bar.

The kid with the shaved head showed up at ten-thirty. He was wearing the same leather outfit he had on when I met him. He was accompanied by a young lady with dyed black hair, chopped short in a bob. She was sporting a floaty black skirt, a scruffy vintage brown coat and heavy work boots. Her makeup was garish and the stud in her nose looked like a big metallic pimple. "This isn't Joe," I said to the kid as they sat down.

He gave me a funny look which wrinkled the crossbones on his forehead. "This is Ariana, a friend of Joe's—"

"He ain't no friend of mine!" Ariana piped in.

"Shut up!" the kid said, giving Ariana a menacing look. He turned away from her and she made a face at his back. "ANYWAY, as I was saying, Ariana's going to come too. Did you bring the money?" He held out his hand.

"Not until you show me where Joe is. Let's go."

I put on my coat and my new friends followed me to my car. After a brief scuffle over the front seat, I was directed to a decrepit yellow Victorian house with missing shingles and broken windows on the edge of Northwest Portland. All of the other houses on the block were in the process of being razed—

probably for row houses. There was an orange bulldozer in the middle of the lawn next door and the area was fenced in. We got out of the car. The lawn of the Victorian was overgrown with weeds and choked with bottles and garbage. The boards on the front porch creaked as we walked across them. A notice on the front door said in big black letters that the house was condemned. The kid opened the door without knocking.

"The house is condemned," I whispered, in case he couldn't read. "Are you sure that Joe's here?" I was ready to bolt.

"Yeah, yeah," he answered. We went inside. The entryway was dark. In front of us a staircase with tattered red carpet twisted around to the second floor. To the left was a living room illuminated by candlelight. A dark blanket hung over the window facing the street. The room was like a cave. I could see a group of six teenagers dressed in black studded leather and denim huddled inside around a makeshift milk crate table. They were passing around a joint. The sickly sweet smell made me want to gag. A broken mirror smudged with white dust lay on the floor next to some extra large bottles of malt liquor. With what little light there was I could see there was no furniture—only card board boxes, litter, and a rusted out shopping cart stolen from Safeway. The fireplace was stuffed with trash. The walls were decorated with spray paint and some music was playing on a small battery operated CD player. The music grated on my ears but I found the scrabble of little rodent feet even more appalling.

The kid approached the group, clearly one of them. I hung back in the shadows, standing still so the rats wouldn't feast on my feet. Ariana went over and sat on some guy's lap, then she took a hit off his joint. She looked at me as she blew the smoke into the air. Her face was dreamy. The other kids didn't pay much attention to me until I heard the kid tell his friends that I was willing to pay fifty bucks for "fire boy." Guess he was going to keep the other one-fifty.

One of them stood up. It was a boy, sixteen, I guess, and he was holding a candle. The light made his skinny face and sharp nose look ghoulish. He was wearing a big sweatshirt and droopy jeans with ragged holes in the middle of his legs. "I know where Joe is," he said to me in a solemn voice. "C'mon, I'll show you."

Somewhat reluctantly I followed him through the living room into a foul smelling kitchen. The sink was black with grime and the counters were cluttered with rotten food. There was a stove without burners or an oven door. Something streaked across the floor as we walked in. The boy walked over to a door and pulled it open. "Joe's down there," he said, holding the candle away from the door. I walked over and peered down into the blackness of the stairwell that led to the basement.

"In the basement?" I said doubtfully. This was not a good idea.

"Yeah, go on." The boy made a gesture to urge me down the stairs. My attention was diverted by the thundering of footsteps coming from the second floor.

"What's that?" I asked, stopping in my tracks. He didn't answer. Instead he reached out and pushed me hard. I plunged down the rickety stairs, breaking one on the way down. The door slammed shut and I heard the snap of a lock. I lay still for a moment on the concrete floor, mentally checking for broken bones. I seemed to be okay. Little shits. Outside I could hear a car start up. My car! They must have hot wired it.

I scrambled to my feet, lurching forward into the stairs. "LET ME OUT!!!" I screamed. My plea was greeted with silence. I tried to look around but everything was dark except for the shine of my coat. I felt my way up the stairs and tried the door. Locked. I started banging away on it anyway. "LET ME OUT!" I screamed again.

Footsteps crossed the floor and I could hear the lock turning again. The door creaked open and Ariana stood there, holding a candle.

"What the hell is going on here?" I demanded.

"Sorry," she whispered urgently. "But we've got to get out. Joe's coming back. He's going to set the house on fire."

THIRTY-TWO

ARIANA HURRIED THROUGH the house, pausing only to grab the little CD player on her way out. I stumbled after her, breathless.

"What do you mean Joe's going to burn down the house?"

"He's on his way out to get some gas or something." She flung open the door and we went out onto the porch. It was dark. And lonely. There were no lights on in any of the abandoned houses on the block. The backhoe at the construction site next door hovered over an open pit. It looked like some kind of metal monster.

"Where's my car?"

Ariana was midway down the stairs. She stopped and scrunched up her face. "Joe took it. He said you wouldn't be needing it anymore. Look, I gotta get out of here. When Joe finds out I let you go, he's gonna be really pissed off at me."

"Why?"

"He said DeOrca hired you to kill him."

My jaw dropped open. "That isn't true!"

"Whatever. See ya." Ariana started to run. I watched her go down the street, her dark clothing blending into the night.

I took off my stupid silver coat and turned it inside out. No need to hang a big "KILL ME" sign on myself. I jogged six or seven quiet streets until I hit a residential area. There was a convenience store at the corner. I ran over and used the pay phone to call the police. They were kind enough to patch me through to Dermott.

"Dermott here."

"Dermott, this is Jane Lanier," I panted. I was still winded from my unplanned exercise. "A kid named Joe Arnim is on his way to burn down a house in northwest Portland."

"What does that have to do with me? Why didn't you just call 9-1-1?"

"Well, he thinks I'm in it!" I quickly explained what had just gone down.

"Where is this place?"

"Northwest Portland, by a construction site. Shoot, I didn't get a good look at the name of the street." I described the location.

"All right. I know where that is. They're putting up new housing there, right? We'll get on it. Where are you now?"

"At a Stop and Shop store," I gave him the address. "The kid stole my car!"

"I'll come pick you up."

I stood outside the store and shivered for a good fifteen minutes. Dermott pulled up to the curb in an unmarked squad car. I opened the door and got inside. It was nice and toasty. Dermott was dressed in a pair of slacks, a shirt and a leather jacket.

"You okay?" he asked.

"Yeah, thanks." I was freezing but glad the kid didn't have the chance to burn me alive.

"Tell me why this Joe Arnim fellow is trying to kill you."

I exhaled loudly. "His girlfriend said he thought DeOrca hired me to kill him. I don't know where he got that idea. Maybe that was DeOrca's intention, I don't know. I never got a chance to speak to the man."

"Where's the girlfriend now?"

"She took off after letting me out of the basement. Her name's Ariana. I think she's homeless. You might be able to locate her though. She hangs out at the teen nightclub near Old Town. There were several other kids at the house tonight too. I assume they're all out joy riding in my rental car. What's the plan now?"

Dermott started the car. "We're staking out the house to see if the Joe kid comes back. When and if he does we'll be ready. I'll take you home."

"Thanks. I want to be there when you question him."

"We'll see."

Dermott merged into the traffic on Northwest 21st. The stores were closed but you wouldn't know it by all of the cars parked on the street. We reached the Lovejoy intersection. Music from the Blue Moon restaurant blared into the night. Stand up comedians were surely bombing at the Silver Dollar Pizza amateur night. Shoppers pushed carts out of the Trader Joe's store. Dermott turned left and drove up the hill to my apartment building. He double-parked near the entrance. I got out.

"Thanks. Remember, I want to be there when you talk to Joe Arnim."

Dermott nodded. "Maybe," His radio squawked and I turned away. I was near the front door of the building when I heard Dermott call out.

"Lanier!"

I walked back to the car.

"They picked up your boy."

"Already?"

"Maybe he was in a hurry. He had a five gallon container of gasoline with him—and a gun. He was in the process of dumping the gas onto the floor when they arrested him."

I opened the car door and got in. "Let's go!"

Dermott sighed. "I can't promise you anything. We're going to talk to him first."

"Yeah, yeah."

I cooled my heels back at the police headquarters while they processed paperwork. Finally, a police officer summoned me to the interview room. He opened the door and I stepped inside. Dermott was there, and the arresting officer. Joe Arnim was seated at the table. He was in his early twenties, with blonde hair cut so short it looked like fuzz. He was wearing a ragged gray sweatshirt and jeans. He looked up and narrowed his eyes as I came in.

"It's you." Joe Arnim leaned forward as I sat down next to Dermott. "Why is she here? The bitch was hired to kill me for Christ's sake!"

"Who told you that?" I asked.

Arnim was silent.

"Theresa?"

Dermott looked over at me. I could tell this was the first he had heard of her.

"Theresa told me that you were the one that killed DeOrca." I lied. "You took the money, didn't you, Joe? Two million dollars. Of course, DeOrca was looking for you—and the money. Theresa told you that DeOrca planned to hire me to track you down. So all you had to do was wait for him to show up at my office. And when he did, you shot him."

"You are so full of shit," Arnim hissed. "I didn't have his damn money. If I did, do you think I'd still be hanging around here?"

"So, who took it, Joe?"

"I don't know." He shifted in his chair. "DeOrca gave me a key to a locker at the airport. I went there about a week ago to pick up a briefcase to deliver to his business partner, Brute—I mean Bruce Mortimer. I picked up the briefcase and went to the airport Sheraton to meet him. He was waiting for me in the parking lot in a limo. There was a driver, and another guy in the back seat. I got in and handed over the suitcase like I was supposed to."

"Did Brute open the briefcase?"

"Yeah," Joe admitted. "It was full of paper, not money. Brute was pissed off. His friend grabbed me by the throat and stuck a gun in my mouth. They kept on asking me where the money was. I knew then Fat Freddie had set me up."

"And they let you go?"

"I told them I had been set up. They musta known I was telling the truth."

"Did you know what the money was for?"

Arnim folded his arms. "I'm not saying another word until my lawyer gets here. I want immunity."

"For burning down the warehouse?"

"Yeah," Arnim blurted out. He turned red when he realized his mistake. "You bitch!" he muttered. I smiled and got up. Dermott followed me outside.

"You're good."

I shrugged modestly. "Find out if the little jerk blew up my car. I think he did. Also, you should take a look at his parent's house. Or what is left of it. Somebody torched it."

Dermott nodded. "Who's Theresa?"

"Friend of Joe's—and of Federico DeOrca. She used to work at the Starlite Lounge as a singer. We had coffee and talked yesterday. She was on her way out of town."

"We'll want to have coffee—and talk. Where can we find her?"

"Try Hollywood. I honestly can't tell you. She was scared. She said someone had tossed her apartment."

"Who?"

"I don't know. Maybe the same person who broke into my place." I frowned. "So, what are you going to do with Joe Arnim?"

"We're going to wait for his attorney and ask more questions. We'll lock him up for tonight."

"Did you find my rental car?"

"We impounded it. The perp set it on fire. Near as we could tell he stopped off and stole some gas from a service station, then abandoned the car near I-405. We found it just a few blocks from the condemned house they were using to squat in."

"Well, add that to his rap sheet," I said dryly.

"We'll probably charge him with attempted arson and

grand theft auto. We can hold him for a few days on that while we look into the other fires."

"What about the DeOrca murder?"

"I don't think we have our guy. Unless we can lift a print from the scene or find some evidence tying the shooting to Arnim, I would say that the murderer is still at large."

THIRTY-THREE

THE INSURANCE COMPANY sent a check for my car over by messenger at 9:00 a.m. Earlier that morning I notified them of the stolen rental car and mentioned I was on my way to rent another. The smiley voiced agent quickly transferred my call to the manager. He got on the line and told me very emphatically—not to rent another car, they would send a check—in an hour! He also named a generous price for my battered VW, so I didn't even dicker.

Now I had to buy a damn car.

I hate car shopping. It ranks right up there with root canals, pelvic exams, and IRS audits. The last time I bought a car, I tried to do everything right. I visited 18 car lots, read back issues of Car and Driver, and got a pre-approved loan from my bank. I wanted to be an informed consumer. What happened is I irritated the hell out of every smarmy salesman I met. One of them called me a whore of a dog when I tore up a bogus sales contract. Another took to obscene calls late at night after I questioned the need for optional upholstery insurance. I ended up buying my car from the first salesperson to show me a shred of kindness. I also ended up with empty pockets.

My friend Kelly agreed to loan me her 1984 Honda so I could make the rounds of the car lots. She works in the same building I do, for a community development organization. She was going to be in an all day meeting but she agreed to slip her car keys in the mail box at my office.

I walked to the Galleria, a thirty minute trek. It was drizzling out. Not enough to put your umbrella up, but enough to ruin your hair. I arrived at work with a halo of frizzies around my head. I picked up the keys from my office and walked out to the parking garage. Kelly's car was parked near the sky bridge on the third floor.

It was blue with a bullet hole in the back. I noticed the passenger side was missing a door lock. Kelly's car is a vandal magnet for some reason so she's reluctant to trade up. I know from experience the clutch slips and the car needs a new muffler but hey, it runs.

I chugged down the parking lot ramp and paid the fee of two dollars and twenty-five cents. Zeke, the parking attendant, was on duty. He's about sixty years old, with white hair and a big smile. He wears his uniform—maroon pants, white shirt, and a baseball style jacket with "Smart Park" emblazoned on the back—like it was a tuxedo. He's the friendliest man in the world and he likes to flirt with all the ladies. I was no exception today.

"Here's your change, beautiful." He touched my hand as he gave it to me.

I smiled. "Hi Zeke, how are you doing today?"

He leaned out of his little hut. "Wonderful, wonderful. And you?"

I sighed. "I'm not so good. A man was murdered in my office last week. A Galleria security guard named Peter Sundstrom was hurt too. Did you hear about it?"

Zeke frowned and clucked in sympathy. "I did, yes. The police came by to ask me if any cars left my lot around the time the man was murdered."

"Did any?"

"No, it was a slow night. The lot was practically empty." Zeke's eyes strayed behind my car. Several cars had zoomed to a stop behind me. It was time to go.

"Well, thanks. Have a good day."

Zeke pushed a button and waved good bye. The yellow and black striped wooden traffic arm swung up. I edged into the traffic and headed over to Portland Toyota on Broadway Street in northeast Portland. I had a reason for starting there. I remembered the name from the plate holders on Peter Sundstrom's brand new truck.

I parked my car on the street in front of a row of shiny new cars. A big sign draped over the showroom windows screamed "END OF THE YEAR CLEARANCE. BUY NOW FOR BEST DEALS!" A salesman standing outside the showroom caught sight of me as I left my car. He was twentyish, with black hair, cut short and slicked back. His suit was a little cheap looking and not so clean. He tossed his cigarette to the ground, stubbed it out with his shoe, and reached into his pocket. He pulled out a breath spray, treated himself to a squirt, then ambled over to meet me.

"Hi! Can we get you into a brand new car today?" He looked at Kelly's car then at me. His eyes had dollar signs in them.

"Maybe," I demurred, looking at the trucks section. There was a football field sized lot of them but they all looked the same. Which one had Peter bought? A red one?

The salesman walked me through the lot, chatting animatedly about the features of each vehicle. "So, how much are you willing to spend?" he said, pausing.

"Well," I hedged, as I tried to formulate a plausible lie. "I'm not really sure. My neighbor bought a truck here recently and I wanted to get one just like it. I think he spent around twenty-five thousand." I remembered the price as being a little lower than that but I thought throwing around the twenty-five grand figure might get his attention.

"We can get you in a great truck for that kind of money," the salesman said in a jovial voice. "Which one do you want?"

"I want one just like he had. But I don't see it here…"

"We can order it if you'll just tell me what you're looking for."

"I told you—one like my neighbor's." I was beginning to enjoy this. It's kind of fun to turn the tables.

"What did your neighbor have?" An edge crept into his voice.

"I would tell you but I don't know. He bought it here a few days ago, then he left town to go back to school at Oregon State. Maybe you remember him—his name was Peter and he had a bandage wrapped around his head." And a smashed nose, I thought as I remembered the struggle in my office the night of DeOrca's murder.

A smile lit up the salesman's face. "Oh, I remember that guy all right. I didn't help him but I remember him. He paid cash. Nearly twenty-five thousand dollars! We don't see that here very often."

"He doesn't trust banks," I explained.

"Yeah, okay. Look, I'll just run inside and pull his sales contract. Then we can see about finding you a truck just like his. In the twenty-five thousand dollar range, right."

"Right," I said, scanning the lot. "I'll just look around."

The salesman hurried inside. I watched him go into the showroom and approach the front desk. I walked quickly back to Kelly's car. I had no intention of buying a truck. I wanted a car just like the one I had. Besides that, I had a feeling that this place had a "females pay full price" policy.

I cruised the lots but didn't find anything in my price range. Finally I headed over to St. John's Honda. The place isn't particularly cheap but it seems to be honest for a car dealership. The salespeople will let you know up front if the engine is missing and stuff like that.

The salesman on duty let me wander the lot by myself. I lingered over some Honda Accords with only forty thousand miles on them, but instead I found a used maroon VW Cabriolet, just like my last one, tucked in the back. It was even dent free. I went back to the office. The salesman was the trusting type. He handed over the keys for a test drive—and let me go by myself. The man had obviously not spoken to any insurance agents associated with me.

After trying the car out on the St. John's bridge with the top down, I decided to take it. I wrote a check for a down payment and promised to pick it up later. I still had to take Kelly's car back downtown.

I drove back downtown, dropped off Kelly's car in the parking garage, and slipped the keys in her mailbox. Then I went to my office and called my insurance company to register my new car. They weren't happy to hear from me and the tone of the agent's voice foreboded a BIG premium increase at renewal time. I hung up and checked my voice mail messages. I had another one from Eddie Dickerson, my least favorite colleague. I was tempted to blow him off but in the PI business you never know when you'll need a favor. Even from a slime like Eddie. I called him back. Might as well get it over with.

"Hi, Eddie. This is Jane Lanier returning your call." My voice was professional. Didn't want to sound too friendly.

"Hi, Jane." Eddie sounded irritated. So what. I was still irritated over his boorish behavior at the Northwest PI Convention in Seattle. Then I thought of the toothbrush trick and grinned. We were almost even.

"So, Eddie, what can I do for you?"

"I'm looking for a guy named Nick Panillo, an appliance salesman, been missing since last Friday morning. He drove up to Portland to meet a private eye. And nobody has heard from him since."

"So?"

"Well, his mother is worried. This so-called private eye called him to say he was due an inheritance from a long lost friend he didn't even know he had."

"Oh, that's not good." It was the oldest PI trick in the book. It's hard to get someone's attention unless money is involved.

"Exactly. Must have been some sort of scam. The strange thing is, his car hasn't turned up and he seems to have disappeared into thin air. And this was one big fella."

"So, what do you want me to do about it? Maybe the guy just wanted to get out from beneath his mother's thumb."

"Yeah, probably. But look for him, okay? I've got my hands full with a case down here. I drove up to Portland over the weekend to ask some questions but I didn't turn up anything." Eddie lived in Medford, a five hour drive from Portland.

"All right. Do you have a picture or something I could go on? I could make some calls—when I have time. But I have an errand for you to do in return." I told him about Stan Oscram's missing wife. "I'll Fed ex you a picture of her."

Eddie agreed to Fed ex me a picture of Nick Panillo and to look for Stan's wife—when he had time. I chuckled and hung up.

A quick call to the Tri-Met information line told me which bus to take to the St. Johns area. I hurried out to the bus mall on Sixth Avenue to catch it. I wanted to pick up my car right away because I was about to take a road trip.

To Corvallis. Home of Oregon State University and home of Peter Sundstrom.

THIRTY-FOUR

THE TRIP TO CORVALLIS took an hour and a half. It's a straight shot on Interstate 5. I put my mind on cruise control, barely noticing landmarks such as the signs for Salem, the State Capitol, and Albany, a rather pungent smelling mill town. When I reached Corvallis I threaded my way into town, past a lot of fast food restaurants and Avery Square. My stomach rumbled noisily and I made a quick detour at McDonalds. It was time to christen my new car with French fry salt.

Once fortified, I followed the signs for Oregon State University to 9th Street. I had been a visitor at OSU several years ago when my school, the University of Oregon Ducks, had played the OSU Beavers in a civil war football game. It was a freezing cold day and the benches in the stadium were covered with ice. I dimly remembered sitting in the stands with my friends and drinking hot chocolate with peppermint Schnapps until I puked in the parking lot at half time. I also remember that rabid OSU fans had waved frozen dead ducks around in the air every time their team scored, which thankfully wasn't very often. I hoped to avoid puking and dead ducks entirely this trip, if that was possible.

I passed a Safeway, a liquor store, and an Italian restaurant, and pulled up in front of the OSU Administration building. It's a big brick building that spans half a block. Young people with backpacks were going in and out. Across the street there were three large dorms, also in brick. Young people with beer bottles in their hands were leaning out of the windows yelling at passersby on the street. The dorms were like a people zoo. I dropped my car off in the Visitor's parking lot and walked a block to the Administration building. I had no idea of where Peter Sundstrom lived but this seemed like a good place to start.

A big black sign at the entrance directed visitors to the Admissions area, and the financial aid office. The Admissions area was on the first floor. It was set up like a bank, with a rope herding folks to the counter. There was no one in line. I walked up to the first teller. An engraved name plate told me I was being helped by Aida Pinassi. She was a scrawny woman, about sixty, with hair pulled tightly away from her face. It gave her the appearance of having a do-it-yourself face lift.

"How may I help you?" she asked flicking her eyes over my outfit. I was wearing my uniform—a pea coat and jeans. I glanced down to see if I had lettuce left over from lunch hanging on my coat. Luckily it was produce free.

"I'm looking for a student named Peter Sundstrom." I spelled the name. Aida tapped on her computer keys and looked at the screen.

"Yes, I can verify that he is a second year student here at the university," she said in a tight pickle sucking sound of voice.

"Great. Where does he live?" I reached into my purse for a piece of paper and a pen.

"That's private information. There is no way I can give that information out," she said pursing her lips together. "Why do you want to know?" Aida asked suspiciously as she yanked a tissue from a nearby box and honked loudly into it.

"That's private," I said in a snotty voice as I stuffed my pad of paper back into my purse.

"WELL!" Miss Picklepuss flounced away from the counter. I heard someone laugh. I looked over at a man, about twenty, with long brown hair pulled back into a ponytail. He was wearing a rumpled flannel shirt and working on a computer next to the one Aida had vacated. He winked at me.

"You need an address?" he asked, fingers poised over his keyboard.

Two minutes later, I knew that Peter Sundstrom was a resident at Wilson, a dorm across the street. I also knew that he was an Agricultural major and that he didn't have financial aid or an outstanding grade point average. I walked across the street to the dorms.

There were three in all, on this block. Wilson, an all boys dorm, was situated next to Callahan, a girls dorm. The dorms were about four floors high and spotted with windows. I followed a walkway to the entrance of Wilson. The door was propped open with a rock to let the heat out for the rest of the OSU campus to enjoy. I walked inside and crossed the lobby area to the stairs. About a dozen people were sprawled out in front of the television, watching a Brady Bunch rerun and eating a large, sloppy pizza. There wasn't a textbook in sight. The decor had a prison feel to it. Walls of cement and broken-down furniture.

Peter Sundstrom's room was on the third floor. I was slightly out of breath as I climbed the stairs and walked to the end of the hallway. Some of the doors were open, and I caught a glimpse of students, two to a cell, laying on their beds, talking and studying. Peter's door was open as well. He was alone.

"Hello," I said as I knocked on the door frame. Peter looked up, startled. His head was still bandaged but he looked to be in good spirits. He was at his desk hooking up a new computer. A big cardboard box dominated the space between two small beds. Computer manuals littered the floor.

Peter dropped some wires and stood up. "I know why you're here." His voice broke a bit, as if he was trying to hold his emotions in check.

"You do?" I said, trying not to sound surprised. I wasn't even sure why I was here. I just had a feeling that there was something he wasn't telling me.

"I know about Detective Vance already. I saw a copy of the *Oregonian*." He shook his head in disbelief. Then he remembered his manners. "Come in, sit down. You want a beer or something? I think I'm ready for one." He pulled open the door of a small refrigerator near the window. I could see that it was jam-packed with Bud. There was a loaf of bread on top of the fridge, a jar of peanut butter, and a couple of packages of Top Ramen. Dorm staples.

"Sure." I crossed into the cramped quarters with two steps and Peter handed me a beer. "Vance's death was quite a shock." I sat down on one of the beds and twisted off the cap on my beer. Peter sat down on the other and took a pull on his beer.

"Yeah, it's a damn shame," Peter said, his shoulders slumping. His face was scared and sad. I averted my eyes to his clothes. He was wearing an OSU sweatshirt with creases in it like it had recently been purchased at the student bookstore. His jeans and ragged Nikes however, were ancient.

"Can you talk about it?" I prompted. I didn't want to make the drive for nothing. What in the hell was the matter with Peter? Why was he so broken up about Vance?

He paused. "Well, I wasn't supposed to say anything, but I guess it doesn't matter since Detective Vance is dead." He leaned back against the wall. "After I got hurt," Peter gave me a meaningful look as if to say it was partly my fault, "Detective Vance came to visit me in the hospital. I was unconscious most of the time, but one of the nurses said that he stopped by several times to see how I was doing. When I came to, Vance was right there. He asked me a couple of questions about the murder, but he seemed more concerned about me. He acted like a dad." He laughed a little self-consciously. "Well, not my dad, but that's another story."

"What kind of questions did he ask you? About the murder I mean?"

Peter thought about it. "He wanted to know exactly what had

happened. And I told him just what I knew—nothing. I made my rounds that night at 8:30, like I usually do, once an hour, and heard the commotion coming from your office. I went to investigate and the next thing I knew I was knocked out. Someone bashed me with a bookend when I unlocked the door."

"The killer," I said out loud.

"Yeah," Peter agreed. "Anyway, Vance asked me about my job, stuff like that. I told him I was trying to earn enough money to fix my truck and go back to school. The next day, he showed up with a scholarship fund for me! I was blown away. It was incredible. Vance gave me enough money to buy a truck and go back to school. I really owe the dude. Man, I can't believe he's dead." Peter drained his beer and set the empty bottle next to his collection on the desk.

"Was the scholarship in cash, Peter?" I asked thinking what the man at Portland Toyota had said. Peter had laid down twenty-five grand in cash for his new truck.

"How did you know?" Peter said in surprise.

"A guess." I changed the subject. "Peter, did Detective Vance impose any conditions regarding the scholarship? Did you sign any papers?"

"Well," Peter hesitated, "he said I shouldn't talk to anyone about the night of the murder and finding the fat guy's body. He also insisted I enroll in class here right away. He said it was important that I get a fresh start after what happened to me." Peter glanced around his dorm room. "So here I am. Winter term won't start until January, but my friend let me move in early. He's at his girlfriend's place most of the time."

What a goof. Did he really believe that the Portland Police Bureau handed out cash scholarships to victims? I took a sip of my beer. I had one more question.

"Peter, if you made your rounds at 8:30 p.m. that means you were knocked out cold for about an hour and a half. Do you remember anything about the murder at all? The sound of gunfire?"

Peter shook his head. "Nope, the guy was already dead when I got there."

"You mean when you came to after being attacked—"

"No, the body was on the desk—it looked like he was dead." Peter stopped and patted the bandage on his head ruefully. "But I got whacked in the head before I could check."

"You mean you lied to me before?"

Peter looked sheepish. Something here was not making sense. I had seen Federico DeOrca get out of a cab at 10:00 p.m. the night he was murdered. Hadn't I?

THIRTY-FIVE

THE WHITE LINE STRETCHED out into the darkness. I rubbed my eyes, temporarily driving into the bumps dividing the lanes. I was on Interstate 5 again, on my way home to Portland.

I had questioned Peter over and over again about his story. There was simply no way that DeOrca could have been bleeding on my desk at 8:30 p.m. and getting out of a cab at 10:00 p.m. One of us was wrong and I was pretty sure it was Peter. The blow to his head must have knocked something in his brain loose.

Peter's admission about the cash scholarship brought new questions into play. Where had Vance gotten the money? Had he been involved in some way in the DeOrca murder?

I checked my gas gauge. It was low. I stopped in Woodburn to fill up the tank. The gas station had a little mini mart where you were forced to go to buy your gas. I went inside to pay and get a Diet Coke. The clock on the wall showed it was nearly seven-thirty. Forty-five minutes and I would be home. In forty-eight minutes I'd be relaxing inside a hot tub...

An accident near Wilsonville slowed traffic to a crawl. It was after nine before I got home. Severe crabbiness had set in. I fumbled for my keys outside the door. As I did so, I could hear the telephone ring repeatedly. After unlocking the door, I lunged for it. The answering machine kicked on and I was greeted by my outgoing message. I punched a button, turning it off.

"Hello?" My voice was breathless.

"Jane?" I recognized Violetta's voice.

"Yes."

"It's about time you got home. Put your coat on, girlie. We've got a lot of work to do."

"What?" I whined. "I'm tired, my butt hurts from sitting in a car for two hours and I need a drink. You're on your own."

"All right." The voice on the other end was somewhat cheerful. "But don't say I didn't give you any warning."

"Wait a minute. Warning for what?"

"I'm gonna take out Brute Mortimer tonight."

"Take him out?"

"Whack him, knock him off, send him to hell in a hand basket…"

"I get the picture. Where are you?"

"I'm at a pay phone by some red apartments. There's a nice little grocery store here. It's by the river. Look, I gotta go. My cab is waiting."

"WAIT! Where are you going? I'll meet you."

"I tailed Brute to a burned out warehouse with a dock."

"I know where it is. Don't go—"

"Meet me there." The phone hung up abruptly.

I yelped out a naughty word in sheer frustration, and back-tracked to my car. The damn seat was still warm. I pulled away from the curb and took off down the hill to 23rd Avenue. I hung a left, drove to Everett and took another left turn in the direction of Naito Parkway. Once on Naito, I headed north to the warehouse that Howard Kirkwood showed me the other day.

I almost drove by it. The streetlight was broken and the massive charred structure was hidden by the darkness. Screeching my brakes, I pulled into the lot. The cab was nowhere to be seen. The lot was deserted. A large yacht was moored by the dock. A man on the deck trained his flashlight in my direction. I put the car in reverse to back up. A second later I heard the explosion of gunfire and my car sank to one side. I screamed in fear and surprise. The bastard had shot out my tire!

Still screaming, I hurled myself out of the car and took off running for cover in the warehouse. My only chance was to find a weapon. I was an easy target running down Naito.

The gunfire had stopped. My tennis shoes slipped in the gravel, propelling me to the ground. I cried out as a layer of skin was removed from my elbows and knees. The warehouse entrance was in sight a few yards away. I could see the outline of a late model Cadillac inside. Someone moved out of the darkness. It was a small man, clad in black, with a ski mask over his face. He ran toward me with a gun in his outstretched hand.

"Get up. Put your hands above your head," he ordered.

I stood, with my hands in the air. My bloodied knees were weak and my heart was beating furiously.

The man's cohort from the yacht ran over, his gun aimed at me. He was also wearing a ski mask, dark clothing, and heavy boots.

"Quien es?" he asked the short man in an angry voice.

"Who are you?" The short man cocked his gun. For the second time in a week I got ready to die.

"I'm here to warn Brute Mortimer. He's in great danger," I improvised.

"La mujer esta aqui para el Señor Mortimer. El esta en peligro." The short man spoke in labored Spanish. I felt a gun shoved in my back. A volley of rapid fire Spanish erupted from the man behind me. I could see the confusion in the eyes of the first man as he struggled to understand.

"No comprende," he said finally.

"Put the *puta* on the boat," the Hispanic man said in broken English.

The *"puta"* apparently was me. I was patted down, then frog-marched in the direction of the boat. Yet another man with a ski mask emerged from inside the vessel and appeared at the rail.

"What the hell is this?" He spat the words as we approached.

I took stock of my options. The night was quiet and cold. Across the river, the city lights twinkled. A train snaked by on the tracks. There was a ship moored about a half mile down the river. If I screamed would they hear me? I closed my eyes. It was more likely they would hear the gunfire used to cut me down. I opened my eyes again as we boarded the yacht. On the side of the vessel I could see green lettering that read: "The Natalie."

It was Sam's boat.

Once on board my heart was chilled by the sight of blood streaked on the deck. I was led down a narrow stairway into the cabin downstairs. It was warm and I could hear the hum of conversation. There was a teeny table heaped with plastic bundles of white powder. Sam was seated there with another man. They both had shot glasses filled with an amber fluid in front of them. Sam's drinking buddy was a white man, late thirties, with dyed black hair and a furry beard. He wore a windbreaker and jeans. He was puffing on a cigar and the cabin was polluted with smoke. There were dark curtains over the windows, trapping the stale air inside. Five other men in ski masks and dark clothing were crowded into the cabin. Out of courtesy for my presence, they pointed their machine guns in my direction.

"Christ!" I sputtered. Sam looked at me without a flicker of recognition in his eyes.

The man with the furry face spoke. "Who are you?"

"Jane Lanier." My voice was trembling. I hoped I wouldn't wet my pants. "I got a call a few minutes ago that led me to believe Brute Mortimer was in great danger." I avoided Sam's eyes and looked into the cold ones of the stranger.

He puffed on his cigar while he considered my answer. "You're too late. Somebody already shot him."

"Oh," I said, my voice forlorn. That explained the blood on the deck. "Is he dead?"

The man shrugged. "Who called you?"

"A little old lady."

I felt a gun smack me on the back of my head and I lurched forward. The edge of the table broke my fall.

"I'm not kidding!" I protested. The gun cracked my skull again and the room started to fade to black. I heard someone say: "Kill her. We'll dump the body on the way back." The last words to filter into my consciousness were Sam's.

"I'll do it."

THIRTY-SIX

IT WAS LIGHT, then dark again. A forceful wind buffeted the boat from side to side. I moaned and thrashed around but I was wrapped in a plastic tarp. Overhead I could hear the whirr of a helicopter. Sam's voice was in my ear as I struggled to wake up.

"Hang on, Lanier. And keep your mouth shut. Dead women don't talk."

I opened my eyes. Sam was crouched next to me, holding a gun. I was on the deck. The blinding light swung overhead again and I heard a voice boom from the sky.

"FBI. Hold your fire."

Footsteps thudded on the deck and gunshots exploded into the air. I sat up and tried to shed my plastic cocoon. I freed my arms and felt the back of my head. A big goose egg was forming. The helicopter moved away. I could hear the screech of gravel in the parking lot, accompanied by the symphony of sirens.

Inexplicably, Sam was muttering under his breath. "Six men downstairs, two drivers in the warehouse. Mortimer got away. He's wounded."

The rat tat tat of gunfire filled the air.

"Speak up," I demanded weakly. "I can't hear you."

"Can you swim?""

"Yes, why?"

"I'm gonna throw you overboard. You're right by the dock."

"But I'm injured!"

"You'll live—if you're lucky."

Sam swept me up in his arms. I kicked free of the plastic and he dumped me into the water.

I plunged down into the icy darkness and frantically dog paddled my way to the surface. I spit out a mouthful of foul tasting water from the Willamette River. The strobe light shone in my eyes as I emerged from the water. I swam by the bank and struggled to climb up the slick surface. A bullet whizzed by my shoulder. I stopped, then scampered over the bank into the glare of a huge light. In the shadows I could see men crouched by cars with weapons pointed at me.

"DEA, drop your weapons." The voice came from a megaphone.

"It's only me," I whispered as I held my hands up. The helicopter hovered by again, the wind whipping my wet clothes.

A man moved swiftly in the darkness. As he approached I could see he was carrying a gun.

The gunfire from the boat started again. I ran for dear life in the direction of the light. As I got closer I could see the men by the cars were dressed in DEA helmets and dark jackets.

Someone wrapped me in a blanket and helped me to the back seat of a car. A female agent spoke into a radio. "The hostage is off the yacht. We have one man down. We could be here for a while. There's an arsenal on the boat. Not to mention two tons of cocaine."

My head sank against the back seat of the car. A middle aged African American man with close cropped hair leaned in the back seat.

"Are you okay?"

"I think so. I'm just cold. And I have a nasty bump on the back of my head."

"We have an ambulance on the way."

"All right."

"Can you answer some questions?"

"I guess so."

"What were you doing here?"

I hesitated. "Umm, I got a call from a pay phone."

The man interrupted. "We know that. Who called you?"

"You bugged my phone?" Of course. There was no other way on this earth to explain the super fast repair service.

"We had a court order. Who called you?"

"A little old lady." I wrapped my blanket around me tighter. "What's going on here?"

"Drug smuggling. We've been tracking this thing for three years. You nearly screwed everything up."

"I'm sorry."

"Ron!"

The man turned away from me and leaned out of the car. "What?"

"They're gonna surrender!"

"All right. Have them disembark one at a time. I want everything done by the book so nobody gets hurt."

I scooted over to the side of the car to watch. One at a time the smugglers walked down the dock towards the parking lot. In the bright light I could only see the silhouette of each man. Agents cuffed them and searched them for weapons. Finally, Sam appeared.

"Wait." I got out of the car. Sam was being cuffed. I tugged on Ron's sleeve as he spoke into a radio.

"What?" He turned around.

"Go easy on him." I pointed to Sam. "He saved my life."

Ron chuckled. "Okay."

An ambulance pulled into the parking lot with flashing lights. One of the agents guided me over. Without arguing, I got on the stretcher. I was starting to feel woozy and frankly, the idea of a bed appealed to me. I was strapped in and two paramedics heaved the stretcher into the ambulance. I closed my eyes.

When I opened them again, Sam was standing there.

"Are you okay?" he asked.

"OMIGOD! SAM! How did you get in here?"

"I'm gonna ride with you to the hospital so you can get checked out."

"I thought you were going to jail."

"Well, Ron said you put in a good word for me." He laughed softly and the ambulance pulled away with a squeal of the siren. "Actually, I'm an undercover agent for the FBI. Our agency and the DEA have been working together on this operation for years. We arrested more than fifty people tonight in Portland, Nevada, California and Mexico. Mostly on money laundering charges."

"They funneled drug money through the restaurants, right?"

"And the Lucky Lady Casino. I believe you're familiar with the place."

"You had me followed?"

"We needed to keep tabs on you, after the DeOrca murder in your office. We didn't know if you were in on it. Incidentally, that agent saved your life at the Reno airport. We arrested a guy named George Krantz there. You might remember him. He was dressed up as a maintenance man."

"Really?"

"Yeah. He had a rifle stuck in his garbage can. He admitted someone had put a contract out on you. He wouldn't tell us who, but I'm guessing Mortimer did. He would've been successful if you hadn't won that jackpot and created a fuss."

I smiled. "So, I won twice."

"Yep."

I didn't want to think about that now. "Sam, where were the drugs coming from?"

"We traced them to the Cali drug cartel of Colombia and the Juarez cartel in Mexico. DeOrca Enterprises was responsible for distributing drugs in the Northwest. Quite a slick operation. Too bad the bastard died before we could put him behind bars."

"What about Brute Mortimer?"

Sam clenched his jaw. "He got away. We'll find him sooner or later. He was bleeding too much to go too far. But we need your help. Who shot at him tonight?"

"DeOrca's mother."

"You're kidding!"

"I wish I were."

THIRTY-SEVEN

I WAS TREATED and released from Good Samaritan Hospital. It was after three in the morning before I got home. I popped a few pain pills and climbed into bed. My dreams took me back to the night of DeOrca's murder. I opened my office door and I could see his body sprawled on my desk. I had black leather gloves on, I remember, so I wouldn't get blood on my hands. Otherwise I was stark naked. I moved through the room and approached DeOrca's body. This time he was lying face up and he smiled at me as I came near. There was a silver briefcase near the body. I reached for it and DeOrca seized my hand. The leather glove slipped to the floor and DeOrca's pinky ring burned into my palm. I gasped and pulled my hand away. The initials "FD" were branded in my flesh. I screamed.

And woke up.

It was morning. The sky was still dark with clouds and the rain was tapping on my window. I sat up in bed, my heart racing. Would this nightmare ever be over?

I showered, dried my hair, and applied makeup. The bump on my head was tender, but for the most part all of my injuries were mental. Rather than lounge in my flannel nightie, like I wanted to and deserved, I got dressed in jeans, a big black turtleneck sweater, and black leather loafers. I was anxious to talk to Dermott and to tell him about Peter Sundstrom's "scholarship." I also wanted to go to the office and put together a final report to give to Elana.

It was clear to me Brute Mortimer had killed Federico DeOrca and Roger Vance. Now everything was up to the police.

I put on a long, black winter coat and looked in my purse for my leather gloves. As I put them on I thought of my dream and my encounter with DeOrca's ghost. The leather gloves were tugging at my memory. Wasn't he wearing them as he entered the building? Time had passed and I couldn't be sure. If he was, then where did they go? Did the killer take them?

A door slammed across the hall. Must be Stan Oscram. I opened my door in time to see him leave. He was still wearing that damn orange sweatshirt and he was eating a pop tart. When he saw me he crammed the rest of it in his mouth as if I might make a jump for it.

"Stan! I need a picture of your ex-wife. I have a PI in Medford looking for her." I grabbed my purse and umbrella and shut my door.

"U mply mv un," he replied, exhaling a bit of pop tart dust from his stuffed mouth.

"What?" I waited for him to swallow.

"I only have one."

"Well, give it to me. I need it."

He gave me a woeful hound dog look. I returned it with a pit bull one. "Do you want to find her or not?" I said somewhat crossly. I was in no mood to be messed with.

"All right." He dug into his pants pocket and pulled out his battered wallet. Then he turned away slightly and extracted the photo. I walked over and snatched it.

"Thanks." I shoved the photo in my wallet and walked quickly to the side door so I didn't have to listen to Stan whimper. Once outside, I realized I was carless once again, so I walked to the Kinko's copy shop on Twenty-third Avenue. I photocopied the picture and faxed it to Eddie Dickerson in Medford. When I was done, I walked downtown, a thirty

minute trek. I stopped at Starbucks for some coffee and a rasp-
berry scone and took them up to my office.

My desk was free of bodies. Thank God. I sat down and
ate my scone before I called Eddie to see if he got the fax. He
had. He told me he had already sent the photo of Nick Panillo
by Fed Ex since I was too poor to have a fax machine. I
wasn't too poor—I was saving for a Fendi bag. I gritted my
teeth and bit back a salty reply. "Thanks, Ed. I'll get back to
you." I hung up and tried to call Dermott. I was told he was
out but expected to be in later on in the morning. I turned my
computer on and got busy on Elana's report.

What had I learned in the week since DeOrca's death? I
knew from Theresa LaSalle that DeOrca had been looking for
Joe Arnim and a large amount of money. Jackie Crombie had
revealed that DeOrca and Mortimer had been partners in some
past drug deals and she believed they were both responsible for
the murder of Everett Crombie, her late husband. I presumed
Detective Roger Vance had been blackmailed into spiriting
away evidence that would have convicted Federico DeOrca of
murder. And where was the missing money that Brute
Mortimer was looking for? DeOrca didn't have it. He was
dead. Joe Arnim was in jail. Detective Vance had turned up in
the river… and then there was the weird Widows Inc. thing.

There was a sharp rap on the door. I went over and opened
it. It was the guy from Federal Express. His dark hair was
ruffled, his cheeks were red and he was breathing hard. He
handed me a clipboard to sign.

"The elevator out again?" I asked as I scrawled my name
on line 13.

"No. I'm parked outside in a loading zone. I gotta hurry."
He handed me a big cardboard envelope.

"Well, thanks." I took the envelope and returned to my desk.
It was from Eddie Dickerson. I opened it. There was a letter and
another envelope inside. The letter had a few cursory details

about Nick Panillo. He had been missing since last Thursday when he went to Portland to collect an inheritance from a PI named Robert Riley. Robert Riley? The mysterious Robert Riley who stood me up the night of the murder at the Marriott?

I looked at the letter again. Nick Panillo hadn't returned home or to his job as a washing machine salesman since. His mother was worried. Nick was about 5′6″, 300 pounds, fifty years old, dark hair, a moustache… I opened the envelope. There was a photo inside. I took it out and looked at it. I recognized the face staring at me.

I had seen him a week ago, sprawled on my desk with a bullet in his throat.

THIRTY-EIGHT

"PAGE HIM! TELL HIM it's an emergency! I need to talk to him right now! I'll be waiting by the phone." I slammed the receiver down. Detective Dermott was out in the field. I pulled out the phone book and looked up the number and address for the Medical Examiner's office. The phone rang as I was about to make my call. It was Dermott.

"What do you want?" He sounded a little annoyed at the way I had summoned him. I took a deep breath and told him what I knew. I also told him about my trip to Corvallis to see Peter Sundstrom and the drug bust on the Natalie.

He was silent for a while as he absorbed the news. "There isn't a scholarship fund for crime victims," he said finally.

"I know that." I tried to be sympathetic. Dermott was finding out about his former partner's transgressions the hard way. "I'm going to call Elana DeOrca and have her meet us at the morgue."

"Us?" Dermott asked.

"Yes, us," I said impatiently. "We need to talk to the Medical Examiner who performed the autopsy. They must have pictures of the body. I can prove that the body in DeOrca's grave is not DeOrca. I want DeOrca's wife to look at the pictures."

"All right," Dermott said wearily. "I have a copy of the ME's report. I think it was performed by Dr. Anderson. I'll see if she is in the office. At any rate, I'll meet you there in thirty minutes."

"Wait! Can you pick me up? I don't have a car."

"Why not?"

"A drug smuggler shot the tires out."

There was silence on the other end.

"Never mind, I'll get a cab."

I hung up the phone and grabbed my phone book to call Elana DeOrca. The only problem was, I didn't have her damn number. Sam had given it to me once, and I lost it. The woman at the dry cleaners had pointed out the way to the DeOrca mansion. But still, I had no number. Stupid of me. I called a cab and took the elevator down to the street to wait for it. Better a ride with Fresh D than with Dermott anyhow.

A Rip City cab dropped me off at the Medical Examiner's office twenty minutes later. The office is located in an old funeral home on Knott Street in northeast Portland. A hearse was parked on the side of the building and two attendants were unloading a body. I averted my eyes and walked up to the front door. I could see Detective Dermott through the glass doors standing by the receptionist. I knocked and she buzzed me in.

"Hi, Dermott."

"Where's Mrs. DeOrca?"

"I wasn't able to reach her. I realized I don't have her number. Anyway, take a look at the photo of Nick Panillo that I told you about." I pulled it out of my purse and handed it to Dermott.

He looked at the photo, his face grim. "It looks like the body we found, but we'll need to talk to Dr. Anderson to be sure."

A few minutes later, Dr. Helen Anderson entered the room. She was an attractive woman, late thirties, with blonde wispy hair and small wire frames perched on her nose. She wore a black rubber apron with lace sewn around the edge at the top and scrubs underneath. On her feet she wore rubber duck shoes. They were bloody.

"Hello, everybody." She extended her hand to Dermott and smiled at me. After Dermott made the introductions we followed Dr. Anderson to her office. It was a small room on the first floor with a view of Knott Street. Medical degrees and licenses adorned her walls. The furniture was functional but not fancy; since most of Dr. Anderson's visitors were of course, dead. We sat down in chairs facing her oak desk. Dermott passed her the photo of Nick Panillo.

"Does this look like the man who was brought in late last Friday night?"

Dr. Anderson studied the picture. "It does." She picked up a file and read from it. "The man brought in last Friday was a Caucasian male, age fifty two, 312 pounds. I performed the autopsy early Saturday morning and concluded that he died as a result of a gunshot wound to his trachea. It is my opinion that the manner of death was homicide." She sighed. "Normally, I would have waited until Monday morning but I received a call from Detective Vance. He said it was important." She paused and looked at Dermott. "I'm sorry, Tom. They brought him here earlier this week. I know you guys worked together."

"Did you take fingerprints?" I interrupted.

Dr. Anderson nodded. "Yes, prints of his thumbs. Vance was going to run them through AFIS." AFIS, I knew, was the Automated Fingerprint Information System. The FBI maintains the database.

"Did you get a chance to talk to him?"

"I did. Vance said they matched the ones on file for Federico DeOrca. I have a copy of the report." She flipped through the file and frowned. "Where is it?"

"Who was the last person to have the file?" I asked helpfully.

She looked up at me, concerned. "Roger Vance. Oh, God. Poor Roger."

Dermott shifted in his chair. "Can you order an exhumation of the body?"

Dr. Anderson picked up the phone. "I'll do it now."

THIRTY-NINE

"DERMOTT, I NEED MY GUN." I hurried after him as he left the Medical Examiner's office. Birds squealed in the distance, carrying my voice away with the blustery wind. The sky had darkened while we were in our meeting with Dr. Anderson. The clouds looked bloated, like it might pour. I needed my gun and also an umbrella.

"What?" He turned around, an expression of surprise on his face.

"My gun. You guys took it the night of the murder. For evidence. You must know by now it hadn't been fired. I need it. I don't feel safe with DeOrca and Mortimer on the loose." Not to mention Violetta.

Dermott signed heavily. "C'mon down to the station. I'll see what I can do."

"I need a ride."

"Of course you do." He moved over to the passenger door of his unmarked Chevrolet and opened it. "Where's your car?"

"It was towed to Les Schwab on Broadway. The tires are being replaced."

We drove back to the station. I waited in Dermott's office while he went to see about getting my gun released. While I was there, I took the opportunity to use his phone to check my voice mail. Henry had called. I smiled happily, not bothering to jot his number down. I knew it by heart. I also had a call from a Ms. Elizabeth Weston, my banker at the Portland Teacher's Credit Union. Elana's check had bounced.

Dermott returned with my gun. It was in a plastic evidence bag. When he saw my face, he stopped in his tracks, alarmed.

"Who died?"

"It's worse. Elana DeOrca's check bounced." I fumed. After all I had gone through! The body on the desk, the bomb in my car, my tossed apartment, near death by fire and water… That woman had a lot of nerve!

He held up the gun. "Can I trust you with this?" It was not a rhetorical question, given my present state.

"Yes," I said grudgingly. I signed for it while Dermott checked the chamber.

"No bullets," he commented.

"Can you loan me some?" It would be the neighborly thing to do.

He scoffed as his phone rang. "See you later." He leaned over to pick it up.

"Bye." I stuffed the gun in my bag and left the station. Damn Elana. I was furious. If it weren't for my Reno winnings I would be in serious financial trouble. I had charged the trip to Nevada and I hadn't settled up with her for the damage to my place, not to mention my fees. I thought about the car I had just bought and I started to feel sick. Insurance hadn't covered all of it. I had spent an extra two grand for a working clutch, new tires, and fewer miles.

A cab was cruising by as I was trying to decide my next step. On impulse I hailed it and got inside.

"Where to?" the driver asked as she pulled away from the curb.

"I'm not sure of the address," I replied. "But I can show you. It's near Northeast 33rd and Fremont.

If Elana thought she was going to get away with the stiff on my desk AND stiffing me, she had another think coming. By the time the cab dropped me off at her house I had worked myself up into quite a hissy fit. Today I was full of contempt for the manicured lawns, the three story pillars, and the naked cherubs dancing in the fountains. I marched up three sets of stairs to the front door and rang the bell.

Violetta answered the door. She was dolled up in a fake fur mink coat complete with a fake dead animal hat. A cigarette dangled from her fingers. My jaw dropped open.

"Violetta! You nearly got me KILLED last night! The police are looking for you—and Brute Mortimer. What in hell were you thinking?"

"Jane Lanier! Come in!" She was obviously in high spirits from her murder attempt the night before. "You're just in time to say good bye. Me and my grandson are getting ready to blow this joint."

I stepped in the house. The floral arrangements from DeOrca's funeral were still on display. Only now, the heads of the flowers were drooping. Shriveled leaves were scattered on the big polished table. There were several suitcases and a backpack on the marble floor. Violetta's duct taped suitcase was among them.

"Yoo Hoo! Elana! You have company." She sang at the top of her lungs. "I'm gonna go see what's taking Sean so long. Nice chatting with you, Janie." She hurried up the stairs, a bit wobbly on three inch heels.

After a moment, Elana emerged from the door of the study. She was dressed in black again: a sleek floor length cashmere coat and Manolo Blahnik slingbacks. A Chanel purse was slung on her shoulder.

"Hello, Jane. I didn't expect you. I was just about to leave. I have to take Sean and Violetta to the airport."

"This won't take long. It's about the check you gave me. It bounced."

"Oh dear." She frowned.

"Is there any way you can pay me with cash? I've got a lot of expenses and time invested in this case. Not to mention a

hospital bill. But I suppose I have Violetta to thank for that."
I told Elana about Violetta's escapade the night before and the
drug bust aboard the Natalie.

"Oh dear," she said again. "I'm afraid I don't have the
money right now. My husband's business partner has seized
all of our accounts. I can't even pay the mortgage on this
place. He said it was to pay off my husband's debts."

"You mean the missing money from the insurance scam?"
It was hard to work up sympathy for a woman with a purse
that cost as much as my car.

"I don't know anything about a 'scam' as you put it, but
yes. Federico received two million for the warehouse. Then
there were other things too…" Her voice trailed.

"Why don't you have your husband pay for them himself?"
She looked at me, flustered.

"He's alive. You knew that didn't you?"

"I need a drink." Her voice was faint. "Will you join me?"

I followed Elana to the study. The room was frosty cold.
Probably couldn't afford the heating oil bill. I glanced around,
trying to determine the garage sale value of her belongings.
How much would the green leather chairs go for on the
auction block? A tenth of the retail cost? Elana picked up a
crystal decanter from a tray near the big polished desk and
poured a shot into a glass.

"Jane?" She held it out.

I shook my head. "How long have you known?"

Elana sat down behind the desk, and put the drink down,
untouched.

"Federico told me before he disappeared that he was in
serious financial trouble. He borrowed money from Brute to
build six new Mexican restaurants. Unfortunately, they
weren't doing very well. The Multnomah County Health Department closed four of them down. So, it was very lucky that
the warehouse burned down when it did."

I looked at her face for a trace of irony, but I saw none. I was in the presence of a great actress, but her performance was wasted on this audience.

"Did he tell you what he was going to do?"

"No. He merely said that our 'ship' was coming in and it was a temporary problem. I had no idea he would—" She hesitated. "Kill someone."

"Well, the ship was busted by the Feds, and old Freddie will be soon. The Medical Examiner is going to have the body you buried last Friday exhumed. You could have saved them a lot of trouble if you had spoken up."

"I didn't know until the day of the funeral."

"How did you find out?"

Elana blinked. "He showed up at the house right before the service. He said that he faked his own death so he could buy himself some time to find the missing money. Otherwise Brute Mortimer would've killed him."

"What about the man that he killed? Nick Panillo. Why him?"

"I didn't ask. I was afraid."

"You were weak."

"Yes," she admitted. "I was. But who are you to judge me? Do you know what it's like to live with a man like DeOrca? I was afraid to stay and afraid to go. I've been waiting for years for a chance to leave. Remember the bullet holes in the living room? They're a souvenir from that night. I said I wanted a divorce."

"Hmm." I didn't know what to believe.

Elana stood up. "Look, I need to go. I have to take Sean and Violetta to the airport. Sean is going to stay with his grandmother for a while. It will be good for him to get away."

"About the check—"

She sighed. "I'll pay you later. Until then, take my car. It's worth much more than what I owe you." She opened a desk drawer. "The title is here somewhere."

"I can't take your car."

"If you don't, Mortimer will find a way." She leafed through some files and extracted a slip. Then she picked up a pen and signed for it.

"It's in your name?"

"Everything is—not that it means anything. Brute owns it all now." She handed me the title and the keys. There were a bunch of them on a dainty silver key chain. "Here you go. Could I trouble you for a ride to the airport?"

"Oh, sure." Was I really getting a Mercedes or was this another trick?

"Thank you." She picked up her purse.

Violetta appeared in the doorway. Sean was standing behind her with a scowl on his face.

"Elana," Violetta said. "Time to chop, chop. I don't want to be late for the plane."

"Violetta," I piped in. "I hate to be a wet blanket, but the police want to talk to you."

She laughed. "And so does a big bully named Brute. I shot the bastard twice in the ass! I'm getting the hell out of here while I still can. Me and my grandson are going to do some traveling. Maybe Italy. I've always wanted to see the leaning tower of Pizza." She turned around to Sean. "Sonny, can you get the suitcases?" He rolled his eyes, suffering.

"I'll help." I moved past Violetta to the hallway. I had the keys to the car after all.

Sean clomped on his heavy boots into the entryway and picked up a suitcase. He was dressed in a thick blue parka and jeans. He acted a little pissed off.

"What's the matter, Sean? Don't you want to go on a trip with your Grandma?"

"Not if she's going to steal my cigarettes. Can you run me by the store before we go?"

"Sorry."

We gathered the suitcases and went out through the back door in the kitchen. There was a cappuccino colored 450 SL Mercedes parked in the driveway. I held my breath. Not my favorite color, but it was beautiful. When I went by I noticed the interior was done in soft buttery leather. I couldn't wait to take this baby through the drive-thru at Taco Bell.

Sean dumped the bags by the truck. "Did Mom give you the keys?"

"Yep." I walked over and unlocked the truck, after going through several keys. I made a mental note to remember to give Elana back the rest of them when I dropped her back off. We loaded the bags and got in the car. Elana and Violetta emerged from the house a moment later. Elana got in the front passenger seat and Violetta sat in the back with Sean. She was a little huffy, it seemed, because she was booked to travel coach. "I hate coach!" she whined. The drive to the airport was quiet and tense. I wanted to flip on the radio to fill the silence but I didn't dare. Raindrops splattered on the window and I pretended to concentrate on driving. When we approached Portland International I looked at Elana.

"Do you want me to wait for you?"

"It might be a while," she replied. "Do you have time to come in?"

"Sure." I was a little tempted to take off myself until Brute Mortimer and Federico DeOrca were in custody. "Let me park the car. I'll meet you by the United ticket counter."

Double-parked, I dropped everyone off at the departure level, then zoomed down the ramp to the short term parking lot. After searching for fifteen minutes, I located a spot somewhere near the State of Washington. A shuttle van took me back to the airport. Passengers swarmed through the entrances, loaded down with an assortment of luggage. Elana was waiting by the United counter. When she saw me come in she moved towards me through the gauntlet of travelers with rolling suitcases.

"Hi," I said, a little breathless. "Sorry it took so long."

"It's all right. Violetta and Sean are at the gate."

"Are you going to see them off?"

"No. But I wanted to give something to you. It wasn't safe to talk about it in the house."

"Oh shoot! I forgot—it's bugged, isn't it?" That explained her odd behavior earlier.

"I assume so."

I followed Elana down the escalator to the lower level baggage claim area. Six carousels filled with an assortment of luggage were rotating, while hopeful passengers waited to snag their bags. We walked past several car rental counters to a wall of lockers. Elana stopped and took a key out of her purse. She unlocked one of the lockers and struggled to pull two identical large silver briefcases out. One of them she handed to me. It was heavy.

"What's this?"

"It's the insurance money. I want you to take it to the police."

"Christ, Elana! People have died over this money. How did you get it?"

"I switched the briefcase that DeOrca gave Joe Arnim, the deliveryman. Without the money there was no hope of me ever leaving him. I saw my chance and I took it. When Joe showed up to the meeting with Mortimer all he had was a suitcase full of paper. Federico thought Joe stole the money, Mortimer thought Federico did. I planned to slip away in the confusion, but things didn't work out."

"What's in the other briefcase?"

Elana smiled sadly. "Papers, credit cards, a passport. Things that I need to make a fresh start. I've had this here for quite some time. Once I even bought a plane ticket. But I didn't go. Freddie had me followed. He used to do it all the time. But he has other worries now. So this is it. No more dress rehearsals."

"That key you gave me. What's it for?"

"The briefcase." She pointed at the one I was holding. "I realize it might be tempting to keep it, but you need to take it to the police right away. Mortimer thinks you killed DeOrca for it."

"Oh, God. He must have been the one responsible for tossing my apartment."

"Was the key there?" Elana looked concerned.

"No. It's in a safe place."

Elana looked at her watch. "I have to catch my plane."

"I guess this is good-bye then. Good luck."

"Thank you, Jane. I won't be coming back. Enjoy the car."

I smiled, knowing that I might have to hock it soon to pay bills.

A crush of passengers from an arriving flight flooded through the aisle way. Elana turned to go.

A thought occurred to me and I grabbed her arm. "Widows Incorporated—was there ever such a thing?"

Elana looked at me with dead eyes. "Ask Violetta Sharkey, ask Jackie Crombie, ask Dorothy Vance. It's real enough to them."

FORTY

A NEW MERCEDES SEDAN. A suitcase with two million bucks. My life had changed dramatically over the last week. The rain started to pound on the windshield. I flicked on the wipers and pulled into a metered spot in front of the Galleria. Lightening zig zagged across the dark sky.

I had every intention of turning the money over to the police. But first I wanted to get the key, open the suitcase, fling the money in the air, and maybe roll over it with my naked body. I felt giddy—and dizzy from hunger. I needed some food. The scone I had eaten earlier in the afternoon had long since worn off. It was past dinner time!

The Galleria was fairly deserted. I dripped a trail of water on the marble floor to Roberto's. The clock by the escalator told me it was after six o'clock. I went inside and looked at the menu board. A hotdog, that was what I wanted. And fries. I set the suitcase down and opened my purse as the counter person excused herself to answer the phone. I looked in my wallet, and came up with coins and a coupon for laundry soap.

The irony of the situation cracked me up. What would the waitress think if I whipped open the suitcase and threw a couple of hundreds at her for my hot dog? I hollered something to her about coming back later, then I left.

I took the elevator to the fifth floor and walked to my office. Before unlocking it, I picked at a bit of adhesive on the nameplate next to my door. What the hell was that from? I went inside my office.

Nature's fireworks were in full display outside. Thunder rolled and the rain came crashing down. I stood in the dark and listened to the storm. A jagged streak of silver came dangerously close to the Multnomah County Library. I moved across the room to the window. As I approached, the chair in front of my desk swiveled around.

A scream died in my throat as I saw the gun pointed at me.

The man that held it was none other than Federico DeOrca. He was dressed like he had been the night of his "murder." A black suit, an overcoat, and dark gloves. A gun in his right hand. Only tonight, I was the one holding the silver briefcase.

"Don't kill me." I breathed, sure that he was going to.

"Give me the briefcase."

"How did you know—"

"I followed my lovely wife. GIVE ME THE BRIEFCASE NOW!"

I set it on the desk and stepped back in fear. The glow of the street lamp outside slashed across his face, spilling a pool of light onto the desk. His greedy eyes gleamed with satisfaction and his jowls quivered. He reached for the suitcase and pulled it toward him, setting his gun down on the desk. With difficulty he tried to open the lock. I started to inch my way back to the door, wondering if I could make a break for it. My heart was pounding and my knees were shaky. I jumped as he slammed the suitcase down in frustration.

"Where's the key?" he demanded. His voice was rough and I knew he wasn't fooling around. He was going to kill me. I put my hand to my throat.

It's stuck in a wad of gum underneath the desk you're sitting at! I thought. Instead I answered in a weak voice. "It's in my purse."

"Well, give it to me."

I slipped it off my shoulder and handed it over. He pulled

out my gun, grunted and set it down out of my reach. Then he pulled out Elana's key chain.

"That bitch." He spat the words. "I'll kill her."

He obviously recognized the keys. I had forgotten to give her the rest of them, but it didn't matter now.

"Like you killed Nick Panillo."

"Yeah," he said, examining the keys. He fingered the smallest one. "How did you figure out who that was?"

"A private investigator from Medford called me, looking for him. Why Panillo? How did you lure him to my office?"

A grin snaked across DeOrca's face. "The asshole sold me thirty crappy washing machines for my laundromat. He wrapped them in plastic and said they were brand new. Damn things didn't work. I found out that they were junked from a hotel chain. When I tried to get my money back he just laughed. He wasn't from here, otherwise he'd of known that he couldn't get away with it."

DeOrca stopped fiddling with the suitcase for a moment. "So, I didn't say nothin. I let him think that everything was okey dokey. Then I dummied up some business cards for a private dick and sent him a letter telling him that he was gonna inherit some money. All he hadda do was show up here. I made sure that you were out of the office—"

"So, you're Robert Riley."

He chuckled, pleased with himself. "I put up a sign over your nameplate outside. I shoved your business cards in the desk. Panillo showed up right on time. He knocked on the door, and I told him to come in. I was sitting in your chair then, like I am now."

I knew what happened next.

DeOrca tried to force the smallest key in the suitcase lock. It got stuck. "So I turn the chair around, Panillo walks over, sits his fat ass down and I blew him away. Then I put the plane tickets in his pocket. To throw off Mortimer." He shrugged.

"Why did you shoot him in the throat?"

DeOrca pulled the small key out of the lock. "Damn thing don't work." He muttered, his frustration rising. He tried a second key. I repeated my question.

"Cause dead men don't talk."

"Like Roger Vance?"

He looked at me irritably. "You ask too many questions. Shut up and open this."

"You wanted the police to think that Brute Mortimer killed you. And you got Detective Vance to help."

"Yeah. I got to Vance through his grandkid. I had to kill him. He went by my house after I killed Panillo and took the account books for my business. The bastard was either gonna blackmail me or turn me in. As for Mortimer, it was a matter of time before he had me whacked. He knew it and I knew it. Two million is too much money. Hell, two grand is too much money. It's about respect. If you let a guy shit on you once—" He stopped and threw the keys against the wall in an explosion of anger. I saw an arc of silver then they disappeared into the darkness of the room. "None of these damn things WORK!"

"It's okay," I cooed, trying to calm him down. He was acting like a three hundred pound infant. "Let me try."

He shoved the suitcase across the desk to me. I moved closer and slowly turned it around so the locks faced me. "I need the keys," I said.

DeOrca moved to his left without thinking, to get the keys. I pounced on the gun on the other side of him. He whipped around and smacked me on my arm. I was swept to the floor, still holding the gun.

He picked up the other gun as I scrambled behind the desk, knocking the chair over. I looked up to see him looming above me, sprawled across the desk. Black hair, angry eyes, bared teeth. Rage. His gun aimed at my face. I drew my gun up to my chin and we fired in unison.

Only it wasn't my gun that I held. It was his.

EPILOGUE

FEDERICO DEORCA WAS buried a second time on November 7th. He died again of a gunshot wound to the throat. This time nobody came, as far as I knew. The Feds shut down the remaining Mesa del Rey restaurants, the laundromat, and the Lucky Lady casino, so there were no salaried employees to attend. Most of them were arrested. As Sam Madsen had suspected, DeOrca and Mortimer were using the businesses to launder drug money. All assets were seized—well, the ones they could find, anyway. I'm still driving the car Elana gave me. I think I earned it.

The insurance money was never recovered. The suitcase that I was supposed to turn over to the police was packed with a second set of books for the DeOrca Enterprises. The businesses were a vehicle for hiding Brute Mortimer's and DeOrca's ill gotten gains. Using this information, officials confiscated an additional twenty million dollars in U.S. and foreign bank accounts. Two million was never found. I kept my mouth shut. If I hadn't, I could've told them the story of a banker's daughter and a phantom company named Widows Inc. Regardless, the Secretary of the U.S. Treasury declared the case "a battle won in the war against drugs". Defendants were taken into custody in Portland, Reno and Los Angeles. Brute Mortimer was arrested in town, while on the operating table. A surgeon was taking the bullets out of his behind.

I don't know what ever happened to Theresa LaSalle/Sarah, the missing juror. I wouldn't be surprised to see her on the silver screen someday. The woman was a talented actress.

Eddie Dickerson drove up from Medford to settle the affairs of Nick Panillo on behalf of his family. We met for coffee at Jamie's. Eddie was able to provide me with an address for Patty, Stan's wife. She's no longer following the Grateful Dead. She works as a fund raiser for the Republican National Committee and is quite good, from all reports. Stan and Patty have been trading phone calls and plan to reunite in Disneyland soon.

As for me, I'm doing all right. After I shot Federico DeOrca I spent a lot of time giving statements to the Portland Police and the Feds. The District Attorney's office declined to press charges, calling the incident a clear case of self defense. I gave Henry Sullivan the exclusive on the story.

One thing eludes me still. It's peace of mind. Late at night, when I'm getting ready to drift from the waking to the dreaming world, I'll see the face of my would be executioner. My eyes fly open and I remember once again, the question I asked myself at the beginning of the case. Who killed Federico DeOrca? I know now.

I did.